CRITICAL ACCLAIM FOR
THE RETURN!

"Maynard possesses a pyrotechnic narrative power: his combination of vivid description and crackling action elevates some . . . material to almost sublime heights!"

—*Kirkus*

"A worthwhile exercise in 'suppose' and 'what if' science fiction!

—*UPI*

"A dark parable of humankind's headlong rush toward progress!"

—*Library Journal*

"Maynard has breathed new life into . . . a vibrant first-person narration . . . a compelling portrait of this alien Earth!"

—*Providence Sunday Journal*

"Well written and thought provoking!"

—*Science Fiction Chronicle*

"A science fiction thriller . . . *The Return* is gripping in its portrayal of seven men trapped in a place that is both familiar and horrifyingly unfamiliar. More than that, it is a chilling vignette of an all too plausible fate that may await us!"

—*New York Times Book Review*

BACK TO THE FUTURE

Haunting in its imagery and utterly compelling in its narrative power, *The Return* depicts a post-catastrophe Earth inhabited by a primitive people who resist relearning civilized ways.

Forced to make their way through this world are seven astronauts who return from an aborted space flight that they believe has lasted sixty Earth years. What has happened to make humanity reject advanced civilization? Gradually the crew discovers clues among the savage hunting tribes and in the crumbling ruins of technological man.

Reminiscent of H. G. Wells's *The Time Machine* and Pierre Boulle's *The Planet of the Apes*, *The Return* offers both a warning and a hope for regeneration.

RICHARD MAYNARD'S first novel was hailed by critics as a "literary tour de force" *(The Sunday Telegraph)*, and "a gripping adventure story" *(Daily Telegraph)*.

By the same author

THE COCONUT BOOK

RICHARD MAYNARD

THE RETURN

LEISURE BOOKS　NEW YORK CITY

For Nick

A LEISURE BOOK®
Published by Special Arrangement with Donald I. Fine, Inc.

October 1989

Published by

Dorchester Publishing Co., Inc.
276 Fifth Avenue
New York, NY 10001

Contents

BOOK ONE

An Alien Land

Chapter One

I am the last. And I am afraid. The fear is not a physical thing, for I have experienced so much of that now that it barely affects me. The fear is for my offspring, the apprehension for their future without me. They can stand alone; I am sure of that, but the apprehension remains. Perhaps it is less fear than sadness. The sadness that I shall not see them mature, shall not see them conquer. And the fear is that they might fail. Their world of their own oncoming discoveries, their own inevitable challenges, is so different from mine in my growing up, and their responses to their world cannot be taught from the limited experiences that I have had within it, indoctrinated as I was and undoubtedly still am with the social values of my youth.

That ordered world of my generation, that world of governments, of industry and commerce, of science and research, automobiles, aeroplanes and spaceships, is now just an unclear memory, sometimes so vague that I, who lived and loved and laughed in it, can hardly believe that it existed. I had a wife, and it is difficult now to recall her name. There was a time when I loved her, and I knew her utterly, every indentation of her body, every sensual tremor of her muscles; yet I cannot recall any of it. Why is memory so fragile? I cannot now remember the sensation of her, of being totally absorbed within her, although those feelings must have been intense at the time. It has all gone. It was the past. A dream. Years have become moments. The great accumulation of knowledge of which mankind was so justly proud has become a scrap of unrecorded history, meaningless and, with my death, lost for all time for the use of future men.

The cities stand yet. I can see one from where I sit and write, its skyline exactly as it was then, though perhaps more ragged now as vegetation has been uncontrolled for so long.

How long? I do not know. Barry, who was the cleverest of us, made a guess of four hundred years. I find that hard to credit, but it must be as good a guess as any. There are tall edifices configurating the skyline, exaggeratedly tall and unseemly in the low, rounded form of the countryside. But at this distance, in this grey light, they seem sound and powerful, testimony to a race now past, a race beyond recovery. The sounds of the city come as the gentle calls of birds, confident birds, unfrightened in their occupation, and the city smells are the soft, green smell of grass and the dank, heavy smell of moisting leaf mould. If I were closer I would be able to see the cracking masonry and the haggard façades, and I could wonder, as present man wonders, at the ambition and the arrogance of the builders of those mournful monuments. Yet I shall never go near again, for cities have no power to move me now.

To recall that dead world requires considerable mental effort. It is there, a sediment in my brain, but the recollection is spasmodic. I have to probe for it and only drab pictures surface. The sensations felt then, the humour, the agonies, the thrills, are less than mild hues on the spectroscope of memory. It is as if I had just read it all. There is no reality. Only the more recent years are vivid. They are real. I cannot erase them. I suppose the past has no importance at all now. The crises then are irrelevant. That is all prehistory, and it will all be gone before mankind discovers a willingness to study the past again.

This history, then, must begin when we blasted off in our spaceship, for that was the moment when we left our own world behind for ever. The actual event has little bearing on history itself, and, really, its only bearing on this part of it is that it made me and the others of the crew players in it. No more than players, even though we did attempt to influence its course. That was a preposterous vanity; it is easy in retrospect to see the futility of it. Soon, when I am gone, we shall be forgotten. A legend or two will remain, but they will not be truth and, other than the legends and this record, history will be indifferent.

*   *   *

It was the 17th of June when we left the Earth. It is odd that such trivia remain in the mind when so much else is lost. I also remember that it was an overcast day, and cold as we entered the door in the side of the great craft that was to be our home for the next several years. There must have been some very tense and overstretched moments, just before we blasted off. There were seven of us alone with our thoughts as we strapped ourselves into the launch position, waiting for that moment of finality. My own thoughts then elude me now, but surely they were less thoughts of excitement than of heartache. Below us, in some reinforced subterranean chamber, were our families and friends, wondering, as we were, how many years of longing and doubt, of pain and loneliness, would pass before we embraced again. We were expecting to be three years in space, but travelling as we anticipated along 'Schroeder's flattened curve of light' and using his formulae, it was generally accepted that we would actually be away from Earth for a period closer to twelve years. Bartholomew Mann, our physicist and architect of the whole venture, admitted that there were several unknown factors that could affect the space–time syndrome and was less specific than most about the probable passage of time. Our destination was planet M2 in the Alpha Centauri system, suspected to harbour quite advanced forms of life, perhaps even intelligent life. Our object was to reach it and observe its life forms at close quarters. We were to be the first manned spaceship to travel beyond our own solar system, very much publicised as a great British venture and triumph of British science, but without the use of Schroeder's theories such a voyage would have been unimaginable—although, as Bartholomew maintained, there were probably more imponderables than absolutes. We were all aware of the possible hazards, all resigned to the expected disparity of ageing between ourselves and our loved ones, all conditioned to the years of monotony that lay before us.

Right on schedule the huge ship moved. I am sure there were some uncomfortable moments then, but I do not recall them. The memories of such minor discomforts are wholly submerged beneath the endless agonies of more recent years. Soon we were free of gravity and the simulated gravity system took over. It would remain operative until we were within the pull of planet M2.

We failed in our mission. We discovered that in space, beyond our familiar planetary system, in the depths of the limitless void, there was a factor that Barry termed 'cosmic refraction', meaning simply that our destination was not where we had thought it to be at all. So for years we searched, within the limitations of the 'flattened curve' which enabled us to travel the vast distances in a relatively brief period of time. However, this principle, founded as it was on the relativity of time in space, meant that for every year we spent on the ship, some four years passed on Earth. Or so the theory supposed. And our loved ones were ageing at a far greater rate than we were. After six years had passed it became increasingly clear that we were lost. We abandoned the mission and headed for home. But that blasted 'cosmic refraction' still played its tricks upon us and it was a further nine years before we found Earth again.

It was Major Waters who first caught sight of our home planet; the rest of us were asleep. He woke me first. 'Commander, Commander, wake up!'

'What's up, Terry? What's the matter?'

'Earth, sir. It's visible through the screen.'

'Is it, indeed? Wake the others, then, Terry, we must all share this moment.'

Soon we all stood before the viewing screen and were strangely silent as we caught our first glimpse of Earth for fifteen years. Even Pip, undoubtedly the most loquacious man I ever knew, was unspeaking for several minutes. He was in front of me and I looked down on his bald head, for he was a small man, the smallest of the group. This was Philip Quincey-Jones, comic, chatterbox and brilliant biochemist, and he made up for the hairlessness of his head by the abundance of growth on his face. He could not remain quiet for long. Soon he turned his face up to me, eyes twinkling in fat-encrusted wrinkles, and said: 'Jeez, I feel randy!'

Lucky laughed. He always laughed at Pip's remarks. Luciano Cragnolini, our systems engineer, a warm, friendly man who, so far as I can remember, never voiced a single complaint. He was a man who took life in his stride, a man without anxieties; he had brown eyes creased from constant smiles, a swarthy face with a thin, immaculate moustache, for he shaved regularly, and the body of a boxer, which indeed he had been: wide, muscular shoulders, heavily knuckled hands. He was the first of us to die, and the guilt of that is still a pain within me in spite of all the excuses. 'You'll have to shave off that great black mat,' he ribbed, 'the girls will think you're a bear.'

'They'll know I'm a man, all right,' averred the little man with a grin. Then, voicing a common sentiment: 'Hell, it'll be good to get home!'

'I wonder just how long has passed on Earth,' mused Barry.

'If one assumes it's sixty years,' I said, 'our wives will be very old or dead and our children could be older than us.'

'I suspect even our children will be dead,' he answered rather quietly. 'You see, Schroeder's formula would not really apply any more. It didn't take refraction into account, for that was a totally unexpected effect. That four-to-one ratio was based on a fairly rigid postulation which we have long since abandoned.'

'Perhaps it could be less than sixty years, then,' suggested Lucky.

'No, I'm afraid not. The world will be a different place from the one we knew.' But even Barry did not realise just how much of an understatement this was. He looked at us bleakly over the tremendous hook of his nose. He had a big, powerful face. He was a big, powerful man. He continued in a clear, contained voice: 'I want you all to be quite definite about your expectations. You should have none for your children. None at all.' He turned away, wavering slightly at the last word. He had had a small daughter whom he had loved dearly.

I think we had all accepted such a situation in our own minds for many years; but suddenly, with our homecoming so imminent, the impact of that realisation became more immediate, dominant in our thinking, so that the silence then was introverted: six men withdrawing into themselves. Not Pip. He was unmarried. He had no family that I knew of, though I think there had been a brother. He never spoke of him. He made no comment then and it was Paul who finally broke the silence. 'Well, we'll just have to build new lives for ourselves,' he said in his slow, solemn fashion. He had a tendency towards solemnity, Paul St Denis, our doctor and the eldest of us. A tall spare man, starting to grey. A quiet man. Serious and gentle. I cannot hate him. Not any more.

'Will they be expecting us, do you think?' asked Lucky.

'Yes, I would think so,' responded Pip. 'They would have been tracking us through our wanderings, no doubt, and their equipment is surely considerably more sophisticated now. I expect we'll be in all the newspapers.'

'Right. Try to re-establish communication straight away,' I said. 'John, you check out the radio.' John nodded. He and Terry made up my service crew; both highly trained men, yet John had as many emotional ties on Earth as any of us and was visibly reluctant to leave the sight of it. 'Well, it's probably too early yet,' I pointed out, 'but we'll keep trying in relays from now on. We should be picking up return signals in a few days.'

John left the viewing screen and, one by one, the others drifted away. Only Barry remained. He was particularly quiet, immersed in thoughts into which it would have been tactless to intrude. He stood there, shoulders hunched forward, his spade beard jutting out as he stared through the screen to the distant, cloud-skirted ball that was home, still too far away to discern the continents clearly, but not too far to hear the words: 'Goodbye, Daddy. Don't be away too long.'

Our re-entry into Earth's atmosphere was accomplished without trouble. We had continued trying to establish communication for several days without success. That was the first seed of unease, I suppose, but there were many explanations for such silence at that stage and the unease was no more than disappointment. But they would see us. A ship would be standing by to pick us up.

We splashed down in the Atlantic Ocean. There was no ship. We dressed ourselves in our warmest clothing and took to a life raft. We headed for the European coast which we estimated to be less than two hundred miles away. That was a bad trip. It took us eight days. Tossed around in wild seas. Cold. All of us sick, except Barry. He sat at the tiller and steered. Soaked. A huge and indomitable man. Eight days he sat there, apart from brief hours of sleep when John or I relieved him, both of us pale and vomiting. I navigated. Barry would always nod assent at my directions as if already fully aware of our position. Indeed, I was convinced that he was. But at last it ended. We landed on a rocky coastline somewhere south of the Gironde. It was nearly dusk, but we located a beach and came ashore. For the first time in fifteen years we stood on land, on our native Earth, and we celebrated with an impromptu dance on the beach, calling out and singing in our relief from our wanderings in space and the greater relief from the sea.

There were no signs of life: just sand dunes and rocks. It was a deserted stretch of coast. I sent Terry and John to locate some of the local inhabitants. I had no premonitions then, in fact, we were all somewhat elated, and the immediate future seemed bright. I cannot even recall giving them a warning to be cautious; there was no reason to do so. Meanwhile the rest of us busied ourselves with pulling up the life raft to the top of the beach where it would be safe from the tide, and pegging it down in case of wind. Then we gathered driftwood for a fire. Soon it was dark and we sat around the pile of blazing sticks, little realising the precedent we were setting; and we waited for help to arrive.

I remember that first fire. There were many, many fires in the ensuing years, but that first one remains in my mind. The crisp flames in the cold, grey evening. The silence emphasising the rising surf. And Pip talking. 'Quite a welcome home!' he remarked.

'Well, it's clear that we weren't expected,' responded Paul. 'They are probably still trying to work out who we are.'

'The world situation could have changed,' Barry pointed out. 'Who knows? Perhaps America is at war with Europe.'

'We'll find out soon enough,' I said.

'It will be good to see a woman again,' continued Pip. We all smiled; it was a common feeling. 'From tomorrow I'm going to spend two whole weeks in bed with the loveliest girl in all of France. What is the nearest town to here?'

'Bordeaux, probably.'

'Ah, Bordeaux. There are some really lovely women there. Just think . . .'

'Just think we could be at war with them,' interrupted Barry with a smile.

'Oh, you said that already. Whatever put that ridiculous idea into your fat head?'

'Just trying to calm you down,' replied the big man, and he began to laugh. He had a peculiarly high-pitched laugh for a man with so deep a voice.

'Calm me down, you great oaf!' Pip cried in mock indignation. 'After fifteen years of listening to your snores I need something tender to sleep with.'

My mind drifted away from their chatter. I was awaiting the return of my two crew members, and suddenly I felt anxious. It may have been the wind in the night making my back cold, or it may have been the smoke in my eyes, but elation left me and it was replaced with an unaccountable apprehension. Why hadn't they returned? Perhaps they had had to walk several miles before reaching a village, but surely not so long, and their return would have been much more rapid in a vehicle. So I waited for the sounds of a motor in the night, but I heard only the crashing of the surf and the chatter of my comrades.

The night was mostly still. Eddies of wind disturbed the fire, but it was a dark, oppressive night. There were no stars and the sky felt like a great weight upon us. It was oppressive and it was cold. The moon was a hidden patch of light without definition in the west. There was going to be a storm soon, before morning. We would need to have shelter before then. Where were Terry and John?

We had no means of telling the time, for wrist watches were fairly useless articles to space travellers, but it must have been about midnight by my estimation, about five hours after our arrival at the beach, when I decided too long had elapsed. Even Barry had volunteered the remark that the two crewmen had been gone a long time. 'And it's going to rain,' he added.

We decided to leave the beach then to find some sort of shelter. One of us would have to remain behind to await the return of Terry and John, and Lucky volunteered. We left him lying stretched out beside the fire, his head upon his rolled-up jacket. 'Bring a car for me,' he called out as we left him, 'I don't feel like walking.' Even then we have no premonition. My thoughts of danger were only of my crewmen.

We followed their tracks from the beach. That was easy enough, for the terrain was quite wild, covered in dense shrubbery—thistles mainly, and bramble bushes; but there were other shrubs, too, such as oleander and privet growing rank and untouched, so that it was difficult to trace a pathway. We must have landed on the wildest part of the coast. But Terry and John had forced their way through and our following behind them must have been a little easier. After about half a mile we came to the ruins of a roadway that had clearly been unused for many years. We wondered about that and our unease began to grow. Barry was scowling in unvoiced puzzlement. Pip had to voice his: 'What the hell has happened to this place?'

No one offered a reply and we continued on our way, unsure, on the road surface, whether or not we were following the same track as the crewmen. In places the weeds had almost succeeded in concealing the road, and in several spots the roots of trees had lifted the surface completely. It had been a standard macadam type of road without kerbing and, judging by its width, must have been at least a secondary highway at some time in its past. Why had it fallen into disuse? I suppressed my increasing apprehension at the strange desolation to voice a more immediate concern.

'There's no evidence that John and Terry came this way,' I said. 'It's possible they went in the other direction when they reached the road. Should we go back?'

'I think shelter is what we need most right now,' suggested Paul, 'and, if I'm not mistaken, that's a barn just ahead of us.'

There was indeed the bulk of a large shed-like building less than fifty yards away and we went towards it. It had once been an iron structure, with steel portal frames and sheet-iron cladding, but the sheeting now was little more than tatters of rust and the frame was so corroded that the whole edifice was in danger of collapse. The wind was now beginning to gust in warning of a much stronger blow to come and it was making the derelict building creak and rock alarmingly. Still, we approached the doorway in some curiosity, as if we expected some revelation in response to our questions. All we received was the menace of a dog aggressive in defence of territory. It was not a big dog, just a scrawny, dug-hanging bitch, but she bared her teeth and snarled, legs stiff and a raised mane of hair down her back. By the condition of her dugs it was clear that she had pups within and we willingly gave way to her territorial claim. We went on our way. That initial confrontation with hostility should have been a portent, but we did not see it as such. Yet even if we had, I fail to see how it would have affected our immediate behaviour.

Our next halt was at a row of cottages which had obviously not been inhabited by human beings for a long, long time. The gardens were tangles of matted vegetation; tree limbs grew through window openings; the roofs were overgrown with moss and grass. Yet they were of brick construction so had withstood the ravages of time and weather far better than the barn. They looked weatherproof enough to afford us protection from the imminent storm. Already the rain had started, coming with the gusts of wind. We chose the nearest cottage and went in. We lost no time in lighting a fire from the decaying floorboards. The light from the flames revealed mazes of footprints in the thick layers of dust. Feline footprints for the most part, though there were also footprints of naked human feet. It seemed that the area had not been completely deserted by man. The place stank of cats. There were cobwebs everywhere, and huge black spiders skulked in corners. But at least it was dry and warm.

'I think I'll go back and get Lucky,' I said. 'We can't leave him outside with such a storm coming.' But I admit to some reluctance as I left that temporary haven and headed back down the road.

It had taken us a little over twenty minutes to reach the cottages from the beach. With the wind howling continuously now, pressing against my body, and the rain driving hard and stinging my face, it would probably take twice that long to return. It was pitch dark. I was soon wet through and shivering violently. But I thought of Lucky exposed on that beach and struggled grimly on. It was raining so hard it was quite impossible to detect our point of entry onto the road. Keeping to the left-hand verge I peered constantly through the blanket of rain. Surely I should have reached the point by now. Consciousness of my utter weariness came home to me. The toll taken by eight days of minimal sleep, sickness and exposure, plus the normal physical debility experienced by all astronauts upon return to Earth's gravity, had caught up with me. I knew that I was close to collapse, and that storm would have defied the strength of a fit and rested man. Where was that blasted opening?

At last I found it. Once within the undergrowth the wind was reduced considerably. Now half a mile due west. The rain teemed down. It seemed an eternity to the beach, but when I reached it I could barely see it. But the white froth of a demented surf and the sounds of a violent sea were plain enough. But where was the life raft? Had I struck the beach at a different point in the darkness? Should I turn north or south? There was no way of knowing. 'Lucky!' I called his name several times. 'Lucky! Lucky, where are you?' But my words were wind-wasted and futile. I decided to try a hundred paces north—I could hardly be further out in direction than that. If I did not locate him, I would return and go a hundred paces south. It took me perhaps five minutes to traverse the beach up and down. Nothing. No sign of Lucky or the raft. It was too dark to recognise any spot and the wind had long since destroyed all trace of our intrusion in the sand. It was possible that Terry and John had come back from another direction and the three of them had headed for their own shelter. I might have missed them by a few feet in the blackness of the storm. But the life raft should still be there. It had been pegged down securely and should not have blown away. I struggled on further south, then north again. Exhaustion was a weight on my plodding feet. The shivering was constant. I searched for what must have been half an hour and finally came to the conclusion that the raft had blown away after all and Lucky had left with Terry and John.

By this time I was virtually strengthless. The continual battering of the wind and the ceaseless rain had defeated me. I stumbled back towards the road, falling over more than once and lying with my face in wet mud, unwilling to move. But the shivering would become worse and I would force myself to my feet once more and forward again on reluctant legs and with an even more reluctant mind.

I found the road again at a different point and had to crash through a hedge to reach it. I fell into a ditch on the other side. I remember lying in icy water wondering if I would drown if the level of the water rose. That was my last coherent thought of that night although I must have dragged myself from the ditch some time before the morning.

I regained consciousness in the early hours. It was dawn. A red sky, grey clouds lurking in the sunrise and I was lying on the road. Paul was leaning over me, examining me. Above him were the concerned faces of Pip and Barry. Pip's bald scalp was bleeding from a number of deep scratches. There were dried bloodstains across his brow where he had rubbed them. I was aching all over, soaked through and shivering still. 'You're okay,' Paul said.

I did not feel at all okay, but he was the expert. He helped me to my feet. I felt weak and found it difficult to think clearly. Paul said: 'You'll get a bitch of a cold out of this.'

I nodded and asked Pip: 'What happened to you?'

'I was attacked by a bloody cat!' he scowled.

'A cat?'

'Yes, a cat.' It appeared that the cottage we had chosen to spend the night in had been the lair of a wild cat which, returning home in the early hours of the morning, had promptly sprung upon the fire-bright scalp of the sleeping scientist. Pip had awakened in something of a fright and had had to wrench the creature from his head. It had immediately returned to the attack and Pip had had to kill it. 'Which was no easy matter, believe me,' he muttered, 'it was the most ferocious cat I've ever met. And all these baboons could do was have hysterics. You would have thought grown men would have more control.'

Barry smiled again at the memory. He said: 'It wasn't till the cat arrived that we realised you hadn't come back. We all flaked out, I'm afraid, and just fell asleep.'

'We came as soon as we realised you hadn't returned,' added Paul.

'What happened to you?' Pip asked.

'Well, I couldn't find Lucky in the storm and I must have

lost my way on the path back. We'd better go and see if we can discover what happened to him now that it's light. I suspect that Terry and John must have collected him before I arrived. They must have gone north. I couldn't find the life raft, though. It either blew away or I missed it.'

We were soon back at the beach at the exact spot where we had anchored the raft, easily relocated in the daylight. It had gone, but the stakes that had pegged it down were still embedded in the sand.

'It wasn't blown away by the wind,' remarked Barry solemnly, 'or there would be tatters of cord still hanging on the stakes. It must have been untied and carried away.'

'Who would have done that?'

'The rescue team, perhaps. Look, there's a lump in the sand there. I bet it's a message from them under a stone.' Barry bent down and brushed the sand away from the lump.

He did not say anything. There was no gasp, no exclamation. He simply remained still, his hand not moving from the thing. Pip said: 'Oh, my God!'

I felt sick.

Barry moved at last. With the same hand that touched the thing, with visible self-control, he grasped the hair of Lucky's head and lifted it free. Of the body there was no sign. He placed it gently on the sand. It was a mutilated thing, the ears and the nose cut from it and the eyes missing. There were great slashes across the face as if whoever had done the deed had hacked at it rather wildly. The stump of the neck was a shredded mess.

It was still just recognisable as Lucky's head. A gold tooth glittered in the morning sun.

'One trusts they killed him first,' said Barry.

'What sort of world have we come back to?' muttered Paul.

I just stood there in total emptiness, staring at the thing on the sand, and the emotion that finally came was guilt. It had been my responsibility to ensure the safety of my crew and comrades. It had been my carelessness that had caused Lucky to die. I could not have known. That was my excuse, but it was not enough. The thought came also, that Terry and John must have suffered a similar fate or they would have returned before now. We had been ashore less than twelve hours and already our numbers were down to four. Barry must have sensed something of my thoughts, for he touched me on the shoulder and said very gently: 'Don't blame yourself, Captain. The world is obviously a very different place from the one we left. You were not to know.'

'We can at least give what's left of his head a decent burial,' I said.

Chapter Two

The village looked just like any other in this part of France. There were more crows perched on the roofs, perhaps; the road was broken and rubbish littered the streets, although we were not to learn this until later. We had hidden ourselves in an old mill on a hill about a mile away, viewing with cautious and wondering eyes the cluster of once-white cottages and the single tall-spired church that had formed the community. The fields around were mere thickets of thistles and bramble patches with, here and there, little oases of green corn. It must have been summer, although it was really too cold, the sun not exposed at all in a saturated sky.

We had headed north after the discovery of the butchery on the beach, and then east at some crossroads. We had become not only extremely wary, but totally puzzled. There was little sign of animal life on that first day, just many birds, easily alarmed, but once the still smoking embers of a campfire. That made us proceed with even greater caution, keeping to the hedgerows and skulking like fugitives along the ditches. We were unarmed, not even a knife between us, and we were unwilling to share the fate of Luciano. When we saw the village ahead of us from the top of the hill on which stood the old mill, we felt a great reluctance to approach it. It was Barry who suggested that we remain in the mill for a time while we kept the village under surveillance. It was an ideal spot for such a purpose.

Other than safety, our most pressing need was for food, but Paul was also anxious to obtain drugs, particularly for me as I was already feeling the effects of my night-time ordeal. I was feverish and had a pounding headache, presaging a virulent attack of the common cold. We took the precaution of scouting about the vicinity of the mill prior to our occupation but it was totally deserted. It was actually a ruin, but it did offer some protection from the elements when the rain came again, and that prospect was clearly imminent. But its greatest asset was the boost it gave to our jaded sense of security. We had territory, we had a defined spot on the face of the land, a base. Our initial apprehension had increased to alarm; unnamed fears, magnified spectres, flitted and loomed in our imaginations. Lucky's shredded throat was still vivid and startling in our minds.

To say the mill was totally deserted is not strictly accurate. It was a haven for rats—great grey scurrying shapes, bold, aggressive and numerous. Our few hours' stay there was not pleasant. We must have killed a hundred of them, but this seemed to make little appreciable difference either to their numbers or their aggressiveness. We had to perch ourselves on rotten beams to avoid them, and even then, occasional ones would climb up to attack us so that we had to kick them off. They were tenacious beasts—it was not easy to dislodge them. It was as if they had no fear of humans, as if their species had unlearned any innate wariness of mankind. They were certainly the boldest and most hostile rats any of us had ever experienced.

Yet that time in the mill served to provide us with our first clues to the sort of world we had come back to. They were our last hours of innocence. From that time we had to face the reality of a new social order for which we had no training at all. We could see people in the village, and it was the sight of them that increased our apprehension as well as strengthening our resolve to be cautious. They were not people from an age of technology. They were primitives, people of a Cro-Magnon age, dressed in untanned hides, with naked chests, untrimmed shaggy faces, necklets of animal teeth, crude spears; no bows, no steel weapons, just carved wood and bone. If it were not for the houses of the village with here and there a television aerial still attached crookedly to a roof, we could have been watching an encampment of our very own ancestors. They wore no footwear of any sort and, in spite of the unkindness of the elements, on that day all the children were stark naked. We could see no sign of the stolen life raft among them nor any indication of the presence of our two comrades. All we could deduce was that something

26

quite incomprehensible had happened to this part of the world, some odd reversal of evolution, and even Barry was unwilling to hazard a guess at its nature. 'Wild dogs, wild cats, wild rats, and now wild men,' was his only comment.

'Everything that we've met since we landed has been hostile,' said Paul.

'We don't know that those people are hostile,' replied Pip. 'They are not necessarily the group that murdered Lucky.'

'I don't think we'll take that risk,' I said. 'We'll stay here and just observe for a while.'

It was soon apparent that the village was not the permanent home of the people there. The women were gathered and busy around a fire lit in the middle of the main street. They were scraping hides and making spears while the children collected firewood by the simple method of breaking up the floors and walls of the cottages. The toddlers played in the street, never far from the women. The men sat idle most of the time, perhaps whittling away at a stick. Occasionally one would wander about the village, always carrying his weapons, one spear in his hand and others slung across his back. Soon after midday the women threw water on the fire and we watched them rake out large stones from the centre of it, and then beneath that the carcass of some animal, possibly a pig or a sheep. The tribe ate. We counted about twenty-five adults, nine of whom were men. It was painful to watch them eat. Our own stomachs were aching at the sight and our mouths were dry with longing. That roasted meat, with the fat dripping from savage hands and teeth tearing great mouthfuls from the flesh, looked so tantalising, so succulent, that we could almost smell it. We could only watch and drool.

The light was weak in the mill. My comrades were just dark shapes bulked about me. Barry stomped a rat's head against a beam. Pip was intent on watching the activities of the savages. He licked his lips for the hundredth time. I remember sneezing and my head wanting to burst apart. After some time the village slept; even the children were somnolent after that meal.

It began to rain.

'I'm going down there,' decided Barry.

'No, at least wait till it's dark,' I exclaimed.

27

'They won't see me, not in this rain,' he declared. 'They're all asleep anyway. We must have food of some sort, even if it's only a few apples. I can see some trees down there and there should be fruit on them at this time of the year. I dare say there's even some wild vegetables in those gardens.'

I was not up to argument. 'Well, be careful,' I insisted. 'Those people are clearly not bound by our social considerations. Just remember Lucky.'

'I'll remember,' he said grimly.

'I'll come with you,' Pip volunteered. Barry nodded and the two of them slid to the floor. Kicking rats aside as they ran out, they were soon lost to sight in the blurring rain.

'And then there were two,' muttered Paul.

'They'll be back, never fear,' I reassured him. 'Barry is as indestructible as a mountain.'

'Just like Lucky,' he murmured.

The rain grew steadily heavier. The village was no more than a grey blur, a group of murky silhouettes just within our scope of vision, the church steeple clearer than the rest, rising like a great sword from a lake of shadows. The mill was far from water-tight, and we shifted several times trying to find a spot free from the constant drips. I finally wedged myself against a post, hooked one arm around it and allowed my legs to hang free on either side of a beam. Paul found himself a similar spot a few yards away. Fortunately the rain had forced the rats into shelters of their own and for the moment we were free of them. I suppose two hours went by. I slipped into a sort of coma of sniffling misery, shivering and sneezing and aching—whether from the oncoming cold or from the discomfort of my perch I do not know. I believe my spirits were at as low an ebb then as during all the months that followed.

I heard voices. I must have slept. Barry and Pip had returned. The rain was then a solid curtain of water. I was quite amazed that the two scientists had managed to find their way back in such weather. They were to continue to amaze me in the future. They were saturated.

'I'm going to have you all down with pneumonia at this rate,' grumbled Paul, but his smile was one of relief. Their spoils from the expedition were meagre. A dozen undernourished potatoes, a scrawny rabbit that they had forced a hawk to release, already half disembowelled, and an axe head so corroded it was only just distinguishable as such.

'Light a fire, quickly,' said Paul. 'Let's get you dry and I'll cook us a stew with that little lot.'

'One fire coming up,' cried Pip, water dripping from him all over the place, but his spirits undampened. He began to peel off boards from the very structure of the building. It could have collapsed about us at any moment but no one stopped him. In fact Barry began to assist him with considerable vigour while Paul worried away at a dome-shaped piece of machinery that would serve as a pot. I just sneezed and ached and shivered in my personal misery. But the fire helped and a semblance of interest in life did return to me as it blazed and the food was pitched into the makeshift cauldron. Paul braved the rain to gather some nettles which he added to the stew, despite our grimaces.

'Good for you,' he said. 'It's the only medicine I have.' Soon it was done. The rats were scurrying around in the gloom of corners, but the fire kept them at bay. We could see their eyes glittering all about us. It was of no importance. Nothing mattered, only that soup. We took it off the fire. It would take some minutes to cool. The aroma wafted about our nostrils, and the saliva ran in anticipation. We were never to eat it.

'Don't move, Captain,' cried Pip suddenly, 'there's someone right behind you.'

Even as he spoke I knew the truth of it. My crawling neck sensed the presence before my mind did. I felt sweat trickle down my back. Whoever it was was very close to me. Something touched my shoulder. I jerked. Impossible to control that instinctive reflex. It was the fire-hardened end of a wooden spear. I turned my head slowly and looked up. I saw a filthy hairy face. Two sardonic eyes; they were golden in the firelight. I had a sense that there was more of curiosity in them than hostility. He had lean, muscled shoulders. And there were four more shadows in the gloom. I remembered Lucky's grisly death and every sinew of my body tensed. I was afraid, afraid with a fear born of a hovering vision of an eyeless head; a fear born from the thousand unanswered questions we had asked ourselves, the unknown, phantoms from the darkness of the days of caves. But this was no phantom despite the absolute soundlessness of his approach. This scornful, arrogant head was the head of a man, and my fear was soon more of a cold anger, an emotion under control. I would sell my life dearly. My head would cost his life.

The mill was full of men. They were all around us. I turned back to the fire, reached in and picked up a brand. Then I stood up holding the flame high. Turning round I counted them. Nine. There had been nine men in the village. Clearly we had underestimated their alertness. '*Bonjour,*' I said as amicably as my weeping nose permitted.

The one who had touched me with his spear raised the weapon and held its point a few inches from my stomach. I bent my arm so that the firebrand fell slightly towards him. We stood thus for a minute in silence. Only the sputters of the crumbling fire disturbed the hush. I looked at a strong and handsome face. About thirty years old, I guessed, though we were to learn that their apparent ages were deceptive. He was hard, thin lipped, without fear. Not as tall as I, but strong. Strong and young and unflinching.

Then Barry was beside me. He folded his hand around the spear. The man thrust. His shoulder lurched, knotted veins and muscles like ropes. The spear barely moved. Barry's arm was like a rock. Then his other hand grasped the spear and he snapped it like a twig. Barry dropped the pieces on the floor. And the savage did a foolish thing, a deed of extraordinary courage or extraordinary arrogance. He sprang at the scientist. Barry's speed was astonishing, even to me who knew him well and knew of the athletic prowess of his younger days. He bent low and caught the fellow by the leg. His great arms heaved. In an instant the savage was swept off his feet and raised high in the air, and Barry held him there. The savage remained still. Below him the fire crackled. The other eight men stood silent, just watching, still encircling us but making no move. The moments of tension stretched. Heartbeats echoed in the stillness. Beyond, the eyes of the rats were intense, glittering in the glow of flame.

Barry looked up calmly at his captive. '*Comment vous appelez-vous?*' he asked. The response was a grunt. Impossible to tell if he had understood. Then he began to talk, a torrent of words, almost comprehensible, almost standard French, but we did not understand it. The other savages knelt then, slowly, first one then another, and they bowed their heads and pushed their spears harmlessly in front of them. Barry lowered his captive, landing him on his feet. The fellow looked at the big man. There was puzzlement in his eyes, some animosity still, but above that there was a respect. The tension had gone. We all realised instinctively that there was no more immediate danger. The savage said something that could have been: '*Venez!*', and he led the way out into the rain.

'I think we should go with him,' said Barry, and we all followed him out. Pip stooped to pick up the axe head. The eight other savages brought up the rear. I stopped to look back once, my training exerting a reluctance to leave a burning fire unattended in a building. But immediately I consciously quelled the habits born of another age, another order. It was my first step in entering a new world, a world of a different ethic, of a different morality. I allowed the fire to burn. The soup bowl was overturned and lumps of rabbit lay on the floor. Rats were already squabbling over them.

Chapter Three

Another fire. Flames leaping up as high as a man. Faces all around. Eyes dreaming. Thirty savages and four space-age men returned from the stars. It was three weeks later. Night. There was no village here, just heath and the night sky. And the fire. It was a warm night, yet there was a fire. There was always a fire. The night was vast beyond the plains and the men were near. We were disturbingly aware that there were women near, too. All around us there were golden, grime-streaked skins, nipples violet and pimpled in the ceaseless flicker, shaggy heads, the odour of unwashed hair, sweat-drenched hides, and the stale blood of slaughtered beasts. Conversation was limited. There were grunts and coughs, but little laughter. They were a singularly grim people. Suited to their way of life, admirably so, but melancholy. We were living in a neolithic culture, surviving on wild fruits and the spoils of the hunt. The game was domestic cattle gone wild, horses and pigs and sheep, and also deer. They were excellent hunters with their simple weapons. They dug pits, built traps, snared rabbits and fished with spears. They had no concept of fishing lines, nor of bows and arrows. They had no realis-ation of the potential of horses other than as a source of meat, and not favoured for that. It was as if all technological expertise had been erased from human culture, and was beginning again at the very elementary stage.

We soon learned to speak their language. It was really only a much simplified and distorted version of the French we knew, but simple as it was, it was adequate for their needs. Complex communication was not necessary in their life-style. This consisted almost entirely of hunting and chores connec-ted with it: the making of spears and snares and the digging of traps. It was raw subsistence living; life's only concern seemed to be the obtaining of food. We were to learn that

that was not the whole truth, but those first weeks revealed no other prospects in their existence. They carried fire with them, but they could make it rather arduously when necessary by means of striking flints together and assiduously blowing on the sparks as they fell onto dry leaves. We still had matches but reserved them for our own future use. The man Barry had overpowered in the mill was their leader. His name was Oa. The men of the tribe were all closely related, for it was really an extended family group, and most of the women were also part of the clan, but some of them were from other tribes, apparently captives. We learned later that there were several similar clans in the neighbourhood and the territories of each were clearly defined. Defined but not always respected, especially when a tribe was following game. Such trespass frequently resulted in conflict. There was no friendliness between the various tribes at all. In fact it appeared that they were in a perpetual state of hostility, and the stealing of women from each other was common practice. But we were yet to learn all that. Our initial stay with Oa's tribe was peaceful if not exactly idyllic.

As our skill with their language increased, we questioned them on the death of Lucky, but it was clear that they were not responsible. That area was not within their territory. It was the domain of a tribe they called the 'Mekans'. They also knew nothing of my missing crewmen.

Our position in the tribe was never clear-cut. We were tolerated and fed, and allowed to sit around the campfire, yet we were not accepted as guests. It seemed really that we were captives; rather free captives, but not free enough to leave them of our own free will. Our wanderings, of casual intent on our part, were restrained not with direct use of threat but with a sort of implied menace. When we drifted too far in their eyes, or at least in Oa's eyes, one of the men would come and hover about us, his spear looking anxious in his hand. We did not challenge that in the early weeks. We had decided between ourselves that we needed to learn as much as we could of the society we found ourselves in before making our own way within it. In truth I do not think they really knew what to make of us. Our clothes were strange. Our speech was different. We made new and awesome weapons. Oa was

33

wary of us. We often caught him looking at us strangely. For our part we did not know his reasons for constraining us, but it was quite obvious he put some value upon our presence.

Barry had fitted a handle to the axe head and had sharpened it into a worthwhile tool—a far superior tool to their axes of stone and bone. We found lots of rusty metal, ploughshares, engine blocks, girders, railway lines and the like, and we built a huge fire in an oven fashioned from rocks. Then, with the aid of bellows made from cowhide and wood, we had a forge. Barry was the epitome of a blacksmith. He would stand for hours wielding the back of his axe as a hammer, remoulding the rusty steel into other axe heads, and hammers and knives. The picture is still clear. A giant of a man, black with hair and smoke. Naked to the waist, a massive body, steel being moulded by muscle and mind. Sweat streaming off him, his eyes glistening, white teeth in a constant grin born of strain and striving. The greatest scientific brain of his nation; an astronaut; a blacksmith.

We made bows, too. Spears were too clumsy for our sophisticated minds. They made no attempt to copy us. They had no reason to, their success with their own familiar weapons was far greater than ours with our new devices. Pip once managed to shoot a wild chicken, and I shot a rabbit after four hours of stalking. We had much to learn.

We had stayed in three other villages besides the first. They had all been looted long before and there was little left from the civilised world that we could have used other than the dwellings themselves. We needed to get to larger settlements, a city such as Bordeaux, which we knew could not be too far away. We reasoned that if John and Terry still survived, that would be where they would head for. The tribe cared little for the villages except as sources of easy fuel after rain, and it was only after rain that they went to them. Paul had been disappointed in not finding any drugs that he could use, but he had an encyclopaedic memory of medical lore and amongst his vast store of knowledge was the understanding of herbal remedies. In a way he welcomed the opportunity to put such erudition to good use. Yet he still expressed the hope that we would find modern medicines when we finally got to Bordeaux. Bordeaux became a sort of goal in our thoughts, almost the be-all and end-all of our confused aspirations at that time. We discovered by careful questioning that there was a 'big village' in the territory of their neighbours, the Mekans, but Oa's people never went there. To them it was an evil place, and they could tell us little of it. It was apparently some thirty miles to the west. After three weeks with Oa's tribe we decided to go there.

Unfortunately we could not just up and leave unless we were prepared to do battle. And we were not. We desired neither to risk our own lives nor to place any threat upon the lives of Oa's people. We decided that guile was preferable to force.

After fifteen years in space, the women of the tribe appeared utterly desirable. They were lithe and strong, with quite beautiful bodies for the most part, perhaps inclined to be more rounded in the stomach than our twentieth century tastes preferred, and the breasts of the older ones tended to sag onto their bellies, but actually there were not many older women in the group. That puzzled us a bit. The men, too, were all seemingly less than forty, certainly all younger than us, but that could be readily understood, whereas the dearth of mature women seemed to be without reason. Most of the women were probably under thirty, with golden skins and naked breasts, big hipped, and to women-starved men as we were, quite delightful.

There were two who were really exceptional and would have been so in any society. One was a wife of Oa (he had several), and her name was Lian. She had a young child still nursing at her breast; hair long and straight and fair. She was statuesque in her pride and her womanhood. A deceptive impression indeed. Her face was striking: full lips, a large mouth, but with narrow cheeks and prominent bones; and eyes very large. Brown eyes they were, with unwavering, unfathomable looks. She never spoke for she had no tongue. I learned later that Oa had cut it out when he had captured her in order to stop her screaming. She hated him, that was very clear. Oona was younger than Lian, one of the tribal group. Perhaps sixteen then. She was smaller than the average girl of her age, and slimmer in the hips than most, but she was a truly lovely creature. Shy eyes; a pointed delicate chin;

small and smiling mouth; dark hair that curled around her ears and rambled across her shoulders, uncombed and unwashed as was all their hair. They all had long hair. They all had big feet and work-hardened hands. And they were all submissive, even Lian in her hate; they had to be in their society. Yet they sang and chattered and loved their children as women have always done. We thought that they were almost like slaves, but they had a great deal of freedom, and although they were beaten on occasions, their men mostly treated them with kindness.

We desired them. Barry grew veritably dreamy over Oona. But we were never permitted opportunities to be alone with them and they were abruptly scolded if we merely attempted conversation with them. Pip did try to get one of them alone one night and there was an angry scene. Pip apologised and pretended innocence but the women was still beaten by her man. In order to avoid friction we determined to restrain our urges for the moment.

Barry's efforts at the forge soon had us equipped with a steel knife each and an axe. We also made ourselves a bow each and a quiver full of arrows. We adopted the practice of carrying them about with us as part of our dress. And so the first three weeks passed. We were as far south and west as the tribe permitted themselves to wander. We would never be closer to Bordeaux. It was time for us to depart.

The fire cast strange shadows over Pip who sat at right angles to me, his jacket pulled around his shoulders for it was cold at our backs. His bald head was patterned in flickering reflections of the flames, his eyes just smudges, his nose changing shape constantly in the alternating pattern of light. His beard was a black beast hanging from his face. Barry sat beside him. They were always together. Inseparable. They had long been friends, but it seemed that the present circumstance had made them even closer. Barry was speaking.

'There is no evidence of any nuclear fallout,' he intoned. The most marvellous man that I ever knew, but he sometimes spoke as if he were giving a lecture. Still, I listened. I was opposite him, next to Oa. Oa had singled me out as the leader of our small band and so accorded me special privileges. Just behind him, and behind me also, sitting on her calves between our shadows, was his favourite wife of the moment, Lian. I was acutely conscious of her presence. I could smell her and it excited me. A part of her, probably her knee, though it may have been her hand, was touching my thigh. I knew no part of her was touching Oa. Even in the relaxation of the fire she shrank from him. I tried to think of my wife. That was no help at all, so I concentrated on Barry's discourse. 'I observe no evidence of mutation in any man or beast or any plant. It is true that most living things have reverted to a wild state, including our own species, but to claim a nuclear cause for such a condition cannot be supported by the visual evidence. It is worth noting that the villages we have come across so far, though in ruins for the most part, are only so because of disuse, not in any way due to war damage, nuclear or otherwise. No, we have to discount the "bomb" theory for the current state of affairs. A world thus destroyed would still retain a certain degree of technological inheritance—the wheel for instance, the use of metals, oral traditions, religion, the domestication of animals, any number of facets. Here we have nothing at all, not even the beginnings of scientific knowledge, elementary mathematics, nor the use of script. They cannot even make a clay pot. It's as if man was evolving all over again. It is most intriguing.'

'But we have only touched a small part of France,' I put in. 'That doesn't mean the whole world is the same.'

'I think we must assume that it is. If any other portion of the Earth had retained twentieth century culture the present state of France would not have been possible. Sea and air travel would soon have revealed the conditions here to a more advanced culture and they would have been intruded upon. We have a culture here that has obviously had no contact at all with what we call civilisation.'

'That doesn't necessarily indicate that all existing cultures are as primitive as this one.'

'Oh no. But it would seem that whatever remnants of civilisation still exist elsewhere in the world, their technology doesn't include the means of sea travel. That would make it quite primitive, wouldn't it?'

I remained quiet. I was reluctant to accept that idea at that time. It meant that all I had held dear, all that I had loved on

Earth, had vanished. It seemed inconceivable then, in spite of the fact that I was living in a Magdalenian level of culture. Still I hoped that my own country might have been different. It was Paul who spoke. He said: 'You build quite a powerful hypothesis on rather slight evidence, I believe. These are very aggressive people. Perhaps they have resisted intrusion often enough and successfully enough to discourage it.'

'The North American Indians were a war-like people,' commented Barry drily. 'It didn't help them. Look at it this way: anything other than what I have suggested would mean that this state of primal being is only an isolated case, perhaps just on the European continent, or maybe retained within geographical boundaries. But does that really stand up to examination? All right, so we have made quite an assumption based on the little knowledge we have, and it may turn out that that assumption is wrong. But it won't be far wrong. We might as well accept the fact that we are going to have to live amidst this sort of culture until we die.'

So it was said. For the first time we had mutually faced the only prospect for our future. And I found it a most unattractive prospect indeed, one that drained my soul, that agitated my mind so much it was difficult to hold on to any clarity of thought. I turned and looked at Lian. Her face was shadowed by the bulk of Oa. She leaned forward slightly so that the firelight reflected in her eyes and a dappled glow flickered across her face. She smiled, but Oa moved and she jerked back. I looked away. If one possessed a woman like Lian, the prospect might seem somewhat less dismal.

'That doesn't mean that *we* have to live in this primitive fashion, though, at least I hope not,' said Paul. 'Surely we can re-establish a more civilised life in one of the villages.'

'Perhaps,' murmured the big man. 'Yes, perhaps we can.'

'It's nearly time to go,' I said. Our plans had been well discussed and it was time to set them in motion. A guard was posted every night, although it was unlikely to be specifically for our benefit. Looking back now from a more experienced viewpoint, one can see that such a precaution was vital to the continued welfare of the tribe. Yet it was essential for our purposes that the guard was not aware of our departure. We had determined that violence was to be avoided at all costs.

This meant that the fellow had to be put to sleep, for their night-time senses were far more acute than ours. That night the sentry was one known as Yog, the only one of the savages with whom any of us had managed to become even slightly friendly. Paul had treated an ulcer on Yog's leg that had been bothering him for weeks, using a sticky herbal preparation which, in spite of a foul smell, had cleared up the sore within a few days. Paul had continued to cultivate Yog and had encouraged an evening habit of sharing an apple with him. This was easily achieved for Yog was a simple fellow. Our plans were quite uncomplicated. Yog would be given a compound to induce sleep previously injected into the apple. Fortunately Paul still had some small quantities of drugs in the tiny kit he had brought with him from the spaceship and one or two syringes, so that part of the operation presented no difficulties.

'Okay, Paul,' I nodded at the doctor. It was time to put 'Operation Snow White' into effect.

Paul stood up and yawned carelessly. He wandered over to where Yog lay stretched on the ground resting in preparation for his night's vigil. Paul squatted beside him. We could hear them murmuring together. I could not see them but Pip told me: 'Paul is cutting the apple now. I trust he will give Yog the correct half.' Already some of the tribe were leaving the fire and curling up in their animal skins. They would sleep instantly, we knew that. Barry curled up next, then Pip. Oa had already left, taking Lian with him. Soon I was alone at the fire. I shifted slightly, to be able to see Paul and Yog chatting together. I listened to the sounds of the fire, of dogs barking across the heath, an owl hooting somewhere quite close, and nearer still the dark, sobbing sounds of Oa and Lian grunting together in the darkness. I felt an ache then, a sad and heavy pain, and I felt an unreasonable resentment, too. In my mind I could see Lian's eyes, looking at me and asking me something. Asking what? There was a strong feeling within me that I did not want to leave her. I recognised its futility.

Paul came up to me. 'Yog is asleep. He won't wake up for four or five hours. We can leave as soon as you give the word.'

'Soon,' I said. All was quieter now. Oa and Lian would be

39

asleep already. There were other scuffles behind me. Another couple mating in their rudimentary fashion. It would soon be over, their couplings were very brief. We waited another thirty minutes, silent, watching the fire die down and the grey-bearded embers slowly disintegrate deep down in the heat. There were no more human sounds. I touched Paul's arm and we crept over to Pip and Barry. They were awake, waiting for the signal. There was no need for words. I led the way from the encampment. Soon we were far enough away to stand tall and breathe free. Thirty miles to Bordeaux. With luck and finding a road that led there we should reach it before dawn.

'I'll never make it,' cried Pip. 'I've got holes in my socks. Barry, you'll have to carry me.'

'I'll put you in my pocket,' laughed the big man. They were incongruous as they stood there joking, close to the diamond-studded night with the hesitant dark about, the giant bulk of Bartholomew Mann and little Philip Quincey-Jones; incredible men, scientists out of their niche, and adapting, and taking joy in that adapting. I loved them both. Their loss is an agony to me, even now.

Barry took out his false teeth and slipped them into his pocket. 'Just in case Pip jumps in while I'm not looking,' he cackled. 'They'll bite him.'

'Come on, then,' I said. 'Let's get going.'

The road to Bordeaux was beneath our feet. How deeply I wish we had never taken it. But if we had not, events might well have followed a similar path. Looking back now I can see almost an inevitability about it all. We were aliens in our own world. We were to discover that expediency was to be the governing compulsion of our lives—in retrospective analysis, that was the real measure of our adjustment. The more relevant adaptation, that of becoming as the level of evolution dictated, we never really came to terms with. We were the products of an advanced culture, and perhaps there was no escaping that heritage. Now I see that clearly, but an earlier wisdom would not have made the slightest difference. Yet our night-time flight to Bordeaux was to have far more serious consequences than we could ever have envisaged. Consequences that remain as a guilt in my soul.

Our estimate of the distance to the city was fairly accurate, for we discovered a milestone within the first few miles at the junction of a side road onto a more major artery. It was a granite stone with the number '25' chiselled into its surface beneath the letter 'B'. We passed several villages which we negotiated with caution, but apart from once disturbing a pair of wild dogs which slunk away at our approach and in the same village hearing horses whinny within a hundred yards of our position, although we never saw them, we found all the one-time settlements deserted. Several hours before dawn we reached the outskirts of Bordeaux. Soon there were no more open fields, only a few patches of rank vegetation. There were rats here, and cats killing them, and there were birds twittering and fleas. We stopped to rest in one house. We were going to wait for daylight but the fleas forced us to move on. Paul muttered something about 'bubonic plague', so we carefully disposed of every flea we could find on our persons. But further on into the town there was less life; an occasional grey shape, a skulking dog, and high in the lightening sky the song of a bird, a nightingale I think, thrilling and gorgeous over the extinct city.

Our first impressions of the dawnlit streets were depressing. I do not know quite what we expected, but we had been buoyed up with undefined hopes that dragged behind us like shadows as we wandered through the lifeless alleys. It was a useless and pointless place, with useless and pointless buildings. Great red and grey buildings, cobwebbed in the rising mist; eyeless buildings, eyeless and earless, like a head in the sand. Soundless, so that our shuffling shoes echoed in dejection from indifferent concrete planes. This was a city of corrosion, a surrendered town. Once famed for its life and its colour and its music, now a gaunt and dreary emptiness. Yet it did live still. In patches there was rampant life. There was vegetation growing profuse and wild in areas that had been gardens, and there were parks that had become jungles. Geraniums grew in the gutters. Cobbles and paving stones were outlined in long, wild grass. And here and there were remains of burnt-out fires showing that Bordeaux was still an occasional habitat of man.

'This town's been dead a long time,' remarked Paul.

'Many decades, I'd say,' agreed Pip, kicking at a heap of rust that had once been a motor car, and peering down at the redness.

'At least a couple of centuries,' mused Barry. 'The buildings show considerable damage from the elements.'

Pip picked something out of the rust-heap. He held it up and examined it closely. Rubbing it on his clothes made it glisten. It was a gold ring with a diamond crown. 'Valuable, that,' he proclaimed, and with a titter he tossed it away. 'I always wanted to throw a thousand pounds away,' he said. He may have been clowning, but the sentiment was indicative of our situation. We were in the process of changing our values so completely that wealth as we had known it, and the symbols of wealth, were utterly meaningless. From now on only survival would matter.

We made our way to the waterfront. There were ships jammed in the waterways, not yet completely disintegrated, so great was the mass of metal in them. Barges sitting on the river bed. Gulls sitting on the derelicts. Gull droppings covering the rust with white scale, glistening in the climbing sun. The waters of the Gironde were blue—no oil, no scum, no foam of pollution. The wharves were succumbing to the attacks of time and tide; they were crumbling away, concrete eroding into the river. But they would stand for centuries more, guiding the stream as the mind of long-dead men had deemed desirable.

'A thousand years and it will all be gone,' said Paul. He was always the quietest of us, an observant, listening man, usually keeping his thoughts to himself. His voice was rather sad, as if he felt considerable regret to see these relics of a great technology vanish for ever.

Further along the river bank, where once had been an open park, was a strip of woodland, fairly new woodland, a pleasant place of young trees, grass and summer flowers. There was sycamore and hawthorn, young oaks, hazel and plane. There were also rabbits there, wild chickens, and ducks, too, sedate and unalarmed on the river. It seemed an ideal spot to set up a temporary base for our planned exploration of the city. Behind the copse was a row of tall buildings separated from the trees by a man-high brick wall fringed with broken glass, and between the wall and the buildings a narrow alley giving access to the rear entrances. The mortar in the wall had long since powdered so that removal of sufficient masonry to provide an easy entry to the copse was a simple matter. The buildings behind would serve as our base. They were all four to five storey structures of modern design, and most of them had barred entrances still stout enough to withstand the simple tools at our disposal. However, we found one that was open and entered with some excitement. It had been internally raped of its woodwork on the lower floors, including the lower flight of what had once been a magnificent cedar staircase.

The urge to explore was a powerful stimulus, although our primary requirement was sleep after our night's trek. Still, we felt it necessary to familiarise ourselves thoroughly with our immediate surroundings. We were in a block of offices that must have catered to discriminating and wealthy tenants. The bottom floor had been utterly stripped and there was little left there of timber material, doors and windows no longer existing, but as we climbed higher, having to negotiate the missing flight of stairs, the destruction wreaked by decades of scavengers became less and less. Higher up there were even remnants of carpet on the floors, but these disintegrated even as we stood on them. Timber furniture had been subject to insect attack but seemed still useful. All paper articles, and to our dismay this included books, had succumbed to the ravages of time. Insects had eaten them; mice had used them for nesting material; mould had attacked them. There was nothing there that we could read. Curtains over the windows were just rags. Telephones still hung on walls or were tumbled amid heaps of timber residue on the floors. There were locked safes, the alloy of their construction showing little signs of the passing years. We had no way of opening them nor any incentive to do so. On the top floor, the fifth, a steel ladder led to a skylight and the roof. We explored no further and returned to the second floor which commanded a wide view of the vicinity. I stood first watch and the others slept.

It was nearing the end of my term of sentry duty when I heard the voices. It was still morning. A slow scrutiny of the street revealed nothing. The voices continued, not continuously but at irregular intervals. I woke the others. 'I'm going down for a scout around,' I told them. 'The voices could be those of Terry and John.'

'Be careful!' The warning was sincere, but unnecessary. Any savages would have had no trouble discerning marks of our progress through the town. No doubt discovery of strange tracks could have led any local inhabitants straight to our hiding-place.

Outside the sun was high. It was nearly noon. I had left by the rear door, and I went up the alley to where it connected to the side street. I could not hear the voices from there. Cautiously I looked out and up the street. I saw them. At first I thought they were Oa's people, but there were too many of them and none that I recognised. This was a larger tribe than Oa's although much the same in their general appearance. There were women lighting a fire and men settling down to sleep in the shade. I noticed that one of them had a pair of human ears slung on a thong about his neck. There were bits of orange canvas decorating most of them. I felt a slow and deliberate anger rise in my gorge and made no attempt to suppress it. These were the murderers of Lucky Cragnolini. I had to count them, but it was impossible to see them all from my position. They did not seem alarmed. If they knew we were nearby, and surely they must, they were showing no concern for the moment.

I dropped onto my stomach and wriggled out of the alley to get a clearer view. A man I had not spotted stood not five yards away and he was looking straight at me. Equally startled, we stared at each other. He was very hairy; there was barely any face visible. A tall, lean man, probably blond, but he was so dirty one could not be sure. I wonder why I recall such a detail. His first reaction was to gape, as I'm sure I did. But his reflexes were incredibly swift, far faster than mine. He had reached over his shoulder and had a spear in his hand before I had quite recovered. I sprang to my feet and raced for my life back along that alleyway. It was fortunate that our refuge was not too far along it. Turning into the doorway I risked a glance behind me. He had not followed but was watching my every move while beckoning for his comrades. I paused, wondering momentarily if I should go elsewhere to divert them. A foolish thought. Already four others had joined him and were advancing down the alley. I went inside calling loudly for assistance to scramble up the missing flight of stairs.

Barry and Pip were already descending to meet me. Pip was fitting an arrow to his bow. 'Quick, Jeff!' cried Barry, throwing himself flat and extending a huge arm down to me. As I seized it and he hauled me up I saw Pip loose his arrow. Behind me there came a shriek of pain. I was up on the landing then. I turned round to see one of the savages with the arrow through the side of his face. It had hit him below the left eye and was projecting out of the left of his neck. He was staggering about, both hands held to his face, uttering little grunts of pain. I was elated. It was the fellow with Lucky's ears about his neck. The other savages had stopped behind him. There were looks of stupefaction on their faces. The speed of an arrow was a new thing in their experience. Their reflexes were so rapid, as we were to learn, that they had small trouble evading a hurled spear. We took advantage of the pause to retreat further up the staircase to a point where we had complete command of the only route of attack without being at all exposed. They must have realised this for that invulnerability was not tested. We waited. Paul came down with the information that the savages were grouped at both entrances.

'There is no way out,' he said.

'I suppose they could just sit and wait,' commented Pip. 'They could starve us out.'

'Hungry, are you?'

'Mildly. But if they intend a siege the present state of my stomach becomes irrelevant.'

However, the men of Bordeaux had no intention of waiting for hunger to shift us. Soon smoke began to billow up the stairwell. They had set fire to the place. As the smoke began to thicken we were forced to move upwards. Flames were beginning to follow the smoke. The staircase itself was alight. We retreated to the top floor. 'Out onto the roof,' I coughed. Barry led the way up the iron ladder and through the skylight. We lay flat on the roof for some minutes, trying to still betraying coughs and waiting for smarting eyes to clear. It was doubtful if the building would actually burn down, for there was not much inflammable material left within it. Yet without a staircase our descent was made very difficult. Once our aggravated lungs had returned to normal we rose and crossed without trouble to the adjacent roof. We recalled that all the buildings in the row had been secured against intrusion. 'Which means the wretches can't get in,' stated Pip, 'but it also means we can't get out.'

'The savages will probably assume we have perished in the fire,' I said. 'In that case they are unlikely to stay around too long.'

'I don't know that that reply is too satisfactory. It doesn't answer the main problem,' Pip responded. But in fact the last building in the row presented its own solution to the question of egress, for it had a steel fire escape attached to its rear wall. This was perilously corroded and in several places detached from the structure, but it was certainly a means of descent. Yet just then was not the time to use it. We entered that building through a penthouse door. It was gloomy within and it was not without trepidation that we groped our way into its dimness. Our eyes soon adjusted, though, and we crept down the central stairway realising that this building had remained quite undisturbed through the generations of neglect.

There were telephones on the walls, and while Pip elatedly rang the fire brigade to report the fire, as well as any other authorities he deemed it necessary to inform, the rest of us left him to his clowning to investigate our new retreat. We were to get to know this place very well, but on that first day we were filled with a sense of discovery, while outside the savages were screaming and yelling in great excitement at the fire, and presumably their assumed victory. It turned out that there was little of immediate value to be found. It had been an hotel. There were four floors and a basement, the upper three floors comprising the suites of which there were three to a floor, each with an attached bathroom luxuriously ap-pointed, the ceramic ware and brass fittings being little worse for the passage of time. The suites themselves retained pieces of furniture; there were some odd items of plastic compo-sition, some nonferrous metal articles of no use to us; there were some unbroken mirrors in which we were able to view

46

ourselves for the first time since leaving the spaceship. There were no surprises—we all knew what to expect of our own appearance from that of the others. We were ragged and hairy, much like the savages themselves apart from our manufactured clothes. We each had a hand-forged axe and knife in a cowhide belt, and carried a quiverful of arrows with a bow on our backs. Anything less like a band of astronauts it would be difficult to imagine.

The bottom floor consisted of an office, a bar still with a stock of liquor and wine, a dining-room and a kitchen. We moved about quietly so as not to reveal our presence to the shrieking wildmen outside. It seemed that we were safe for the time being. In the office Pip broke apart a large, once ornate desk. He discovered a number of deserted mouse's nests that had utilised every scrap of paper in the room, shredding it beyond any legibility, and a set of brass knuckle-dusters which prompted some speculative remarks upon the nature of the hotelier. There was also a revolver, rusted into a single lump of apparently homogeneous metal. But Pip toyed with it thoughtfully for some minutes before slipping it into his pocket. And there were skeletons, but surprisingly not as many as one would have supposed. Paul studied these with some care, hoping to find a clue to the manner of their death and the demise of modern man. But there was no indication of violence, no signs of radio-active decay, no bone-affecting disease. One or two of them had false teeth jammed askew in their skulls.

'You don't have to worry if you lose your teeth, Barry,' ribbed Pip, 'there's plenty of spares here.'

But Barry was musing along more serious lines. 'It appears evident that humanity never suffered a sudden all-encompassing annihilation,' he said. 'There are insufficient corpses to sustain that theory. It would seem that mankind was burying its dead right to the very end, whatever that end was. It suggests that the demise was a very gradual thing.' He volunteered no more then, and the discussion was not pursued.

The kitchen yielded some good bone-handled knives, and some oxidised but still serviceable cooking pots. Also crockery, for which modern products we felt a gratitude much greater than their material worth. Ours had been a world of invention and raw material up till then, and personally I was sick of drinking from a cowhide bag or from my cupped and usually unwashed hands. The basement was revolting. It had been inundated by storms in the past and the water had not drained away. It was stagnant and thick, like oil. Its odour was putrefying; we wasted no time searching it. By then I was feeling very weary, having had no sleep earlier in the day. We returned to the first floor to a suite that gave us a good view of the savages' activities, and prepared to resume our interrupted rest.

We noted that the excitement over the fire had subsided somewhat. The men were again inactive and the women were resuming their duties. I was fast losing interest as the need for sleep muffled all other considerations, although I did notice before curling up on a rather decrepit sofa, that the sky was starting to pile up with dark cumulus clouds, rapidly masking the sun. A rainstorm was only hours away. Barry elected to take the new watch.

Chapter Four

Despite my weariness, I only managed to doze fitfully for two or three hours. When I finally sat up the other two appeared to be still sleeping, Pip snoring with a subdued whistle, as I rose to my feet and joined Barry at the window. I studied the scene outside. The fellow Pip had shot was lying quite unmoving on the pavement. No one was paying him much attention, except an occasional child who would go over and gaze at him in curiosity. He was lying on his back and one could have assumed that he was dead, but his wound had hardly been fatal. The other men were sleeping in the shade, exactly as Oa's men would have been doing at that time of day. The women were not particularly active either; they were seated in a group partly hidden from us by an intervening corner. They seemed to be chatting and scraping hides, their perpetual chore. The imminent rainstorm clearly bothered them very little, but as their possessions were few and it was only a matter of moments to retreat to the shelter of a convenient building if they so wished, it really held no terrors for them. Oa's people seemed to sleep as easily in the rain as under cover and it had to be especially heavy or cold to make them seek shelter. Owing to the impossibility of seeing them all at once from our window we were still unable to obtain an accurate count of their numbers, but it looked as if there were about fifteen men and perhaps twenty women. There were also a large number of children including the unbearded youths, at least as many as the women. It was certainly a larger tribe than that of Oa. They were undoubtedly the Mekans.

'They've been like that for quite some time,' Barry told me. 'You didn't sleep long.'

'No.' I sat down beside him on the floor, my back to the wall.

'Worried, Captain?' The scientists had always called me 'captain' although I was actually a colonel.

'Of course. We have to eat.'

'Oh, they'll move off soon, I expect. It was our tracks that brought them here, presumably. Now, believing that they've disposed of us, they'll return to the countryside. They need to hunt.'

'How are we going to fit in to this culture, Barry?'

He shrugged. 'We are outsiders. Hunting people have never accepted strangers; they have an exaggerated territorial instinct. We shall never be accepted unless we can take over from their leaders.'

'The thought had occurred to me. But it could only be done with violence and death.'

Barry nodded. We were silent then. Some minutes passed without conversation. A thought of my wife crossed my mind. I remembered the ashes of love. Then I was thinking of Oa's wife, Lian. I permitted myself the indulgence of a dream. 'Do you ever think of your wife, Barry?'

'Not much.' I had known his wife and liked her. I had always believed that they had been well suited. I waited, expecting him to enlarge upon his reply, but he remained quiet, his blue eyes fixed in a stare at the blank wall opposite.

'And your daughter?' I prompted.

'They're dead!' he said shortly. 'Both of them. I have faced that fact.' And he stood up and walked away.

Paul was stirring. He came over and stood above me, watching the savages as I had done on waking. I thought of Paul's wife, but did not speak of her to him. I wondered, though, whether or not he ever gave her a thought. Probably not. Theirs had not been a happy marriage. She had been lovely once, tiny, blonde. I think her name was Tanya. I should remember. When I had met her their marriage was already beyond repair. She had lived in his house, but had not shared it with him, nor his bed when I met her. She had shared many beds, but not Paul's in the latter years. She had been a very unhappy girl, for the tragedy had been that she had continued to love him. I recall the time she had told me of her life with him. She had been drunk, of course, as she often was in those days. We were at a party. There had been many parties. She had been gay with a deliberate and determined gaiety. 'He is really quite wonderful,' she had said. 'He is never cruel, you know. He is really very kind. He doesn't mind that I drink. He gives me money. Lots of money. He is such a kind man.'

'But you don't love him?'

'Love!' She had laughed at that, gay of course, but disguising an emotional desperation that was revealed only in the glitter of her eyes and the tautness of her mouth. 'He is so damned superior. He is always so right, so bloody right, so bloody good at everything. Including loving!' she added through her teeth. I remember her swallowing her drink then in an ugly gulp. Some of it spilled from the corners of her lips. She licked at it, and I felt very sorry for her.

'Why don't you divorce him?'

'I've thought of it, often, believe me. But I suppose I'm never sober enough for long enough to carry on with it. And besides . . .' Besides I still love him. The drift into silence spoke the words louder than if she had uttered them.

'And he won't divorce you?' He certainly had grounds enough.

'Not him. He knows that it's cheaper to keep me as his wife than to pay alimony. I don't cost much.' It was a most unfair remark, not at all an accurate reflection of Paul's character.

Paul had happened to pass by us then. 'Making a play for Jeff?' he had called jokingly to her without stopping in the crowd. 'Good luck!' and he had moved on. And it had occurred to me with a certain degree of shock that he had not really cared at all. That evening ended with his wife alone with me, almost clotheless and embarrassingly attentive in my arms. She had been disgustingly drunk, and I remember the vomit stains on her chin. I also remember leaving her crying pitifully into her pillow. I had not known how to help her.

But I liked Paul. If he carried the sadness of her with him he did not show it. He was, as she had said, a very kind man. A gentle man. Very serious, sensitive, and quiet. We were to owe much to him in the coming years.

'Two newcomers have joined the group,' Paul informed us,

disturbing my reflections. 'They have a captive. By God! I think it's Opi.'

Barry came rapidly to the window as I stood up. It was Opi, all right, Oona's twin brother. 'How did they capture him?' Barry cried, quite concerned. I thought briefly of his attraction to the delightful Oona and understood his concern. 'Oa must have tried to follow us,' he answered his own question. 'They would never have taken the tribe by surprise.'

'Why would he have done that?' But no one had a reply to my question.

It must have been very close to evening then. It was falsely twilight with a very black sky and something wholly ominous about the scene. The boy—he was little more than that—had his arms lashed behind him and he was thrust to the ground. They clustered around him and he was hidden from our sight then for several minutes. We could see the tension of the mob about him. There were strain-filled faces, the bright and eager eyes of anticipation, the women jostling against the closing backs of the men. We could hear obliterated screaming. What were they doing to the lad? Then the suspended hush of ritual climax. A moment only. The crowd parted and we knew exactly what they had done to him. They held up the head of Opi, blood still gushing from the draining brains. That was how Lucky had died. For an instant horror gripped me, and it was not only the horror of the revolting deed that had just occurred, it was a premonition filling my soul so that I felt more sick with a terrible apprehension than I felt at the scene before me. It was a premonition of a knife in my own hand, the sensations of severing a living human head from its body. My reason revolted. The act was beyond forgiveness. They were not fit to be termed human. The ingrained morality of my own age condemned them.

The two newcomers were talking in a state of high excitement, gesticulating a pantomime of a battle. Even we could gather that the battle had not yet happened. The excitement was spreading as if their ritual murder had stirred up blood instincts beyond the realm of reason. But suddenly there was silence and the band turned to the man still lying with an arrow through his head, supine on the pavement. There were mutterings and one or two unintelligible cries.

Then a tall, axe-faced man raised a spear and, with a commanding shout, stepped out of the throng. There was sudden quiet. We had the feeling that another ritual was about to be enacted. The tall man walked to the injured one and spoke to him in a loud, almost challenging voice. Then there was a little ceremony, quite meaningless to us, when he danced around the wounded man thrusting alternately skywards and earthwards with his spear. The others watched in silence. After a minute or two the dancer became still. He stood high and gaunt above the still form of his comrade, and, planting his spear beside him, slowly and with deliberate dramatic effect drew his knife while holding his left arm outstretched over the fellow on the ground. There was absolute hush. The sky was the grey of a clouded dusk. The man was a silhouette against the shadowed walls. The knife was wielded, a quick slash and the man's wrist was dripping blood, great black drops striking the supine man on his chest. Pip said he saw the latter move his head. I did not see that. But immediately there came a sound like the single note of an organ, breathless and sad, a mass groan from the onlookers, and then, to our absolute astonishment, the tall man grabbed his spear and, with a single thrust, drove it through the chest of the helpless man at his feet.

It appeared then that the rite was over. The crowd broke up and at the orders of the tall man, now clearly in command, there was a swift exodus from the street, the whole band heading north.

'Well, what was that all about?' puzzled Pip, who had joined us at the window.

'I would hazard a guess that it was some form of ritual leadership exchange,' said Barry. 'The man you shot this morning must have been the leader. Remember he had Lucky's ears about his neck and was the first to attack us. Evidently some sort of crisis has developed that necessitated the immediate assumption of a new leader. That tall fellow was the elected candidate.'

'Very democratic, I must say. But why the pantomime bit?'

Barry shrugged. 'Merely a rite. Rites involving the shedding of blood have always been an important facet of primitive ceremonies.'

'But surely it wasn't necessary to kill him.'

'I don't feel very upset,' stated Pip, 'assuming he was the fellow who killed Lucky.'

'Perhaps the tall one could not have assumed command while an existing leader survived,' suggested Barry. 'There was an urgent necessity to have a fit and capable commander. So the other chap had to die.'

'What could such an emergency have been?'

'That's fairly obvious,' I put in. 'Judging by young Opi's body out there I would say that Oa has crossed the tribal boundaries. Opi could have been sent forward as a scout or something and he was captured by those two savages who brought him in. They would have been unwilling to tackle the whole of Oa's tribe on their own. So they came into town for reinforcements.'

'With Opi dead, Oa has only nine grown men,' Barry muttered. 'If Oa is unaware of Opi's capture the tribe could be massacred.'

'Well, he'll certainly be outnumbered. There's seventeen men in this group.'

'You know, I have a strong desire to balance the odds a bit,' said Barry. 'I've nothing against Oa . . .' and very much something for the lovely Oona, I thought, '. . . and after all, it's highly likely that we're directly responsible for his present predicament. Besides, I have a very basic and completely uncivilised desire to get even for Lucky and this horrible murder of Opi.'

'I'm with you all the way,' I said.

'We'll get wet,' grinned Pip, his little eyes bright with excitement. Already huge isolated drops were beginning to fall.

'Paul?'

'It's all very exciting,' said the doctor with a little smile. These unmilitary men were continuing to amaze me. 'Shall we go?'

My mind was full of thoughts about Lian as we climbed to the roof and down the rickety fire escape, and I felt sure that Barry's was full of Oona. It had begun to rain hard by then, though not as forcefully as the day we spent at the mill. It was also getting really dark. We headed north as the Mekans

54

had done; we could only follow the road. If they had turned off it we had no way of telling. Even in the daylight we would have been unlikely to spot any traces of deviation from the road, but in the dark and the rain there was no chance at all. We just hoped the noises of fighting would lead us to them. We trotted along steadily, not too fast for we were anxious to conserve our energy, and we were not as young as the savages.

We found them quite by chance. There were no noises of fighting, just a girl's screams a few cottages away in a suburban street. We raced towards the sound. It had stopped raining, the clouds had been rather an empty threat. An early moon was already fat in the darkness. It was not light by any means, but we could see. And what we saw was a group of men stooping over the writhing form of a girl on the ground. The girl was Oona. Barry went berserk. Somehow his bulk attained even greater speed. Unfortunately he roared his anger. They turned and saw us, naked all of them, their manhood strutting in silhouette, grotesque and ugly, and their faces surprised. But their reactions were only just less than immediate. They stooped for their weapons in an almost united movement apart from the one cradled and preoccupied between Oona's knees. Barry had carried his axe the whole way from Bordeaux. His violence was terrible. As he struck the still kneeling savage he screamed a scream from the very depths of man's beginnings, a scream born in the caves of primeval savagery. It exhilarated. The rapist died, his head cleaved into two parts. There was blood everywhere, all over the scientist, brains spilling out onto Oona's ravaged nudity. But I responded. Every chord of my soul answered to the violence and the scream. There were two spears in Barry. He whirled his dreadful axe. I saw no more as a spear came hurtling for my own ribs. I must have avoided it somehow, then I was face to face with a sweating and hairy form. I remember hate-filled eyes, a pair of protruding nipples on a muscular chest as my knife went in. I recalled my combat training and remembered to turn the knife to make it easier to extract. The smell of blood was strong. It was good. Only later was I nauseated.

There had been six of them. They were all dead. Paul and

Pip had used their bows at almost pointblank range. Barry had killed three with his axe. He stood then head bowed, a little ashamed, he admitted later, but not sorry. The two spears sticking out of his body were drooping since they were not buried very deeply, one in his backside and one in his upper arm. They were painful wounds but not immediately dangerous if treated for infection. He himself pulled them out with no more than a grimace.

Oona still lay on the ground whimpering. She cringed away from us as if expecting us as the victors to continue with the rape. Barry picked up a loincloth from one of the dead men and, bending down, gently laid it over her nakedness. Then he picked her up. 'Steady, little one,' he whispered in a voice so soft that she must have understood. She watched him, not cringing any more but still with the tremors of panic. She was safe, though, and she seemed to appreciate that. But where were the others? Where was Lian?

'Where are the rest?' I cried at her.

'Gently,' remonstrated the big man.

'We must find them,' I insisted, with the bodies of six men about me and no sense of guilt. Oona stared at me, her eyes huge and olive in the clouded moonlight.

'Shh!' uttered Paul. We were quiet. It was then we heard the sounds of fighting.

'It isn't over yet,' I declared. 'Barry, you stay here with the girl. And you, too, Paul. Pip, you come with me and we'll see what's happening.' I had forgotten for the moment that these men were not subject to my commands, not outside the spaceship, but there was no argument, although Paul followed, too, as Pip and I sped away. That was the first time that we left Barry alone.

The smell of blood was still in my nose, a colonel, commander of a spaceship, hunting other men with a bow and arrow. But that thought only occurred to me later. At that time I was completely involved in the desperation and the excitement, the veneer of more than ten thousand years of civilisation had dropped me as readily as an old shirt. I was primitive man out to kill a fellow being. It was an obedience to an instinct as profound and powerful as the instinct to mate. I did not understand it then; I hardly understand it now. At the time it was only the moment that mattered, the responses to latent drives that in more developed societies are better buried beneath the weight of social conditioning. I gave little thought to the time beyond the moment. With one exception. I thought of Lian as we crossed those fields of darkness. She was there, almost in the forefront of my consciousness. Perhaps it was the mating instinct that drove me after all.

We soon came upon them, at first shifting shadows in the heavy night, then suddenly a few more paces forward and we were stumbling over dead bodies, and there were men, leaping and stabbing, screaming and bleeding and brave. I stopped momentarily, and Pip and Paul drew up with me. We were breathing hard, but strong still. We could see them well then. Oa was there and three others of his band. Behind him were two women: Lian and one other, a girl called Wani. Oa was beating a retreat, fighting desperately for the slightest lull that would enable him to gain a yard or two. His strategy was hopeless, but it was the only one he had. He was outnumbered; there were six of his enemies and, some distance away, four or five were herding the remainder of the tribe's women and children into the darkness. Lian still had her infant held clutched to her breast, and Wani had a toddler grasping her legs and staring fearfully at the combat.

I gave my instructions, and the three of us each loosed an arrow. The range was very close, we could hardly miss. There came shrieking gasps of unexpected agony, the tensing and curling of vertebrae, the crumbling of knees, and three of the savages fell dead. It was not possible to shoot the others, they were locked in hand-to-hand struggles with Oa's men. Oa himself stood alone then, without a foe. He looked at us startled. Lian looked, too. There was a croaking cry from her tongueless mouth and she began to run towards me. Towards *me*. My heart leaped. But Oa turned and, seizing her wrist, he fled, half dragging her with him. I saw her face turned towards me. Supplicating. For a moment she tried to resist him until Oa snatched her baby from her and held it to his own bosom. It began to cry loudly, the great gulping sobs of a child in fear, and Lian responded to it, running freely at the man's side, reaching out her arms for her child. Soon they were lost in the night. For a minute all my instincts urged me to follow her. My being yearned for her. I was indifferent to the carnage about me, standing dreadfully alone under the huge canopy of that primal night. But there was another imperative, the powerful constraint of responsibility. I was the commander of a group of men, and in that sense of duty my feet were still.

An instant only had passed. Pip advanced towards two of the swaying figures. Paul stopped him with a touch. 'I think they're both dead,' he said. The two savages were locked together, each still gripping the handle of a bone-bladed knife; the blades were longer than a man's hand and each blade was buried to the hilt between the ribs of the other, their arms clutching each other's shoulders in a mimicry of affection. They were not quite dead; their eyes shone still in a frenzy of effort. Their teeth showed yellow, tight against down-drawn lips. They would not fall, for neither would yield. I could see their knuckles move, and muscles still straining as their life blood pumped from them. One of them was Paul's friend, Yog. A few yards away Yog's fellow tribesman died and his triumphant victor yelled his valour at the cloud-shrouded moon. He was covered in blood, whose we never knew, for before we could intervene he had leapt to the side of his comrade in the one remaining struggle and thrust his knife into the kidney region of his foe.

'*Venez!*' he called, and the two survivors ran together into the darkness. The stabbed man still stood. He was tottering around, reaching behind him for the knife still embedded in his kidneys. He uttered no sound. His fingers writhed helplessly at the hilt of the knife. His mouth was open and his eyes stared at us over the startling white of his cheekbones. It was ghastly. Then he died, keeling over sideways. The other two straining men, still locked together, had also fallen. And I was suddenly sick of the carnage.

'Let's go back,' I said. But before we made a move, a figure came forward, almost out of the earth, it seemed. It was Wani. She was hesitant, unsure of her reception. She stood just a few paces from us, head hanging and hands twined shyly together.

'Where is your son?' asked Paul. She pointed behind her

without looking at us. Paul stepped towards her but she did not move, though her body tensed visibly. He touched her arm and held it. 'Wani,' he said, 'do not be afraid. Call your boy and you can come with us.'

Obediently she called, but remained tense and scared. She was an attractive girl, perhaps in her early twenties, rather short but well formed with the characteristic large hips and full breasts of her people. Her hair was black and straight, and she was rather swarthy, nose a little too large, lips sultry, eyes with long, long lashes and, deep within them, beneath the submission and the shyness, subdued fire. Her child came up, about two years old, a sturdy, brown, big bellied boy. He was very afraid and silent as he renewed his grasp on his mother's leg. She caressed his head. Paul had released her arm. He smiled at her and turned back to us as we moved off. Wani followed. She had nowhere else to go.

As we neared the spot where we had left Barry and Oona, we could see the tracks of other men superimposed over our own. Anxiously we hurried on. Soon we saw the corpses of Oona's assailants. Barry's axe lay where he had dropped it. Of Barry himself and the girl there was no sign.

Chapter Five

We trudged through wet grass. It was raining again and pitch black. Paul assisted the girl who was having trouble carrying the little lad. He had offered to carry him for her, but the boy clung determinedly to his mother's neck, and she was unwilling to relinquish him. She showed visible appreciation of Paul's assistance, though, as he gave her support on a particularly slippery patch of mud, and later voluntarily gripped his arm to wade across a ditch. Pip carried Barry's axe, for once silent, his face grim. He was wondering about the big man, as indeed was I.

There was no means of gauging direction for no stars were visible. We were enclosed in an envelope of night, a thick, damp envelope that was as much the reaction to our recent behaviour as it was the condition of the night itself. We felt clammy and guilty and short-tempered; the smell of blood upon ourselves was no longer stimulating but nauseating, and we trudged on in our enclosed silence until we stumbled on a farmhouse. It was a brick building, partly in ruins but offering some shelter, and there was dry wood inside. There were also many forms of vermin—spiders, mice, starlings, fleas—and in the morning we discovered a nest of adders. But at that time we were grateful for its cover. We lit a fire and spent the remainder of that night huddled around its blaze, sometimes stoking it up, occasionally dozing. Wani fed her infant from her breast although he had long been weaned. The fate of the babe that should have been feeding there we never ascertained. The rest of us went hungry, although the truth was that we had little appetite as the recollection of carnage stayed with us through the rest of the night.

Wani was the first to move at the emergence of dawn. The sun came up damp and wretched and, although the rain had ceased its downpour, the sky was waterlogged and grey. She picked up Barry's axe and began to prowl around the heaps of debris that once were the walls of the farmhouse. Suddenly she grunted, a sound indicative of satisfaction, and she beckoned us over. Paul and I crossed over to her and, looking to where she was pointing, saw about seven snakes in a cavern of rubble. They were very much alive and aware of our presence, slithering and crawling around and over each other, sinuous and silent, their eyes watching our every move. 'Be careful, they're adders!' exclaimed Paul and made to draw Wani away.

She shrugged him off almost contemptuously. '*Manger*,' she said, and, creeping forward, knocked a few bricks aside with the haft of the axe, then, striking down with the blade, killed four of the snakes. It was a lesson in survival. We soon cooked them and ate them with relish.

We had decided previously to regroup at Bordeaux if we became separated, but our spirits were as wretched as the miserable sun as we left the shelter and in the vapours of the early dawn headed back to the city. Only three of us left, then. The loss of Barry was a physical weight upon us, and even Pip, most of all Pip, had no word of cheer. He did voice the hope that we would find the big man at the hotel but it was a hope without conviction. However, to return to the hotel was our only positive course of action. The grey sky gradually receded, leaving a marbled heaven of matt blue and pencil streaks of cloud. It was an empty world as we plodded through the wet grass. A morning without birds. A day without joy. And gloom walked with us. The city was deserted, which was fortunate because we walked openly and uncaring through its decaying streets.

Barry was not at the hotel.

I left the others there and walked back alone to the scene of the battle. There were corpses and crows. Dog-torn bodies. The sun on newly exposed bones. I stood where we had last seen our friend. It was impossible to distinguish his tracks in the mud. Where would he have gone? There were houses around. If he had fled from pursuit, would he have hidden in one of them? Probably not. Barry was well aware of the uncanny ability of these hunting men to hear and track at night, to approach in silence, unseen and unexpected in the darkness. To hide in a confined space would have been a greater danger than flight in the open where there was always the chance of outdistancing pursuers. So if Barry had fled, which way would he have gone? It would have been to the east or the south in all likelihood, not north for that was open country with little cover, but he may not have known that in the dark, and certainly not to the west for that would have been towards the assailants. Without much rationale to guide me I turned and went eastwards.

*   *   *

Barry stood alone in the darkness, Oona cradled like a child in his arms. Indeed, she was little more than that. He was filled with such thoughts of tenderness, this man who had just killed three of his kind, that emotion choked him, surging against his breast so that for some moments he was unaware of the approach of other men. Fortunately, neither did they know of his presence, for the sound of their thudding feet was soon too close not to betray them. Naked feet to make such a noise, so not those of his comrades. He put Oona down saying: 'Allez-vous en. Vite!' and bent down to pick up his axe. Bt Oona had a wrenched muscle in her thigh from the violence of her rape, and she could hardly stand, let alone run. A whimper of pain escaped her as she crumpled to the ground. Barry left his axe, scooped her up again and began to run.

He ran hard and fast, but he was not a young man and the wound in his buttocks hampered him. It was soon plain that the savages were not only pursuing him but also gaining on him rapidly. Another spear hit him in the ribs, striking with such force that it knocked him sprawling. Oona was flung headlong. But the spear fell out. Seizing it, Barry rolled over. The nearest assailant was almost upon him. Two spears flew together, Barry's from the ground, a weapon that he was unused to, and the attacker's from above, hurled with a skill born of long practice. Both spears struck home. Barry rolled away in desperation but the missile pinned him to the ground by the skin of his neck. The savage lurched as Barry's spear hit him in the groin. And Oona attacked. From somewhere she gathered the strength to spring at the reeling man, and he fell. And as he fell she snatched his knife from his belt. They crashed to the ground together and she unhesitatingly thrust the knife into his throat. A second savage rushing in to hurl a spear at Barry was suddenly disconcerted by the girl's unexpected assault. He turned, momentarily uncertain where to strike first, and Barry leaped, tearing his neck from the spear in his lurch upward. He struck the second savage's knees and the fellow was thrown off his feet. Then Barry strangled him, without effort and without thought. A third savage, the last of them, declined to attack at close quarters. He threw his spear hurriedly, so that it missed, and fled into the safety of the night.

Oona crawled over to Barry who was staring blank-faced at the man he had strangled, blood streaming from his neck and the clothes about his left side dark with welling blood. Hesitating and uncertain, she touched him. His face was white and ghastly in the gloom. It was agonised. He looked at her, and she was unable to understand the shock in his eyes. How could she know that he, who had never before even contemplated an act of killing, had this day killed four men, the last with his bare hands, instinctively and easily, and that his soul was in torment? To her death and violence were part of life's pattern; to him they were abhorrent. 'So this is how we must live,' he whispered, but the words were without meaning for her.

He stood up. 'Come, little one,' he said, and he picked her up and marched bloodless into the starting rain.

*　　*　　*

I found him unconscious in a ditch where Oona had dragged him after he had collapsed, and where she obtained the strength for that deed will remain a mystery. Actually Oona found me and led me to him. I had discovered the evidence of his second battle but he had marched an unbelievable two more miles before crumpling, and carrying the girl all the while. To follow his tracks was beyond my skill, I merely headed along an overgrown lane reasoning that Barry would have kept to the easiest path, and then suddenly Oona rose up out of the thickets and waved to me. We were not too far from town. Within an hour I had fetched the others and we had transported Barry's not inconsiderable bulk back to the hotel. To get him up the fire escape was beyond our ingenuity and we did not attempt it.

Paul attended to Barry's wounds. They were not serious, although he had lost a lot of blood. It required seven stitches to close the gash in his neck but it had not severed any major veins, and the wound in his side, though much deeper, just required some dressing and antiseptic treatment. The dressings were merely strips torn from the tails of our shirts, but they served the immediate purpose well enough.

'We'll have to find some proper bandages,' muttered Paul, 'these will need changing tomorrow and goodness knows what we'll need in the days ahead. I'll need some more antiseptic, too.' He held up the almost empty phial that had been in his tiny kit.

Later in the day Barry was able to mount the escape stairs under his own power, and by the evening was once again the subject of Pip's incorrigible ribbing.

Pip had set some snares of copper wire in the wooded area behind the hotel while I had been gone, and even before midday he had caught two rabbits. So with Barry's return and with full stomachs, our spirits were considerably higher than at the start of that day when we settled down to our first night's sleep in the hotel.

Our sojourn there lasted six days that first time. Barry was made to rest for most of that period. Oona attended him solicitously. She still had some trouble walking, but had really recovered remarkably well from her ordeal. It seemed to have left far less of a psychological scar than such a traumatic experience would have left on the women of our own age. It was as if there was a resignation towards assault in these people, a sort of conditioning to it. It appalled us, of course, but our own conditioning came from a totally different social order. Oona adapted willingly to her new society; she was quick to smile and laughed merrily at Pip's perpetual banter. Away from her tribe it seemed as if she left the melancholy of the tribal condition behind her. She liked Pip, that was clear, and there was no doubt that Pip was very much taken with her, for his eyes betrayed his desire. Yet his attentions were tempered with patience and the knowledge of his big friend's feelings.

It was to Barry, though, that Oona's serious attentions were directed, tending to his wants with a degree of devotion that would have embarrassed any woman of our era. And Barry adored her. Perhaps he did not lust as Pip did, not outwardly at least, but his eyes were soft as he watched her, and he would touch her as if she were a fragile thing. Barry was in love. Oona was a clever girl and it was not long before she had picked up elements of the English tongue as well as becoming more sophisticated in the use of her hereditary language by diligent listening to our dialogue. Soon we could hold quite involved conversations with her and in this manner learned a great deal more about the ways of the people in this corner of the continent. She was a gay creature, quick to see humour and ever ready to break into peals of laughter as if to make up for the constraints of previous years. There was no doubt that she brightened our lives in those early days. If I had not constantly seen that last, desperate, pleaful look in Lian's eyes, if the anguish of that moment had not continually returned to me, I myself might have succumbed to her charms. As it was I could not rid myself of the thought of Lian. I dreamed of her, of her face, of her body, of her arms reaching for me, touching me, exciting me. And my need for her was something far more profound than desire.

Wani had quickly established a relationship with Paul, and Paul seemed perfectly happy with her. He had not forced any but the most gentle attentions upon her, but tenderness was something quite new to these savage women, and they responded eagerly. By the time we moved on from the hotel it was plain that Wani had learned to love; it was an adoration, a devotion, simple and genuine and absolute. Paul had opened up for her a new dimension of sensuality and response, of love and tenderness; he had plumbed depths of her being of which she had been but vaguely aware. And she claimed him with a possessiveness which we were not to recognise until some time later.

The first three days were spent in exploration of any buildings in the vicinity that remained untouched by marauders, as well as the necessary food gathering expeditions in the woodland behind our retreat. Both Pip and I were becoming more proficient in the use of the bow, and we managed to shoot two ducks and two chickens between us. And we felt mightily proud. We still depended mainly upon Pip's snares, though. All our expeditions were conducted with an emphasis on caution now we knew the full hostility of the local people. Assuming we had encountered the whole tribe, we estimated the numbers of grown men in it as no greater than seven or eight after the known casualties of the battle. Still, we had no wish to become involved in fresh hostilities. Lucky had been well and truly avenged.

We discovered little of much use to us, with two notable exceptions. We sought out a nearby hospital and virtually ransacked the place, though for some inexplicable reason it seemed to have been pillaged quite extensively at some time in the distant past. We were searching for dressings and medications, of course, and while most of such stock had remained undisturbed, it had deteriorated beyond any service-ability. We finally came across a disintegrating steel cabinet that was readily pulled apart, and within, reasonably undamaged in plastic wrapping, was a pack of bandages, also several bottles of antiseptic and methylated spirits. We took all of it away.

We also managed to enter one heavily secured building that was quite obviously a library. The great majority of the books had succumbed to the assaults of various vermin over the ages, but deep in the recesses of the vaults we located some locked chests which, to our delight, were crammed full of undamaged literature: books, periodicals, magazines and even newspapers. They were a little mouldy from a long and sometimes damp internment and written in French, but it was reading matter, and to our word-hungry intellects it was as exciting as buried treasure. We spent a further three days immersed in literature.

Barry read very fast and became so absorbed that he even ignored Oona, not deliberately, I'm sure, but just from his total immersion in the printed word. There was an occasional grunt, once or twice a thoughtful pause when he gazed frown-ingly at the ceiling, two or three times an indignant snort. He read through all the newspapers first—they covered a period dating almost from the day of our departure from Earth and for about another four years, but as there were periodicals dated later, they had probably only been used as packing for the books. They revealed no clues to the current state of the world. Pip selected the periodicals initially; they were on a variety of topics but he read them all irrespective of their content, ignoring chronology, sequence or subject, whereas Paul was a much more selective reader, choosing his specialty at first, although I doubt whether anything that he read advanced his knowledge to any degree. Still, it was a pleasure to read even known facts in print. I was less fluent in French than the scientists and a book occupied me for many hours. They were among the most pleasant hours we spent in Bordeaux.

I remember Pip remarking: 'Barry, there's an article here on Biocinetrin. Did you know that it was the subject of a debate by the World Science Council?'

'Was it indeed? I wasn't aware that it was so extensively known about. I believed it was restricted information. Is there a date on that article?'

'A few years after we left Earth. You ought to read it.'

'I will,' said Barry. I am sure he did. I think he read through everything.

Chapter Six

The Mekans came back on our fifth day in the hotel. There were just the men, seven of them. Two of them were carrying a stretcher with a sick or injured man upon it, and two others were carrying what appeared to be a wooden cage with some sort of animal in it. They must have known where we were for they deposited their burdens immediately before the hotel and spent a few minutes simply gazing up at our building. They might even have seen us watching them from the window. At that distance it became clear that the animal in the cage was a man, presumably a prisoner, one of Oa's men. He was naked and filthy and we could not recognise him.

'What do you think they want?' I wondered.

'One suspects that our presence in their territory is something of a challenge to them,' said Barry. 'It looks like their leader is still that fellow who killed Lucky's murderer. While we are still here his prestige will be at stake.'

'So you believe they're challenging us to come out and do battle?'

'Something like that.'

Our assumption may have been correct, but their immediate motives were more sinister. They rolled the fellow on the stretcher unceremoniously onto the street. He could not have been one of their own. Positioning him with obvious deliberation so that we were able to view the proceedings, the tall leader drew his knife and, with some exaggerated flourishes, finally knelt down and pulled the fellow's head back with his free hand. 'They're going to cut his head off!' exclaimed Pip. 'Just as they did with Lucky and Opi. It must be some sort of ritual way of killing with them.'

The man from the stretcher was clearly too weak to put up any resistance, but we could see his feeble efforts to struggle and saw his mouth move in unheard moans. What we did hear was the man in the cage screaming aloud: 'You bastards! You bastards!'

I knew that voice. I knew it as well as those of Barry and Pip.

'It's Terry!' I cried. 'That must be John on the ground. Oh God!' And I ran from the room in a crazed and implacable fury. John began to scream, animal screams of pain beyond endurance that came to me high on the still morning air as I reached the roof. I cannot now recall actually descending the fire escape and running towards the sound of John's screams, but in my haste I had forgotten to bring my weapons. I had only my knife at my belt and the urge to kill overwhelming me as I ran.

They heard me coming and turned to fight. The leader already had John's head in his hands. I was oblivious of the others, he was the man I wanted. But there was one in my way. I lunged at him, my knife in my hand and striking upwards. I had his beard entangled in my fingers and his guts spilling down over my other hand. Spears were driving at me. I forced onwards over the crumpling body of my first kill and straight for the leader's throat. There were noises from behind me. Reports. They meant nothing to me then. The leader was smiling strangely as his spear drove upwards for my stomach. There was a crash and an axe cleaved the spear in half. Barry stood between us. 'He's mine!' I called, and Barry stepped aside. The tall man was still smiling as he came to meet me almost with an eagerness. He had no chance really, for he knew nothing of the techniques of unarmed combat. I grabbed him and tossed him flat onto the bloody surface of the street. It was absurdly easy. Then I knelt down and cut his throat with a satisfaction close to pleasure. In that instant I was as primitive as they were, intent only on revenge. In so short a time had I reverted to the basic nature of man. Then something struck my head and I fell forward into his still gushing blood.

I came to within seconds, but it was all over. Violence always seems to be swift in its execution. There were eight dead, the seven savages and John. The reports that I had heard had been Pip firing his revolver. He had been working on it over the past few days and had made it serviceable.

There had been three bullets in the chamber. Each one had taken a life, thereby undoubtedly saving my own. Barry had killed one with his axe, and the remaining savage had, in his excitement, backed too close to the cage, where Terry had grabbed him, reaching his arms through the bars and crushing the savage to them with vicious strength. Pip had performed the *coup-de-grâce* while Barry had hacked the cage to pieces. It had been that savage who had thrown the spear that had struck me on the head, though it had only been a glancing blow and I suffered no worse wounds than a lump and a headache.

We took John's body to the woodland and buried it. That evening Terry told us his story.

* * *

'After leaving you on the beach, we found a road and headed north. We soon reached a village, deserted and in ruins, but apparently inhabited for there was a fire burning in the square and the figures of men huddled round it. We approached it with puzzlement, of course, but with confidence. There was no reason to feel otherwise. Their appearance was disconcerting but we could see no reason for apprehension. They immediately surrounded us and menaced us with their spears. Even that did not bother us unduly then; it was quite an understandable reaction to two strangers suddenly arriving in their midst. We spoke to them in French, but now realise that they would have understood very little of what we were saying. We thought they were unnecessarily aggressive as they prodded us with their spears, but we still put that down to our strange appearance.

'After a while we realised that their language was indeed a form of simplified French and by listening carefully we were able to make out a word or two, enough to understand that they were discussing whether or not we should be put to death. We stressed over and over again our friendly intentions. One man, the apparent leader of the group, finally put a direct question. I didn't quite grasp what he wanted but John seemed to understand better than I. "They want to know where we have come from," he said.

'Unfortunately it seems that we explained too well in our efforts to simplify the story, accurately describing the beach and the fact that we had friends awaiting our return. There was a great deal of discussion about that. We were eventually bound together by our hands and feet and thrown aside while the debate went on. John was able to pick up bits of their conversation. He told me there seemed to be two opinions about our fate; one group wanting to kill us there and then and the other proposing that we be kept alive for some sort of ceremony that sounded like "Noël".'

'Yes, Nowell time,' interrupted Oona, who had been listening avidly to Terry's tale. 'It is still three moons away.'

'And just what is Nowell time?' asked Pip, 'It sounds like Christmas.'

'It is when the North men come.'

'The North men?'

'Oh, they are a very big tribe. They come every winter when the herds move south.'

'So what sort of ceremony would we have been involved in?' asked Terry.

'Not a ceremony, really. You would have been the tribute.'

'A tribute? What sort of tribute?'

'Every year when the North men come, all the local tribes must give them a tribute. Usually it is the two oldest women.'

'What on earth for?'

'To eat. They eat people.'

We did not pursue that discussion any further just then.

Terry continued his tale. 'Well then, that appears to be the reason we were spared. Anyway, some hours later the debate came to an end, and a few youths were left in charge of us while the older men loped off into the night. We didn't know what it was all about at first, and it wasn't till they came back dragging the life raft that we realised our description of your whereabouts had got through. Our hearts sank, especially when we saw a pair of bloody ears hanging gorily from the leader's neck. At first we assumed that you had all been killed, but John pointed out that there was only one pair of ears in evidence and our hopes rose. In retrospect I see that they either arrived at the beach after you had left or else they waited till you had gone before carrying out their murder. I

71

don't know why they killed Lucky, but perhaps he offered resistance.

'It rained that night, and although there was ample shelter around we remained camped in the open. I doubt if we had ever suffered such a miserable night in our lives before, but it was nothing to the misery that was to follow. The rain was cold and our bonds were extremely tight, and you can imagine the state of our minds. What had happened to the world? Everything was crazy.

'In the morning our hands were untied and we were given some food, just their leftovers from the previous night, merely bones with some tattered shreds of meat still adhering, wet and cold and dirty. But we ate whatever our teeth could scrape off. Then we had our hands tied once more, too tightly again despite our pleas, but our feet were freed. We realised in the light of morning that the tribe was bigger than we had supposed, for the women and children could be seen not far away. They forced us to march then. On and on, mile after mile, our heels burning in wet boots on unprepared feet, our hands lifeless and our minds close to despair.

'It was a long, wet day. That night we were bound to two separate trees, sitting up with our hands tied together in front of us. Fortunately, probably because the bonds were tied when wet, they had become somewhat looser and we were able to restore life to our hands although it meant moving our fingers continuously. The men went off to hunt in the evening and the women prepared a fire and cooked some meat. We weren't offered any. Some of them were rather pretty, and we eyed them appreciatively as you can imagine, in spite of our situation. They responded to our winks and smiles with little shy movements of the eyes and lips, but they were more curious than interested. They took great care not to approach us too closely.

'It was not till the early hours of the morning that the men returned with large hunks of meat slung about them, and they ate, then slept. We weren't fed at all that day, but they did allow us some water. We stayed in that spot for two more days. The men didn't hunt again. They idled, made weapons leisurely, seduced the women, played with the children, and only once gave us some meat. Then we moved off again and came to Bordeaux.

'They knew of a cellar with only a trapdoor in the pavement for an entry. The trapdoor was missing. We were flung inside still bound by the hands, and left there. It was twenty feet high, that cellar. Later, once we had managed to free our hands, we attempted to reach the exit by John standing on my shoulders, but it was a waste of time and there was nothing in the cellar to assist us. It contained only wet moss, creeping slime and cockroaches. We lost count of the days we spent in that hole. They came sometimes, very intermittently, and threw food down to us. Often we weren't fed at all for three or four days, and it was always meat, no fruit or vegetable matter. We took to eating the green moss off the walls. It was little more than algae actually, for there was not enough sunlight in there to generate much photo-synthesis. I persuaded John that it must hold some of the minerals that meat alone wouldn't supply and, vile though it was, we forced it down. We were given no water and had to drink from the vermin-ridden, evil-tasting pools of muddy slime on the floor. We lost weight, of course. John became ill and feverish. God! It was hell! That hole will stay in my memory as a symbol of unutterable evil. We had to perform our bodily functions on the floor, the same floor from which we obtained our water. It is small wonder that John contracted a fever. The wonder must be that I did not.

'I could do nothing for John. I would sit huddled in a corner trying to catch any ray of daylight, any vestige of sun that managed to penetrate that dismal hole in the pavement, and watch John toss and moan. Sometimes his eyes would widen and glitter in the gloom. He would often call out his wife's name. His cheeks became hollow. The flesh fell from him day by day. He couldn't eat. I would drag him under the hole whenever the sun shone through, or when it rained and fresh water could wash over us.

'Then one day they came for us. They had the cage made and a ladder of sorts. They came down and hauled John out; he was too weak and delirious to resist or even be fully aware of what was happening. I went out readily enough, eager for the fresh air and sunshine. But they thrust me immediately into the cage. I don't really understand the reason for the cage unless it was a refinement of sadism connected with the coming ordeal. Perhaps it was just meant as a portable cell, although it was a flimsy affair really, held together by lashings. It wouldn't have held me captive for long if that was its intention. John was obviously too ill to walk, but they already had a stretcher prepared and we were carried away.

'As they walked I did overhear a few words of their discussions. It appeared to be the common opinion that it was hardly worthwhile keeping John alive. They were going to use his death towards some end that I couldn't understand at the time. There was some talk of atonement which meant little to me. Now I see that John's death was in ritual retaliation for your decimation of their tribe. There was a long debate on the nature of the ritual but I couldn't understand much of that except to gather that it was for men only, women were not permitted to participate. The women and children were made to stay behind, not far from here, and the seven surviving adult males carted us off. You know the rest. As far as I can tell there are no surviving grown men in the tribe now. You have wiped them all out.'

Terry finished his story and we were all silent. It was hardly an achievement to be proud of. The extermination of the all-important menfolk of a complete tribe, and possibly two, in the brief period of less than a month back on Earth. I think that the silence of the others reflected a kind of mutual despair. We could all find excuses but that did not lessen the guilt. Finally it was Oona who broke the silence with a little postscript. She said, somewhat archly: 'Then the women of the tribe are yours for the taking. They're probably waiting for you.'

Wani reached out and held Paul's arm.

Chapter Seven

Eighteen women and twenty-four children. They had seen the annihilation of their men and, as Oona had said, were waiting for us to assume responsibility for them. It was Pip who went for them, his eyes alive with anticipation. 'After the drought the flood,' he cried, unashamed of his jubilation as he led them back to the hotel. Oona was eyeing him thoughtfully, but her hands were around Barry's arm. My own stomach was unsteady with excitement as I looked them over. They seemed quite unmoved about the death of their men. We assumed at first that this apparent lack of feeling was due to resignation from their familiarity with death and violence, but later we learned that such devastating encounters were really quite rare in their history. The lack of distress was more likely due to a lack of deep affection, of any real emotional commitment to the men. It was hard to accept that, steeped as we were in our own concepts of sexual relationships, but if any of them did harbour grief it was a private thing concealed beneath their new submission.

They stood now, huddled in a bunch, shy, or seemingly so, their heads hung forward so that we could not see their eyes. As with Oa's women, they were mostly young, only three of them appearing to be more than thirty years old. They were half naked and sturdy, with soft, fat bellies, skin the colour of autumn leaves, rounded and waistless and physically stirring. There were two very attractive girls among them. One was a blonde, no more than sixteen years old, with a baby of just a few weeks at her breast. It must have been her first child and her figure was unspoilt, her young breasts full and delightful with lactation. The other was nursing an even younger infant. She was somewhat older, I guessed, though hardly yet twenty; a tall girl of perfect form, red-haired and freckled, quite outstanding in her colouring, and we were to find that it was rare indeed. But I was searching for Lian in a wild hope that chance had put her among them. She was not there.

I attempted to speak to them. The reaction was negligible. Some giggles, one or two quick, coy looks. We were aware that they were sizing us up carefully. '*Vous!*' I called to the nearest one, '*Venez ici.*'

Meekly she came forward. With my hand I lifted her face. She had beautiful eyes, black and large, but in them lurked fear. It was as if they said: 'I am frightened but you are the master.' That sort of deference did not appeal to me at all. It made me feel very ill at ease. She had a large fleshy nose and there was a pimple on her upper lip. She was singularly odorous. Apart from her eyes she was really very plain. Yet looking down into that submissiveness I felt a sudden ache for her, an unaccountable but specific desire. It was nothing but a basic urge, a hunger for any woman after so many years of celibacy. I see that now, but she saw it immediately. The realisation was in her eyes, a hint of mockery, perhaps, almost of triumph, but not enough to overshadow the meekness.

'Don't be afraid,' I said loudly to her and to them all. 'Our people do not harm women or children. You are safe with us.' Then more directly to the woman before me: 'What is your name?'

'Dua,' she said.

'Then tell the others, Dua, that they are welcome to stay here with us, but if they wish to leave that is also acceptable. We are men from far away, but we have come to stay . . .' where else could we go? '. . . and we shall do our best to feed you and defend you as your own men used to do. Our ways may seem strange to you at times, and we may show you new and different arts and customs, but you will find that we are good men.' It was a simple address but difficult to translate into their limited language. I was not sure that Dua or any of them understood. But then Wani took over, talking so rapidly that we grasped little of what she said, though one point emerged plainly enough. She made it perfectly clear that Paul was her man and that he was off limits to any other woman. With love had come possessiveness, and that was an alien concept for these women. After her harangue they started to mutter amongst themselves, which soon turned to chatter and afterwards into laughter. Their demureness left them and they began to gaze at us much more boldly. Whatever Wani had told them it appeared to be favourable. Two of them left to retrieve the remainder of a steer which, much to our immediate relief, would be adequate for a day or two. Others squatted in the road. Babies were nursed. I looked over my new responsibilities and permitted elation to creep over me. We had our own tribe.

That was the beginning. We had a great deal to learn. That night I took Dua to my bed. She was submissive, but utterly unresponsive. At last I turned away, spent but not appeased, defeated, angry, too, and Lian was powerfully in my thoughts.

The early relationship between ourselves and the women was remarkable in many respects, but it was not without some elements of humour. There was no strain in spite of the vast gulf that separated our cultures. They could not cross that gulf, nor could we, despite all our efforts. Yet it was because of that gulf that there was no strain. Their lives had instilled in them a total reliance on their men; accustomed from birth to be meek and obedient, to perform all the chores of everyday living apart from hunting, they adapted easily to new masters. At first we rather foolishly tried to help them, but they considered that to be ridiculous, and our efforts provoked much hilarity. They would never understand our disapproval of the inequalities inherent in their way of life, and in the end we accepted the submission and the subservience, even though we had strong misgivings. They had a group instinct far removed from the liberation and determined individuality of the women of our own time. What we required of them they gave because the thought of defiance never occurred to them. The truth was that, regardless of how we thought, we were not only their men but their masters, and they needed that understood relationship. It was their security. It would have been pointless trying to convince them of the ethics of our own time, that would have disturbed their cohesion and would have achieved nothing. As it was they were disturbed at first, by our unfamiliar approach; they did not understand tenderness, consideration, soft words, smiles. But they responded. In time they responded.

We wondered what had happened to the rest of them, and

the captive women of Oa's tribe that we had seen taken by force. We were told that those women had fled once they had known of the death of the men, presumably back to Oa's territory, accompanied and even led by three of the young Mekans, youths of about fourteen years of age. That was a relief in a way. So many less mouths to feed. We were suddenly confronted with the awesome prospect of feeding twenty-five adults and twenty-two children, with only one month's experience of hunting to guide us.

I voiced my concern to Pip.

'We had trouble just feeding ourselves adequately. How the hell are we going to feed another forty people?'

'We'll have to learn to hunt better, won't we?' he replied, not very constructively, I thought.

'That's easier said than done,' I muttered.

But we did learn.

The early days were constant toil and we relied heavily upon our snares. The tribe endured many rabbit stews. But as time passed our skill with the bows increased and many a wild sheep fell victim to our dexterity. We devised traps and dug pits. Twice we caught a steer in one of the pits. Then we feasted mightily. We attempted to teach the women the basics of spinning and weaving, shearing the dead sheep rather than skinning them, in order to obtain wool. They failed to understand the necessity for all the stages to make a woollen garment when it seemed so much easier to fashion a hide into a cloak or a skirt. They felt no pride in a finished object, no real desire for additional comfort, and certainly gave no indications of any aesthetic sensibilities. Still we persevered. And they did try, if only to please us, with more amusement than enthusiasm.

They were submissive but they turned out to be much gayer and more fun-loving than we had believed from our experience with Oa's people. They would laugh readily, sing all day, tease us when we failed to provide a meal of solid meat —often enough in the early days—and generally appeared to be quite content with their lot.

At first Pip was completely promiscuous. He probably slept with every woman other than Wani and Oona, and possibly Teena, the red-haired girl with whom I formed a sort of intermittent relationship. He finally settled into a more or less stable relationship with Zo, the little blonde girl who clearly adored him. I never grew close to Teena in an emotional sense. I was able to awaken responses in her after many patient nights when she would tremble in my bed like a frightened doe, and in many ways my patience was rewarded. But although she was tender and very loving, and even at times abandoned, I never *knew* her. And I never loved her. For that I feel sad, for she was shy and kind and gentle, and she deserved to be loved properly. Terry never loved either. He formed no attachments. Occasionally he would lie with one or other of the women but he felt little for them outside of his carnal needs. Terry had had a wife who had been all the world to him. He had worshipped her and she had felt the same for him. After ten years of marriage they had been as much in love, perhaps even more than on the day of their wedding. It had been hard for him when she had died. They had had something very special, the absolute superlative of love, people so in communion, so blended, one could not know them without envy. Cancer had killed her exactly a year before we had left Earth or he could never have gone. He could never love like that again, and he was the sort of man who would only love completely or not at all.

And Barry, that big, gentle man, loved Oona. There was no other woman for him. I cannot say whether or not he made love to her. Somehow I suspect not, knowing the tragedy that followed. She hovered about him always, and she loved him, I am sure of that. She certainly flirted with Pip quite openly, and he wooed her in his comic fashion but with a total lack of sincerity. They liked each other but there was no obvious depth to their playfulness. Barry saw that and was undisturbed.

But Paul had problems. He tended the women's injuries, and they were plentiful in such an existence. Cuts and bruises were daily occurrences. There were boils and sores, the illnesses of pregnancy, even broken bones. He was skilful and tender in his ministrations. The women came to trust him, to respect him and finally to adore him. These were uninhibited women, primitive, unrestrained in their passions. Many of them desired Paul and made it quite plain. Paul, no doubt, would have succumbed, but Wani watched his every move. She half-killed one girl with a stone axe because she caught Paul walking with the girl hand in hand. Jealousy had entered her soul along with love. Paul did admit to me later that Wani's assumptions about his intent had been correct, but he was appalled at the viciousness of her assault. He had had to strike her and knock her down or she would surely have killed the other girl. She held no blame for Paul. He could do no wrong in her eyes. That night she actually crawled to him like a dog, whimpering for reassurance. And Paul lifted her face up. 'My Wani, my Wani,' he whispered, 'what shall I do with you?' For the first time in my knowledge of him I saw something in his eyes that surprised me, a true affection for an individual, a warmth, a depth of feeling that was quite out of character. He had always been gentle and kind, but aloof, holding his feelings in check. Wani, in her assault upon her rival, had reached the heart of this compassionate but unapproachable man.

Generally, however, life was unviolent for a time, apart from the butchery of the game animals. We moved from the city; the countryside was where the game was. Our life became nomadic as is the way of hunting peoples, although we insisted on finding shelter at night, in the beginning at least; later it became less important. It was a peaceful period, but it certainly was not dull. Hunting is often tedious but it is never dull. All previously domesticated animals had reverted to a wild state, and cattle were particularly dangerous game. Bulls, never known for their tractability, were probably the most feared and, as we were to learn, the most unpredictable. There were many stories of the deaths caused by these formidable beasts. Without knowledge of medicine, a goring would have meant certain death. Horse were prolific on the plains that had once been vineyards, but they were wary creatures, unapproachable with our limited skills. We had vague ideas of capturing some and breaking them for use as transport.

'Do any people that you know ride on horses?' I asked Oona.

She laughed. 'Ride on them! Of course not. They are only good for eating, but I prefer cattle meat.' She thought such a concept was a hilarious idea. The other women also considered it a huge joke.

'There was a time when people did ride horses,' I tried to explain, but a man riding a beast was nothing more than a fantasy to them.

Barry summed it up in his ponderous way. 'I think we have to assume that man's culture has not advanced to that level,' he pronounced.

'Or has regressed beyond it,' said Pip rather mockingly. He was pulling Barry's leg, of course.

'The opinions of the foolish are of no value,' retorted the big man.

'But we'll listen to you anyway,' laughed Pip.

Sheep were the most abundant, but they were shy and had developed a wariness of men; they were surprisingly fleet of foot, especially if one tried to run one down, but this could be done for they really were foolish creatures. They became our staple food.

There were also dogs on the plains. Wild dogs, often in packs. They were creatures to be avoided, savage as wolves, with the strength and courage of their man-bred ancestors. All the less brave and less savage had long since been eradicated by natural selection; the inevitable process of evolution favoured only the strong. Fortunately they tended to avoid us as willingly as we avoided them. Cats, too, were savage, but their prey was mainly rabbits and birds so they caused us little problem.

Our spare time, and there was not a great deal of that, we spent reading our precious stock of literature from cover to cover in an endeavour to discover some clue to the present state of the world, but no one proposed any convincing theories at that time. Questioning the women on their traditions and history revealed no insights. The only tradition at all appeared to be the season of 'Nowell', which clearly corresponded to Christmas, although now it had become a time of apprehension rather than anticipation, for it was when the North men came for their annual tribute. We were not totally convinced about the stories of cannibalism—it was a ready epithet to apply to any dreaded foe—but suspected the tribute might be connected with ritual sacrifice, perhaps a distortion of the Christmas celebration we had known. What did seem certain was that the North men were far more numerous as a clan than the scattered bands of central France. The tribes there were probably less hostile towards each other and grouped together for the annual trek south, following the herds as winter gripped the north. The one common fact that emerged was that resistance was futile. There were too many of them and they were giants.

*   *   *

'You know,' said Paul one evening, 'these people are remark-ably resistant to disease, well, to bacteria anyway. Have you noticed how quickly their wounds heal? After all, they are quite dirty in their habits compared to the way we were brought up.'

'I'm sure that's just natural resistance due to constant exposure to germs,' commented Pip.

'Possibly. It did occur to me, though, that it might be related to the demise of man. Supposing it was a bacteriological cause that wiped out our race and only those with an inbuilt resistance to the disease survived to continue the species, then one might expect these people to heal quickly.'

'You mean a genetic ability,' I remarked.

'Yes, something like that.'

Pip was shaking his head. 'Look,' he said. He had an inclination to use the word 'look' whenever he was about to enter serious discussion. 'Look, there is no way a disease could wipe out the human species. Not with all its culture as well. Such a disease would have to have been so virulent and sudden that all mankind was killed off within a few years, months even.' He spoke very quickly so that one had to pay close attention to keep up with him. 'But even if one did suppose such a disease, it could not eradicate man's technology, could it? Nor mankind's beliefs. Surely you see that.'

'The only concept that seems to have endured is the feast known as Nowell,' I put in.

'Yes. You know that bothers me a bit,' Pip mused. 'I suppose we shouldn't put too great an emphasis on it, because we don't really know whether it is actually a feast or just a time of invasion.'

'The significant factor of Christmas in my view,' Barry suggested, leaning forward and staring intently at his friend, 'is its association with children.'

Pip stared back at him, his small eyes shadows of concentration. 'Children, ah, children,' he muttered, as if that meant something, as if some new realisation had come to him. Barry nodded.

'But why?' asked the big man, and I, having been left suddenly far behind their intellectual leaps, looked at Terry and grinned. He just smiled back, also perplexed, but the two scientists had retreated into contemplation and we remained mystified.

* * *

Pip became the most proficient hunter among us, although we made it a rule never to hunt alone. Barry and Pip usually went out together for the two were almost inseparable. They were the unlikeliest of friends really, for apart from their super-intellects they had little in common. Pip was small, ebullient and profligate. He was a constant clown, but strangely enough he rarely indulged in laughter himself. It was as if his clowning was a pose, a face presented to others to disguise a truly serious nature. While Barry was a large man, quiet, introverted, and singularly monogamous in his affections; and he loved the humour of others, was given to peals of curiously high-pitched laughter, almost giggles, though he rarely offered a joke himself, and when he did it was a most ponderous effort. I suppose that he was a ponderous man but I was never aware of it. Pip baited him constantly, ribbing his size, his false teeth, his solemnity, but never his opinions. And Barry would laugh his peculiar laugh, and my heart warmed towards them both, and I even felt a little envy at their closeness.

Then there was the incident of the bull.

It was inevitably Pip who stalked the game. When a herd was sighted, he had learned that he could approach to within a hundred yards before the herd took fright, even closer with sheep. So once he had reached this surprisingly constant limit, it was necessary to commence stalking. This could be difficult unless cover was available downwind, but Pip excelled in it. He had perfected a technique whereby he could approach a herd even in the open. His secret was to freeze immediately a single beast looked his way, and stay thus, completely unmoving, until the animal returned to its grazing. In this fashion he could get to within a few yards of a herd. It was as if the animals were unaware of his continuing nearness if they could not actually see him move. Pip maintained that there was a definite and unvarying time syndrome when animals grazed, between the time they lowered their heads to chew on the grass and then raised them in watchfulness. If so, Pip was certainly the only one of us to be able to exploit it. Once close enough for absolute accuracy he would loose an arrow and we were guaranteed a meal of venison or mutton that evening. He preferred not to experiment with the method in the cases of cattle or horses, except on one occasion.

On that particular day he and Barry had been tracking a herd of pigs in open woodland, but the beasts entered a marsh and they lost them. 'Looks like rabbit tonight,' remarked Barry.

'Why not beef?' responded Pip. They had earlier spotted a herd of long-horned cattle, a remarkably shaggy form of the species, grazing less than a mile from their position. We had never ventured to shoot these formidable beasts with arrows, although I recall that Oa's tribe had a technique for spearing them. Our own method, one we knew the natives used, was to dig a pit across a known cattle run—it did not have to be very deep, three or four feet was adequate—and spike the base with two or three wooden stakes. This so injured any beast unfortunate enough to stumble into it that it was either already dead or easily despatched when we arrived on the scene.

'Beef would be nice,' said Barry smacking his lips. He had not taken his friend seriously.

'Well, shall we go and get one?' uttered Pip laconically, and he began to head back the way they had come. Barry told me later that he had not fully realised his friend's intentions until Pip actually began to stalk the herd. They walked swiftly, Pip leading the way to a nest of rocks on the edge of a flat plain. No words were spoken. Pip merely waved to Barry indicating that he should wait by the rocks, and he himself trotted quietly, hunched low, out into the plain. The cattle were then some two hundred yards away. Barry counted seven of them: three cows, two possibly yearling heifers, one calf and a bull. When within a hundred yards, Pip adopted his usual stalking manner, bow loaded and partly drawn, his progress a series of short, quick advances followed by periods of absolute stillness. There was very little wind. The grass was long, well above Pip's knees. Thistles were abundant.

The closest beast was a cow. Just beyond her, some ten yards further away, were the two heifers standing together, and some distance behind them, but no further, was the bull, alone. All the animals faced the same way as was normal with cattle, in this case broadside on to the hunter. The bull was by far the most restless. His vigilance was hardly less than constant. Yet so skilful was Pip's advance that the bull remained seemingly unaware. Barry, then fully conscious of Pip's seriousness, did not stay secluded amongst the rocks; he wanted to be nearer to the action in case of an emergency. He followed Pip's path through the grass, crawling on his belly. He was desperately afraid, he admitted later, not so much for himself as for his friend, and also cross at Pip's foolhardiness. Raising himself onto his arms he could see the scene quite clearly. There were trees on the plain, all large, still hung with the scintillating green of summer foliage—oak and elm and chestnut, beech and poplar, dotted across the pasture. There was one, a great old chestnut tree, very near to the herd. He could see that Pip would have this tree to his back by the time he was within accurate arrow range. At about a hundred yards from the herd Barry remained still for fear of spooking the beasts. Pip was then perhaps thirty yards from the nearest cow. Close enough for a shot, but a few paces more to be sure. A few more paces.

The sun was high. It was a cloudless day and insects droned in constant activity. There were bees seeking clover in the grass and grasshoppers calling untunefully and without pause. There was little heat from the sun for summer was almost gone, but it was pleasant. There were large ears of grain on the grass stalks. The grass was powerfully aromatic. Barry was oblivious of these sensations just then, his concentration entirely upon his diminutive friend whose bald scalp, brown in the sun and peeling, was visible even from Barry's position low in the grass. He was standing still as if he was a piece of wind-deformed sandstone. But not quite still. Barry could see his fingers tensing on his bowstring and the weapon being raised with infinite slowness. The field stretched into a distorted eternity; the trees were quiet in their patient growth. Nothing watched the insignificant defiance of a creature called man. Barry became adream with a sense of the nascence of his kind, conscious of primality. A man born in a city, reared to the sound of automation, supreme in the understanding of the behaviour of molecules and the physical laws of the universe, aware then only of the excitement of a suspended moment preceding violence. His fellow scientist, trained for years in the study of the structure of life, now poised and intent upon the destruction of life. All science was irrelevant at that moment. The only relevance was the smell of foetid hide, warm and thick in the nostrils.

The bull was motionless. Head at chest height, eyes fixed, horns huge. 'Don't move,' Barry whispered, 'don't move yet, Pip. Not yet.'

Pip's bow was high now. He would need to raise himself to his full height to be sure of his aim. He remained unmoving, strongly aware of the bull's unease. And the moment stretched. Barry knew how Pip's limbs would be aching. The insects droned in their indifference. The bull was an object of stone. Pip had to move. It was move or cramp from tension. His arm straightened fractionally. Then the bull charged.

'Look out!' screamed Barry leaping to his feet. Instantly the herd was stampeding. Pip had loosed his arrow. It was embedded in the bull's neck, and its effect was singularly unnoticeable. Pip ran. He could do nothing else. Barry ran, too, faster than ever before in his life, in a sort of leaping gait to clear the long grass and hallooing like a bellowing moose. Pip could not make the tree. Barry was very close. The bull's lowered head was a mere hand's breadth from Pip's fleeing heels.

'Dodge!' shrieked Barry, and Pip flung himself sideways. A

horn struck him and he spiralled, limbs uncontrolled in the air. The bull pulled up with incredible suddenness, almost within its own length, and spun about scattering clods of grass. For a moment it was still, searching for its victim. Huge, violent muscles heaving beneath matted fibres of hair, one foreleg restlessly kicking up bits of soil. Barry hit it with an arrow, in the shoulder. It saw its new adversary and turned to face him. Huge man and huge beast. Barry edged for the tree. Pip lay scrabbling in the grass several yards to the left. The bull exploded into speed. There was nowhere for Barry to go. There was no time. He flung himself headlong onto the bull's neck between its horns and hung onto them, unable to breathe, his lungs shocked still from the impact. He felt dead in the chest and knew ribs were broken.

Then the bull braced itself on the ground and began to throw its head about in an effort to dislodge the thing on its horns. And Barry hung on. To let go was certain death. To hang on was futile. The bull reared and tossed and shook. And Barry hung on. He thought of nothing. Not of the futility of it. Not of the stabbing pain in his lungs as breath began to come in tortured gasps. Not of the bull's colossal might. Just to hang on; every shred of his will concentrating on that frightful task. The horns were huge where he grasped them, his hands unable to encircle them. There was sweat on his palms and blood on one horn. He tried to lock his legs around the bull's nose. That was hopeless. The bull's head was not still for an instant, and every toss jarred his wilting ribs. It was a test of endurance between man and bull. He knew the bull had to win.

Pip reached for his bow. It had fallen from his grasp when the bull had struck him and lay a few feet away. His leg was torn fearfully and there was so much blood streaming out that he was afraid the femoral artery had been severed. The bull was just three yards away as he fitted an arrow. He felt sick and strengthless and quite giddy. He pulled the bow to its maximum extremity. He would only have one shot. Everything was a blur. The bull, Barry hanging impossibly on its horns, the skyline indistinct beyond. He fired the arrow and fainted before he could see the effect of his shot. The shaft flew accurately. It reached the bull's heart. Minutes later its legs crumpled and Barry rolled clear. The great beast made a last effort to stand but its legs would not obey it. It died and silence descended on the plain.

Barry carried Pip into camp later that afternoon. He had bound up the dreadful wound in Pip's leg, which required fifteen stitches to close, but the femoral artery had not been cut. Barry had two broken ribs as he had suspected and he had to have his chest strapped up for several weeks. We had enough beef to last many days, longer than it would keep. But we never stalked cattle in the open again, and the bond between Barry and Pip was cemented even stronger. It was a bond that even the tragedy that was to come could not break.

Chapter Eight

Summer lingered on that first year. We were never sure of the month. The tribe grew sleek and fat, for the territories of two clans were ours to harvest. While Pip and Barry continued to hunt together, Terry preferred to fish. It had long been a favourite pastime of his and he became absorbed in the challenge of fashioning his own equipment. He would spend hours on the riverbank, perfectly content. I joined him frequently because I was also fond of fishing. Fish began to form a common item of our diet. We ate a lot of meat and a lot of fish, but also great quantities of wild fruit and vegetables. Apples were particularly abundant, and although most of them were afflicted with worm, this made very little difference to the enjoyment of them by the women. Initially we were more squeamish but eventually ate them with as much relish as the women, maggots and all. Paul was fully occupied with his medical activities, if not actually engaged in healing, for he spent countless hours gathering herbs and concocting infusions over a small fire. He was surprisingly successful with his primitive potions and totally happy in his preoccupation. As for me, when I was not fishing, I would tramp the woods and fields alone, and I, too, was content.

One day I went alone to the top of a wood-covered slope. Autumn was nearly upon us. Already the trees were scattering their leaves in the pre-winter winds. It was a cold, grey day and the wind was chill upon the sweat of my body as I scrambled upwards. Ahead of me was light through the trees, the sun diffused and beckoning in the bracken between the stems. The ground was stony underfoot, and the leaves danced around my old boots, damp, yet somehow friendly, and there was a good, heavy smell in the air. There were birds singing, darting across my path, wrens and robins and the ubiquitous sparrows. A magpie dropped at my feet and snatched a cricket from my very footsteps, a confident and carefree bird, so black and so white it could have been freshly painted. And yet the sun was really only half attempting to shine. There was no warmth to it in the woods. At last I came out of the trees.

'Before you, you will see a big town,' Oona had told me, for this was her native country, Oa's stamping ground. 'It's as big as Bordeaux.'

And there it was. Perhaps Limoges; I don't really know for sure. None of us knew France well enough to be certain. It nestled in a river valley, a red and white town, though nowhere as big as Bordeaux. It was a pretty town. 'No one lives there,' she had said. 'Beyond is the land of the Enads. Here is our land. They do not cross the river to come here except sometimes in winter when the herds move. Then we fight them. Neither do we cross to their land, only once that I remember when I was a little girl and Oa's father was chief.'

'Is that the country of the North men, then?'

'Oh no, that's much further north. The Enads pay tribute to the North men just as we do.'

I did not stay long studying the town. The wind was strong at the top of the slope and I was cold. But it was not the elements that inspired my descent. In the valley leading towards the town there was a lone figure; no beasts, few trees, grass that was the height of a man's hips, yellow wild grain rippling in spasms with the eddies of the wind. The man stood with his back to me about two hundred yards away, also apparently studying the town. He was tall, with hair that was long and black and straight, tied into a ponytail with a series of leather thongs. I wondered for a moment why he was concentrating his attention on the town, then realised it was actually on the sky beyond, where massive clouds were piling up and rolling towards us, black and urgent with a hurrying anger. There was a dreadful storm coming.

The man began to move, loping with an easy gait for the town, and I began my descent, following him, not then analysing my motives. It was unnecessary. The man was Oa, and somewhere near would be Lian.

*   *   *

I huddled in a doorway. All about me the rain crashed down, driven by a wind of frenetic strength. Already it was dark although the sunset should have been two hours away. I was wet through, the rain having caught me before I reached shelter, and I was shivering. With no matches I had no way to light a fire, but I had stripped off and wrung as much water from my clothes as I could, had redressed hurriedly, fractionally more comfortable but no warmer. The clothes were damp still and heavy. Oa would have a fire. I had to find him. But it was a big town and the rain had reduced visibility to almost zero.

I strained my ears, but above the howl of the wind and the incessant pounding of the rain it was impossible to detect any other sound. So without vision and without the aid of my ears, I set out on my search. The town was of course completely unknown to me and it was impossible to plan a methodical approach in the storm. It was merely a matter of keeping out of the rain as much as possible, ducking from doorway to doorway, and awning to awning. Somewhere, surely I would find signs of human presence. Oa must have at least six women besides Lian, and also several children, and possibly the three Mekan youths who had fled from Bordeaux. In such a storm even the savages would seek shelter if only to maintain a fire. Somewhere. Somewhere in this town. I did not pause to consider my welcome. Oa owed us his life. Surely he would be friendly.

For over an hour I struggled on, once again wet through, yet my efforts had generated sufficient heat to stop the shivering. Indeed, I was perspiring heavily in the wet clothes. The rain had eased but the wind had not let up, and the darkness was as impenetrable as ever. Once I stumbled into a creature, huge and unseen in the solidity of night. It was hot and wet and muscular to touch—a horse. It had not noticed my approach in the sense-smothering frenzy of the storm, but it knew when I touched it. There was an instant response, a whinny that startled the night, sharper than the wind, a spontaneous, muscular lurch, and I was hurled against a wall. There were hoof beats quickly muffled by mere yards of distance. Then again just the wind and the rain. I was bruised and shaken. What on earth was a horse doing in a town like this? Perhaps it, too, had sought shelter from the storm.

Trembling from shock, I sat down. It was a dry spot. I noticed that my arm was bleeding. I waited until my muscles were once again under control before moving on. But I had only taken two paces when arms seized me. My reaction in my surprise was less than immediate, but I broke free. There were two dark shapes beside me, unidentifiable in the lightlessness. 'Oa,' I called out. 'Oa, is that you?'

Then something struck me from behind and I lurched forward, arms flung out, endeavouring to keep my balance. The two dark shapes merged and forced me to the ground, and then there were bodies all over me, grunting and breathing hard. They had my arms pulled up tight behind me, and they lashed them together from my biceps to my wrists, ensuring my helplessness. I lifted my face from the road. 'Oa,' I gritted, 'is that you? Why do you do this to a friend?'

'Stand up,' commanded Oa's voice. It did not sound at all friendly. I rolled over and struggled to my knees. Unseen hands hoisted me upright. I could see light then. Oa came forward carrying a torch of bound grasses.

'It's the Captain,' he said, perhaps recognising me for the first time, and using the only name he knew me by.

'Untie me, Oa,' I snapped at him. 'I come as a friend.'

His face remained hostile. I glanced at the other two assailants. They were just boys, undoubtedly the Mekan youths. But there were three lads, I recalled. Where was the third? I waited for Oa to make a decision on my fate, but he simply turned on his heels and led us away, my own progress encouraged with the very effective incentive of a spearhead. And so I found a fire.

His camp was made in an old stone building, empty apart from its human occupants and a blazing fire, along with some haunches of meat and a few animal skins. There was the third youth, the youngest, hardly twelve years old, but full of swagger and boldness in a consciousness of status. I counted ten women, only eight children and one adolescent girl. Quite a small nucleus for a new band. The scene was dominated by the fire; beyond and around were just shadows, women yes, and children, but faceless then; bare breasts and hollow navels patterned in the firelight. There was the smell of women, the smell of stale blood, and the aching smell of cooking meat.

There was the sound of the wind and the rain beating the walls about us, the noise of the clean and angry fire, fat dripping from suspended meat, a child's whimpering muffled by its mother's comfort. It was stiflingly hot. I looked for Lian but the shadows defeated me. They threw me into a corner and held me face down by means of a foot pressed to the small of my back while they roped me to a stone column, one of several that supported the roof. My arms were cut free and I was permitted to sit up. Then I was left alone. I wanted to talk to Oa but he was on the far side of the fire, ignoring me.

It was not too uncomfortable. The heat from the fire quickly dried me; it was even pleasant to be warm again. It was almost stupefying. I was suddenly overwhelmingly sleepy, but I fought against it, assisted by the odour of roast meat tantalising my stomach. I was silent, and as my eyes became accustomed to the firelight and the shadows I studied the room carefully. It was large, with just one doorway but several window openings; a stone structure some sixty feet by forty, rectangular, and with the columns breaking up the space struck me as most unfunctional. I wondered about the fire for I could see no stocks of fuel for it and it was a singularly large blaze. I could recognise faces by that time. Nowhere could I see the one I searched for.

About half an hour after my arrival, another figure staggered in under a load of saturated firewood, carried on the back and aided in this by a rawhide thong around the forehead, the arms behind the neck helping to take the unbelievable weight by gripping the strap above the shoulders. She, for it was a woman, was plainly close to the point of exhaustion from her efforts, but no one rose to help her as she stumbled to the fire and by actually crumpling at the knees allowed the bundle to rest on the floor. Somebody reached out and grasped a few pieces of the timber, throwing them on the fire, their wet condition hardly affecting the hunger of that blaze. It amazed me that they sat so close. The new arrival stood up and stretched back her shoulders to ease her aching muscles. For a moment she was portrayed magnificently in the glow of the fire. Glorious golden breasts, planes of light across a slim, flat stomach, hands stretched palms out and taut in the ecstasy of relief. Her face clear and sharp.

Lian. I almost cried out, conscious then of my heart like a separate entity in my chest, big, painful, important. What was it that stirred me where this woman was concerned?

There was a moment when her eyes met mine straining for her across the fire. She tensed visibly. Then a child cried at her feet. It must have been her own, having crawled to her from whatever woman had nursed it during her absence. Lian bent down and picked the child up, immediately giving it suckle. She glanced at me only once more before sitting down. She sat outside the main circle, as if deliberately isolating herself from them, conscious only of her baby, just rocking to and fro and occasionally stroking the infant's head. It occurred to me that now Oa was the only adult male in the group he would have the choice of ten women, no doubt all vying for his attention. Lian's position as his favourite wife would have been usurped, probably much to her relief. But it looked as if she had become a menial, an outsider. Pondering on this I fell asleep.

When I awoke the fire had subsided to a pile of glowing embers, emanating a powerful heat. The tribe were asleep around it, except one keeping watch on the fire. It was Lian. She sat cross-legged on the floor, her infant asleep beside her. She must have been watching me. I had fallen asleep with my head supported on my knees. As I straightened up and looked at her, Lian smiled. I had never seen her smile openly before. She looked about her, checking the stillness of the sleeping forms, then, taking something from beside her, she stood up and crossed over to where I sat, making no sound for these people would awaken at the least alien noise. She squatted beside me and I touched her, just her arm—I could not restrain the impulse. She had brought me some meat which she offered like a tribute on outstretched hands. I took the meat in one hand and held her wrist with the other. Tenderly I lifted the small, work-worn hand, palm up, and kissed it. She withdrew her arm quickly and rose to go. I reached for her wrist again and gently pulled, indicating that I wished her to sit beside me. She shook her head, looking around almost fearfully and pulled against my grip. I released her. Then she hesitated. Suddenly, quickly, she reached down, touched my shoulder very lightly, a momentary contact, and she stepped away. Soon she was sitting with her child again.

I ate the meat. Lian fed the fire. The immediate flames lit up her face in all its striking beauty. Her long hair flickered gold and copper in the dancing light. She was looking into the flames, a habit as old as man himself. What were her thoughts? What emotions stirred in her heart? She did not look at me again, I who loved her. I knew that then. Why? I have asked myself that question many times; the answer still escapes me. She was lovely, yes, but beauty alone is not a reason for love; passion perhaps, but that is subject to simple control, whereas love is overwhelming, a drive beyond rational thought. Was it her eyes, so full of clouded emotions, repressed and subjugated? It may well have been, but it was soul calling to soul, a communication uncomprehended, but real, very real, and tangible, and profound, and full of agony, the agony of all men and all women since the dawn of time.

The piece of meat was tough and half raw, but I was very hungry and finished every scrap, fat and gristle and soot. It seemed delicious. Feeling better, I proceeded to examine my bonds. Rawhide rope is virtually unsnappable, so I paid most attention to the knots, but made no attempt to untie them. With only my teeth to use it was clearly futile. I studied the stone column with care, contemplating the idea of working the tether backwards and forwards to wear it through, but the column was quite smooth and I never really held out much hope for success. Nevertheless I occupied myself until dawn broke rubbing the tether on the stone. It was a complete waste of energy. When morning came the tribe moved camp.

The storm had passed. The sky was an untarnished and innocent blue as if declaiming all knowledge of its violence the previous night. They prodded me along once more, but not very far. They forced me into one of the many factory buildings in the area, a place of brown brick, plain and moss-covered, a dreary place of little light and dank air. I was thrust and jabbed into a crevice beneath a piece of machinery. It was full of cobwebs which clung to my face. Things crawled over me. The hole was rank with the odour of mice. My hands had been tied behind my back and my ankles strapped together once I was on the floor. At first I could not see a thing. It was utterly black. A cobweb was in my mouth and there was no means of removing it. I heard them shifting heavy weights behind me. The crevice was very cramped, but I succeeded in rolling over to face the light. They were blocking off the entrance to the hole with massive lumps of corroded machinery from elsewhere in the building and I realised they were effectively hiding me from the possibility of discovery by my comrades. Why was I so important to them? It could only have been the same factor that had persuaded Oa to keep us with him in the early days, the reason that had prompted the Mekans to keep Terry and John in captivity; as human tribute to the raiders from the north. One thing was certain: Oa's present numbers made such a consideration a vital one indeed.

Then they left me. I was helpless. I did try to wriggle back and push at the obstructions, but they were immovable. It had taken all four males to move them individually into position. Perhaps with my arms free I might have had a chance to shift them, but my arms were behind me, quite numb, and my legs were so confined I could only keep them straight out. Pins and needles soon attacked my feet. I was unable even to bend my legs to relieve them. My head was jammed up against the metal support of a huge piece of machinery whose function I never discovered, and when I lay on my back, the only position offering any degree of comfort at all for a few seconds, I looked up at a huge roller just a few inches from my face.

A whole day passed. There was some difference in available light between day and night and I could see reasonably well in the fractional light of day. The hole was a haven of mice. If I turned my head away from the blocked entrance I stared straight into an occupied nest. At first the agonies of unrelieved cramp absorbed my whole mind, but later I endeavoured to disorientate myself by studying the mouse's nest so close to my gaze. There were little cosy, cup-shaped dens of shredded paper, hair and grass, with pink and naked mouselets. I watched them being suckled. The smell was abominable. I discovered that some of the shreds of paper had somehow, through the countless decades, retained a faint and disjointed degree of legibility. I pieced together the name of an actress who had once been familiar to me; part of an advertisement for a brand of toothpaste that had been universally popular; I read of a wonder drug in another scrap of advertising, its

96

name nearly illegible, but 'bio . . .' something or other, which almost triggered a chord of my memory; there were two very clear words, probably from a headline: 'President acts . . .', certainly provocative words in other circumstances; and there were other unconnected bits of words. It was surprising how much those few echoes of the past in printed form assisted my mental state. For the first few hours.

Otherwise the hours were mind-destroyingly tedious, and painful as cramp overcame all mental distractions and took anguished precedence. Several times mice ran over my face, sometimes stopping to gaze into my giant eyes, their little noses twitching and whiskers vibrating continuously. I would shout at them to scare them off. I prayed there were no rats. There were spiders, though, and there were lizards. I learned to loathe them. One spider, fat furry abdomen, thick short legs, lurked not far from my eyes. He was always facing me, his jaws forever working. Once he swung down upon a thread, almost brushing my nose. I dreaded him touching me. Supernatural fears beyond reason and understanding welled up inside me. I stared at him in nameless horror. Sweat poured from me. I screamed. He scrambled back up his thread and resumed his position in the centre of his web, rubbing his jaws up and down, up and down. The lizards scurried boldly over me, over my eyes, over my lips, around my ears. It was as if they had some knowledge of my harmlessness. They were an irritation beyond measure, and I have hated lizards ever since.

Then thirst began to assail me, and that was the worst torment of all. Cobwebs on my lips, dust in my mouth, my tongue dry and raspy. I licked my lips but there was no spittle. I was unable to close my mouth for my lips would seem to grow together. I breathed dust, it was in the back of my throat. My head was enormous and splitting. I thought many times of a glass of cold beer, clear and amber with a band of foam, and drove myself insane with the imagined ecstasy of that first golden, white-lipped quaff.

Eventually the ordeal was interrupted.

About a day after my internment I heard someone approach the hole. The footsteps stopped just outside the blocked entrance. A few guttural noises, an attempt at speech, told me it was Lian. There was a space between the machines and I turned my face towards it. I could see her looking through at me. There was in her expression such agony, so great a distress, so much love, I was moved to croak her name; I was unable to speak. Her arm came through the gap and she wiped my mouth and face with a piece of damp fur. Then followed a skin bag of water which she poured into my craving mouth. The water was muddy and smelled of animal hide, but it was more wonderful than I can describe. She left the bag within the hole and then fed me pieces of meat and fruit, waiting while I ate each piece before feeding me more.

Oa's voice called from nearby, imperiously. She passed me one more piece of food. I was able to kiss her fingers before taking it into my mouth. She responded by touching my lips gently, passing her fingers lightly across them. Then she was gone.

I spent three more days in that hole. Feet dead. Wrists raw from working my fingers to retain feeling. A continual fight against cramp till in the end it defeated me and I lay in pain and despair. It became a semi-comatose state of unrelieved anguish. The water was a blessing, or surely I would have died. I kept the opening of the water bag in my mouth and sucked moisture continually. The mice ran over me, and the lizards. The spider wandered carelessly over my face. But I was indifferent. Twice Lian came with food, but on the second occasion I was unresponsive. Feeling was dead. She came a third time, but there was no food, just an arm through the gap, a knife thrust at me and swiftly dropped. She fled. I cannot guess at the risks she took to bring that knife to me. But how could it help?

I remember lying for hours just looking at it—a thing of bone and wood, no larger than a table knife. It amazes me now to recall how indifferent I was to that knife. The will to survive had almost gone. Thought needed effort, and effort was practically beyond me. I sucked my water bag. There was no more moisture. It did not matter. Nothing mattered. Soon death would come, and in death no more torment.

A mouse bit one of my fingers. I felt the pain above the unrelenting ache of my strained ligaments. Then from somewhere, from some deep, inner part of my unconscious mind, the last remaining shred of defiance came to the surface of a defeated consciousness. At first it was a mere twitch in my dying fingers, almost in reflex to scare the mouse away. Then thought. Reason slowly returning. If my hands were free. My hands free. Hands free. Hands free. The knife. There was the knife. I could do it. I could do it. I *would* do it.

But it took time for thought to convert itself into action. I worked the knife down with my shoulders and elbows to within reach of my bound hands. Then the blade was in my fingers. There was something quite stimulating in the pain of strengthless digits struggling for muscular control. I had become frantic with the desire to live, when minutes before death had been my only wish. Then suddenly my hands were free. I could not reach my feet but my mind was alive. For perhaps thirty minutes, maybe an hour, for time had no meaning, I worked at my arms and hands to resensitise them. Then I explored the bulk of the machinery that was blocking the entrance. One hand stretched through the gap, felt a lever of some sort, possibly an operating lever for the machine. Further fumbling exploration revealed its attachment to the main body by a split pin, corroded to uselessness. I was able to work the lever backwards and forwards, easing it from its spindle until it was finally free in my hands. It was made of a steel alloy and had oxidised superficially, but it was solid enough for my immediate purpose. Using the lever as a crowbar, I jammed the end of it under a piece of machinery and heaved. It was an almost impossible task, almost but not absolutely. An eighth of an inch at a time, the nearest obstacle moved. It was muscle-aching and should have been despairing. But I had already sunk to the depths of despair and had beaten it, and the aching of my muscles was an almost wonderful sensation. All that occupied my thoughts was that I would live, and I would be free.

I do not know how long it took. All I can recall now is my awareness that I would make it. And I did. There came the moment when I pulled myself from that hole and cut my feet loose. It was impossible to walk, impossible even to stand, but my feet had sensation still, the terrible agony of reviving bloodflow. I crawled to the doorless entrance of the building and into the blessed coolness and freedom of a star-sprinkled night. I lay in the street, happy and grateful till dawn, enduring the torture of my feet and exercising my limbs. By then I could stand. I could walk. Returning to the interior of the building, I concealed myself behind the door opening and waited.

After about an hour Oa came, and Lian carrying food. Lian came through the doorway first. She saw me but moved on towards the hole without betraying my presence. I believe she had been confident that I would be free and understood my intentions clearly. Oa followed her through and I hit him with the steel bar across the back of his skull. He dropped without a sound. Lian turned and faced me. I dropped the lever and we looked at each other. We stood, just looking, for many seconds. Silent, but the silence was communication, and we told each other many things. We came together slowly; it was I who moved to her, and I dropped on one knee and put my arms about her waist, pulling her to me. My head was beneath her breast, and she knew that I loved her, was offering myself to her. She clasped my head tightly to her stomach, her fingers moving in my hair. How glorious was the emotion that passed between us then. I felt her tremble, and I was trembling, too. And in that mutual tremor everything was said.

I stood up, took her hand, led her past the bleeding head of Oa and out into the sunlight.

We walked into their camp. It was not far away, just on the outskirts of the town. Three boys—how easy it was to overpower them even unarmed as I was. But I had no wish to kill them. Disarmed, they lay bruised and awed in the dust where I had hurled them. We collected Lian's infant and some food, as well as my own weapons. Then we left that town.

We headed into a blue sky, green grass wet with morning dew, the songs of happy birds and the smell of freedom.

Chapter Nine

Our own tribe had moved on, but where I was unable to pick up their trail, Lian could always find signs of their passage. We travelled leisurely. My ankles were swollen and, for many weeks, walking long distances was to be difficult. Those were golden days, warm and gentle, with carpets of sun-ripened leaves, and wild grain in its harvest colours. The land was mellow and hospitable. There were apples to eat, and peaches, red and full and sweet, and grapes still persistent despite the years of neglect. There were ducks, moving south then, succulent eating in their summer-grown fat; and deer, too, herding together at the coming of winter, cropping their way inevitably southwards. For the first time in my life I was aware of the instincts of wild creatures, attuning, developing an empathy and an understanding. The days were shortening and the breezes, although still mild, were cool. I rested often during those languorous days, drinking peace, revelling in my new awareness of natural things, their simple beauty, their complex loveliness. Here in the sun, leaves fluttering above, the grass alive beneath my conscious flesh, and high up a kestrel, motionless on its serrated wings.

'See,' called Lian with the soundlessness of a pointing hand, 'it stoops.' The incredible plummet, feathers, fierce and sudden death in mid air. In death there is grace. In death there is beauty. I know the absolute ugliness of death now, but at that time, in that transitory paradise, I saw only beauty. Lian looked at me, her brown eyes alive with the excitement of it, eager to share her thrill, and she touched me gently. I loved the days. The nights—I will not share the nights with you. Warm, love-wrapped hours. For her there was wonder—the wonder of tenderness, of gentle hands, of caresses. The wonder of her own emotions. She could not vocalise them but she told me with her arms and her lips and her eyes and her adoration. They seemed like stolen hours. We had no responsibilities, just two people alone, confident in our aloneness and our privacy. The countryside was without mankind, uncultivated, serene and unpossessed. Seven days of tranquillity. Then we found our tribe.

They were heading south when we came up with them. They had searched the town for me, had actually met Oa and his band, but they had kept their distance, despite repeated attempts to converse. It had been a large town and the storm had erased all traces of my presence. As they really had no reason to believe that I had been there, they had decided that I must have gone elsewhere during the storm and had become lost. They had moved on, confident that sooner or later I would find them.

Life resumed its habitual course. We hunted with increasing adeptness, and we fished. We skinned animals and tanned the skins, rather crudely but a considerable improvement on the primitive methods of the savages. We made new bows, modifying them in the light of our experience, and an infinite number of arrows, feathered and tipped with steel. Life was basic, yet it was utterly absorbing, and satisfying, too. Our greatest longing was for more books, and Paul was occasionally frustrated because of the lack of modern drugs, even though he performed herbal miracles. His biggest regret was his inability to create sterile conditions, but even so he managed to keep most infections at bay. Our past life rarely intruded. If we thought at all of our families, of our friends, if memories of our children gave us pain, we did not speak of it.

We had endless conversations around camp fires, usually in the open for the evenings were balmy and the dying light and flickering of flames were hypnotic after a physical day, conducive to talk that was slow, thoughts that came in fragments, were assembled into remarks and gradually moulded into vocal ideas, philosophy, and very often humour.

I recall one such evening. It was raining, not unpleasantly, not even cold as I remember, but steadily, like liquid moonlight. The fire blazed. Pip was eating the haunch of a young deer; the fat kept running into his beard, and his bald head shone yellow in the rain. Terry was sharpening his knife on a stone. He said: 'I wonder if a bone knife could be made as sharp as this.'

Pip answered him, waving his piece of meat, 'Oh yes, I think so, but temporary, so temporary.'

'Man doesn't really need steel, then, does he?'

'Not at this level of development, that's true.' He paused as if contemplating where he would bite next, but he did not take a bite. He held the haunch up like a baton. 'Consider this,' he said. 'If mankind again learns to herd and fence in cattle and sheep, if he again takes up agriculture, then bone implements will not be adequate.'

'You mean man will have to rediscover the use of metals before evolution progresses any further?' I put in.

Pip waved his hunk of meat. 'Look, it's like this. Our past social evolution depended not only on the settlements made possible by agriculture, but upon the discovery of metals. They had to go hand in hand. Agriculture wasn't possible without metals on any reasonable scale, but metals weren't necessary until agriculture became a way of life.' He bit the lump of meat then, tearing a piece off with his teeth. His mouth was not visible through the great black mat of his beard.

'Will that happen again, do you think?'

'Oh yes, eventually. It has a great deal to do with numbers, you see. At subsistence level of living, the hunting and gathering existence that we find ourselves part of, human numbers are very limited. There is a mathematical relationship between the size of tribes and their area of hunting ground. As you have seen here, those hunting territories are fiercely defended, but if a group became too large for its own territory other factors would come into play.'

'Such as?'

'Well, studies have shown that the optimum size of hunting groups is about thirty individuals. When a tribe grows too far beyond this number, rivalries occur and result in breakaway groups. The territory cannot support more than one tribe so hostilities break out, either with an adjacent tribe or with the parent clan. Tribal numbers are limited not so much by summer conditions such as we have experienced so far, but by winter scarcity. We still have to face that.'

'Our numbers appear to be all right.'

'Yes, we are less than thirty adults, but our balance is wrong. We are rather light on males.'

Then Paul spoke. His voice was soft but full of passion. 'The world must never become so full of people again, not with the ethics of humanity that we maintained. Our numbers outstripped the capacity of the world to support them. We raped our own planet. In our egotism we held human life as the most important ethos of our decisions, beyond the worth of any other forms of life, beyond the very order of nature itself. We spent countless millions of pounds and poured endless resources into keeping alive our chronically sick, extending the life of the old, trying to save the lives of babies too severely handicapped to survive. We destroyed our world to accommodate our precious philosophies, devoting our energies and our resources to ensuring no decrease of human numbers, irrespective of the cost to the environment. It's no wonder that technological man was wiped out and only subsistence man remains. One could almost believe in a deity giving mankind its just rewards.' That was a long speech from this aloof man. It was as close as I ever came to his inner thoughts, except once, years later.

'But . . .' said Pip, leaning forward. Rain ran off his nose and dripped onto his naked feet. His toenails were large and thick and black around the edges. He still held his hunk of meat, by then little more than bone. The rain hardly bothered him. '. . . not all men did die.' He did not pursue Paul's theme. 'I think we have to look elsewhere than at divine interference for the causes of such a drastic decline, the total loss of technological knowledge.'

'There is only one sector of society that could have been so ignorant of science and craftsmanship that it couldn't pass it on to its descendants,' put in Barry. It was his first contribution that night. He was huge and ragged and his hair was straggling catstails that merged with his beard as the rain spattered over him.

'Children!' added Pip.

'Children,' said Barry. It was another night, I am sure, though they do tend to merge in memory. Yes, there was no rain at all that night. The moon was wearing a skirt of flimsy cloud, a cold iceberg of a moon. The night was grey. There were no stars.

'Children under eight, perhaps, or even younger. No knowledge of any technology, the wheel only a device for toys. How would they survive? How would they grow up?'

'Would they survive at all?'

'Some. There would be some who were tough, who knew something of catching animals or fishing. There were always children with such an inclination. They would have been the leaders, the providers while the others learned. For a while, whatever the catastrophe that wiped out the adults, there would have been cans and jars of food, but once the last can had been opened and the final jar broken, then a society much as we see here would have been almost inevitable. Untaught children growing up unaided by adult guidance. Think of it. Imagine for yourself the likely outcome. It's not a great leap from a stick to a spear, but a bow is a more sophisticated refinement.'

'The most meagre of clothes without anything but the crudest method of tanning, no traditions or beliefs other than a lingering and distorted memory of Noël,' Pip added. 'A festivity particularly directed at children.'

'But why? Why only small children surviving?'

'Ah! It certainly rules out a nuclear cause anyway, doesn't it? Radiation affects children as much as adults,' was Barry's unhelpful contribution. He was seated, bending over searching for fleas in the hairs of his chest. His words came muffled from his lowered head. I noticed signs of grey in the black of his hair.

Pip elaborated a little. 'Look, I think we all agree that the cause was not nuclear. Not a virus either as Paul has suggested, for much the same reasons. That leaves us with only one other possibility as far as I can see.'

It was Paul who said: 'Drugs!'

'Exactly. Following that train of thought one can see a number of possible answers to Jeff's question, why only children? Assume a drug that had universal popularity, perhaps an apparently harmless opiate. A sort of Aldous Huxley "Soma" if you like. Let us further presume that it would not have been given to children. But the drug turned out to have effects that no one could have foreseen.'

'Surely not a sudden wiping out of the whole human race?'

'No, but there are other possibilities.'

It was another night. It was cold. Icy winds had been blowing for days. Hunting had been arduous and of limited rewards. We had retreated to the hotel in Bordeaux. 'I can't imagine such a drug,' Paul was saying. 'It would have had to be taken by every adult. It would have had to have either a sudden lethal effect, or a universal addiction that would eventually achieve the same effect. Yet every drug that I ever dealt with had to undergo such exhaustive tests before release on the market that such a result would have been impossible. It seems too far-fetched to me.'

'They are valid arguments,' agreed Barry in his best lecturing manner. He was standing up. The picture of him is still clear in my mind. There was an unconscious straightening of his spine. His hands moved as if to tuck his thumbs under his armpits; they touched his sheepskin jacket and moved back to his belt. He frowned and walked several paces away from us, presenting us with a view of his vast back. 'However, I cannot agree entirely that the lethal aspect was necessarily sudden at all, or even recognised.'

He paused and, turning round, glared at us as if we were a group of students. 'Or even recognised,' he repeated, making his point very ponderously. 'It would be far more likely that any effect would have been the reverse of sudden. Possibly everyone was affected at first, from infants to adults . . .'

'In which case it could well have been a virus,' interrupted Paul.

'Yes, but let me finish. If it was a bacteriological problem, say a virus introduced to Earth from a returning spacecraft which had immediate, widespread and devastating consequences, what happened to it?'

'It mutated to a benign form,' suggested Paul. 'But by that time humanity was already doomed to a slow death. Maybe a decade passed before the final extinction of mankind, but in the meantime babies had been born unaffected by the microbe.'

'Well, it's a theory,' said Barry, obviously unimpressed, and perhaps cross that his lecture had been interrupted. 'But it couldn't happen, not from a space-introduced virus, anyway. No, I cannot accept that hypothesis at all. But a drug that had effects similar to that, not suddenly lethal at all, but perhaps cumulatively so over many, many years, possibly in conjunction with some other compound.'

'Alcohol?' I suggested.

'No, no, not alcohol. It would have been tested thoroughly with both alcohol and tobacco, with contraceptives and analgesics, and all commonly used compounds. The effect has to be related to long-term use in conjunction with something unforeseen, perhaps some drug that came on to the market afterwards.'

'Look, it may not have been lethal at all,' put in Pip. 'It may have had no fatal consequences to an individual directly in any way.'

'What are you suggesting?'

'I'm suggesting that the supposed drug may have affected the fertility of the species, not life.'

'But surely that would have been tested.'

Pip shrugged. Barry had gone very quiet, looking at his fellow scientist with great intensity. 'Yes, I see,' he said after a while. If he did, I certainly did not.

*　　*　　*

Winter came gently. We had become a close-knit group and we permitted ourselves some congratulations on the success of our adjustment to our new way of life. Superior intellect had prevailed and we had come out supreme in an environment completely alien to us. Our tribe was happy, the women's only concern their anxiety about the arrival of the North men. We dismissed this as exaggerated. We were not as their men. We would not be tamely cowed by a bunch of roving bandits. From constant questioning we were able to form a picture of these enigmatic northerners. It appeared that they were very large and very fierce. No one really knew where they came from, just from the north which simply meant further north than the immediate neighbours in that direction. Our own territory had northerly limits roughly described by the

Charente basin. We could elicit no stories to give us a clue as to the origins of Nowell time, other than that it coincided with the arrival of the North men on their trek to obtain human food. The women were so adamant about this that we were finally convinced of its truth. We did learn that on one occasion Oa had actually fought the North men rather than accede to their demands for tribute, but his resolution had decimated his band, and he had finally succumbed.

'We had the biggest tribe of this region before then,' Oona told us, 'and we were feared by all our neighbours, even the men of the hills to the east from where Lian comes, and the Mekans would flee at the sight of us. But after the battle with the North men we had only ten warriors.'

'So you don't recommend resistance, young lady?'

'Oh no! Please don't fight them. You are all so strong and very wise, but they are many, and they are very fierce.'

'Then we would have to pay them the tribute.'

'Yes. It's only two women. Two will be enough.'

'No, little one, that we can never do. We will find a way to defeat them, never fear.'

She looked at us oddly. 'You are such strange men,' she said. 'You have such strange ideas. You're not like our men at all.' I found that remark quite disturbing.

Gradually our hunting became more and more unsuccessful. We were still able to snare the occasional rabbit and there were still fish in the river Gironde, but the tribe had an enormous capacity for protein that could only be satisfied with meat. We went too far south and had a minor clash with a southern tribe. There were no fatalities and really no serious harm done, but we did learn the southern limits of our hunting territory. The game grew more and more scarce. We lived mainly on rabbit and winter fowl, fish and harvested fruit from the autumn. We did not go hungry, not then, anyway. We returned to our hotel in Bordeaux, and because of the repeated, almost desperate pleas of the women, prepared the place for a siege. We calculated that after a few days of futile waiting, the northerners would abandon our lands for more rewarding prospects further south.

We closed up the opening that we had made in the rear wall of the hotel as an access to the copse, and we pulled down the complete wall separating the hotel from the strip of woodland. With this masonry we built two man-high barricades thirty yards apart and perpendicular to the line of the buildings, giving us a defendable area for our trapping purposes from the hotel to the river. We stocked up on firewood, vegetables, wild corn with which we sometimes made a tasteless but probably nutritious porridge, and we filled all the hotel baths with water. We also made a huge stock of arrows. I must admit we supervised all the preparations without a great deal of sincerity. We really felt little fear of the North men. We were confident in our abilities, our superior intellects; fawned on by the women, idolised by the children, we saw ourselves almost as gods. Fortunately caution balanced our egotism.

Then the winter truly gripped the land. Weeks passed. Our efforts had been a waste of time. We left our woodland strip alone and trapped rabbits in the countryside. There were ducks to be had, hares and badgers still in the woods. The North men did not come. We became convinced that they would not come.

I enjoyed that period. It was hard and cold, but I have always liked the cold. Heavily rugged in sheepskins, the air sharp in the early dawn, the ground crackling beneath my moccasins, I would do the round of the traps. I liked the trees stark and silver, the occasional pine vividly geometrical against the random grouping of the elms and the beeches and the oak trees. It was silent in the mornings, the birds quiet and few, no dogs then, no leaves to rustle in the breeze, just the frost on the grass and my footsteps muffled in the woods. And perhaps there would be a rabbit strangled in a copper wire snare, often living still, with bulging eyes and feebly kicking limbs. I would be happy then, the struggles of the rabbit meaning nothing to me, its pain not reaching my soul. It was just food, and food was the imperative of my life. There were still deer in the woods, but I rarely saw them, only their tracks. I wondered what they ate, and Pip told me they lived on pine needles. There was grass beneath the frost, but not enough for herds of game.

Lian never accompanied me on my morning expeditions, but she was never far from my thoughts as I crunched through the stillness of the frozen forest, and I would wonder at the depth of my feeling for her. That feeling had not abated now that she was mine, rather it had intensified. It was a love such as I had never dreamed could exist in the heart of man. To her I was truly a god. I was adored as few men have ever been adored by women, and I felt humble before that adoration. I never gave much thought to the North men.

Then came a day when Paul and Terry did not come back from a fishing expedition farther upstream. There were the lights of strange fires on the plains. Then the fears came, born of the stories of the women. There were many fires, and the fear was tangible; solid and real and ugly.

They had come, the men from the north, and we no longer felt like gods.

Chapter Ten

We drew straws to see which one of us would stay behind. Pip drew the shortest straw and with some chagrin remained with the women while Barry and I ran through the first hours of the night. We could run for miles in those days, toughened to a fitness we had not known since our youth. It was midnight when we saw ahead of us the fires of the invaders' camp. We scouted for some time, separating and encircling the camp. Together again, we summed up our discoveries. In spite of the women's tales, the North men were no larger physically than the men of the local tribes, and probably no fiercer as individuals. The danger lay in their numbers, for there were indeed a great many of them. Whether or not that was in contradiction to Pip's theories on the optimum number for a hunting community, or whether there was a banding together of several normally disparate groups, we were never to learn. What we did see was that the North men were certainly dirtier and more rowdy than we had expected. There must have been about a hundred of them, perhaps rather more women than men. There were at least thirty adult males, far too many for any surprise assault by the two of us. Barry observed that some of the men wore necklaces of teeth which he was convinced came from a large carnivore, but we did not discuss this odd detail at the time. Our attention was concentrated on devising a means of rescue for Terry and Paul who lay trussed up like two chickens close to one of the fires, extremely uncomfortable we would have guessed, but alive and not for the moment being molested.

We watched them for some time while planning our strategy. It seemed improbable that we would be able to effect a direct rescue, so we decided that our best course of action was to take hostages. We waited, hoping they would sleep, but they showed no sign of settling down. They were a jovial bunch, unlike the savages we were used to, feasting with much chatter and laughter, shouting and dancing. From time to time groups of men and women performed some fantastic and decidedly erotic steps around the fires, which inevitably ended in hoots of laughter. But for the fact that they held our two friends captive, we might have concluded that they were a very likeable group. It seemed that the women were much more involved in the social structure of the northern tribes than were their southern cousins; they were part of the tribal fun, the intercourse between individuals, welcome contributors to the activities rather than mere bearers of children and bedmates to the men. It was refreshing to see the women enjoying themselves, laughing with the men and indulging in their own badinage. It was clear that this night was one of celebration, perhaps because of the capture of our friends, and sleeping was far from their thoughts.

Barry pointed out that a woman was heading for a spot some fifty yards from our hiding-place, closely followed by two young men. Some bushes grew there and it was dark, just beyond the limits of firelight. The woman had been dancing a few moments previously with the two lads, not touching them, but acting an increasingly frantic parody of copulation. The three of them had jerked and gyrated, becoming more and more excited. It had been hypnotic to watch them as the woman worked herself up into a high pitch of desire. My attention had been diverted for a while by some children approaching the prisoners. The children had proceeded to urinate on the helpless pair. In the meantime the woman had stopped dancing, covered in perspiration despite the coolness of the night, her upper garment long since discarded. She was not beautiful, rather she was a crude animal, her breasts overlarge with immense scarlet nipples, her stomach creased into rolls above a filthy hide skirt, her mouth hanging wet, lust-filled eyes and hair stringy with her sweat. Barry told me that it was she who turned and ran for the bushes, the young men eager on her heels.

I looked at Barry and he nodded in agreement. 'They'll do,' he said. We crept in silence, keeping low to the ground, heading for the grove of love.

We waited for one young man to roll away and the other

to thrust himself, frantic and gross, onto the moaning and urgent female. Barry took the slowly rising, spent young man, and knocked him out with a single blow of his fist. I seized the other by the throat, exerting pressure on his jugular at a certain spot that caused rapid and silent collapse. The woman's eyes opened in surprise, uncomprehending from the bewilderment of another preoccupation, and I hit her very forcefully upon the side of her head. She seemed to be unconscious as we left her there, legs spread and repulsive, carrying the two lads with us across our shoulders.

*　　*　　*

Dawn next day. They were a hundred yards away from the barricade, a mass of warriors, ragged men in sheepskins and beards, looking much like us. They carried shields of wood and leather, and several spears each, as unsophisticated as those of the local tribes. There were more than thirty of them. Either our count had been astray, or there were other encampments close by. They looked formidable. We waited behind our barricades. After some shouting and argument amongst themselves, about half of them attempted a direct assault.

We had three bowmen, but an arrow travels much further than a spear and swifter. Even before they were within spear range we loosed several shafts, and at least four found a target although no serious harm seemed to have been done. That display of the possibilities of our strange weapons disheartened most of them, but three intrepid fellows continued to advance. They were unable to see us behind our brick wall, and three carefully aimed arrows fired through apertures in the masonry at each of the attackers put an end to that first assault. They limped back to their companions, two with a shaft in their legs, and one carrying a shaft in his hip.

For several hours there was no further action. They were probably waiting for darkness. We were not unduly concerned about that, for we could retreat into the hotel, only exposing ourselves on the fire escape ladder for a short time when the chances of a hit would be minimal. It was true that they could pull down our barricades under cover of darkness, and we saw that as the greatest risk, so we determined to light fires in the area between the barricades before we retreated; these should give sufficient light to defend the walls from the hotel windows. With any luck that light would last until moonlight replaced it. They could put out the fires but not the moon. A clouded or moonless night would pose serious problems; we needed that enclosure to supplement our stocks of food if they decided upon a prolonged siege. Our hotel was difficult to attack successfully with their crude weapons and it would not be easy to set a masonry building alight without access to the timber materials inside. We felt sure that they would eventually abandon attempts to dislodge us, negotiate for an exchange of prisoners and move on to more productive pastures. We congratulated ourselves on our foresight, forgetting that it was mainly due to the women's insistence that we were prepared at all. Our immediate strategy was just to wait, to drive them off during the daylight hours with our arrows, and repair any night-time damage to the barricades. All we needed was a few moonlit nights and we would have them beaten. Our food stocks would last several days. We were secure.

It was about midday that first morning when they sent two women towards us carrying a pigskin bag. Why they assumed we would not shoot at women, I do not know, but we allowed them to come to within a few yards of the wall. 'That's far enough,' I called. They stopped and put down their burden. 'What is it you want?' I asked. They did not reply, simply left the bag on the ground and fled back to their men. Pip scrambled over the barrier and picked up the bag. He scurried back and upended it. Out into the sunlight rolled a head. The North men shared the revolting practice of hacking off their prisoners' heads. It was Terry's head, eyes open—brown eyes, fixed and expressionless in the shadows—mouth slightly open, lips tight exposing his teeth unnaturally. There was not much blood, just a bruise on his cheekbone and the hair on his beard congealed into a mat inseparable from the hair of his head. I stared at it, and stared at it, and stared at it. I cannot explain my utter grief. I was empty within a carcass, a shell full of pain—pain and guilt. I picked up the head and held it in my two hands. It was cold and dry and heavy. Pip was saying something. I did not hear the words. Did those fixed and lifeless eyes smile at me? Was that intellect alive still in that skull?

Then a new emotion flowed through me. A resolve, distilling out of the guilt and some lower morass of unthought reason. I knew what I had to do.

Pip was still talking. He was saying: 'Captain, Captain!' in a kind of muted voice, a shocked voice.

I placed the head carefully on the ground. I walked across to the hostages we had taken the previous night. They were still bound and helpless. I knelt down and drew my knife. The lad was no more than seventeen years old. He was looking at me horrified. I remembered cutting the throat of the Mekan leader, but that was in the heat of battle. With the youth it was cold, calculated and merciless. He was gurgling in a cut-off cry as I plunged the knife into his throat. I felt no compassion, just blood spurting over my hands and the memory of a premonition I had had when Opi, Oona's brother, died, but there was no horror within me, just the power of my purpose. I knew with absolute certainty how the leader of the North men would think. I knew there was only one way that we could save Paul from a fate similar to Terry's, and it was not a moment for weakness. There was silence. All about me, screaming silence. Not one reproachful voice. Not one restraining hand. Not one single question. It was very difficult cutting the head off, much more difficult than I had imagined, and I made a mess of it. But at last it was done and I held the bloody thing by the hair. I stood up.

I marched, holding the head at arm's length, up to the barricade and over the top. I carried on to within twenty yards of the savages. Then I swung my arm and rolled the grisly thing at them. They offered no violence as I strode back.

The others refused to look at me. They actually drew away from me, and no one spoke. But Lian came and stood with me. I took her arm and it was then that I began to shake. Barry said: 'Someone's coming.' He climbed onto the barricade. I leaned my back against it and listened to the conversation that took place. Its content was simple enough. They would exchange their captive for ours. Barry agreed and the exchange was promptly put into effect. All that time I remained unmoving. Barry conducted the whole thing. They released Paul and our hostage was then freed. My plan had worked as I had known it would, but I felt no elation, just a sickness. Then Paul came up to me. He said: 'Captain, you look ill.' He was pale but seemed unharmed.

'No, Paul, I'm not ill.'

'They killed Terry quickly, Jeff. He didn't suffer. I promise you.'

'Thanks.' I managed to make my mouth adopt the shape of a smile. 'Welcome back.'

'I didn't think I would ever see you again. I am sure you did the only thing possible to make them release me. Thank you for that. It could not have been easy.'

'I'll be okay in a minute. Just feeling a bit of reaction, that's all.' I could feel the blood greasy on my hands.

'How are you feeling, Captain?' It was Barry who spoke. Dear Barry. I knew then that he had overcome his revulsion.

I nodded. Pip said: 'We had better clean up this mess. Give me a hand, Barry.' The two of them picked up the headless corpse and walked to the river with it, where they threw it in. Pip came back and put Terry's head in the pigskin bag again. He went and threw that into the river, too.

While they were doing this, Paul told me that the two boys we had captured were apparently of some importance to the tribe. 'I believe they were sons of the chief,' he said. 'That will mean we can expect determined efforts at retaliation. In fact, I heard him say that he won't be satisfied till we're all dead.'

'Does he know how many of us there are?'

'I don't know. He probably does. His last words to me when he released me were, "You will all die", and he struck me as a fellow of great determination.'

'We might be in for a long siege, then. Better ration the food supplies. We should be able to make the stocks of vegetables last two weeks. I doubt if we shall get very much from this piece of land. But surely they will leave before two weeks.' Thinking about the immediate problems diverted my mind from the reaction to my deed. I had stopped shaking.

Paul said: 'By the way the chief was talking, I think he would be prepared to camp here all winter if necessary. He wants vengeance, and he has the whole countryside to obtain food from as well as already having Terry's body.'

'There is no doubt about their cannibalism, then?'

'None at all. They discussed it quite openly.'

'It seems an odd characteristic in a country where other sources of meat are so readily available.'

'Who knows if it has always been so. Perhaps there was an especially hard winter when the only ready protein was human beings. It seems that game is not so plentiful in the north in winter time. That's why they trek south, of course. I suppose in earlier times the strong territorial instincts of these people would have meant hostile resistance to that. There would have been a few dead bodies. Oh, I think one can see how such a habit would start.'

'Yes, and I suppose continual defeat by superior numbers made the tradition of tribute a preferred option.'

'That would seem to be the case.'

'Well, they're not going to eat us,' I vowed. 'We will survive.' But the weight of that responsibility was already an oppressive cloud on my mind. The aftermath of the killing had left me empty of joy. There was just my resolve.

Chapter Eleven

I looked around the huddle of cheerless women in the kitchen of the hotel. The great fuel stove was glowing only dimly in its depths; wood to keep it bright was almost gone. Upon its great top a lonely cast iron bowl simmered, containing little but old potato water. Children whimpered in the shadows of their mothers' bosoms. It was night. Hunger was gnawing at my own belly. The last of our food had gone into that iron pot the night before; the copse had been picked bare. The men had not eaten all that day. The women looked at me, not desperately but still with an unspoken plea. The responsibility of feeding these people was mine. They all expected leadership from me, even the scientists, and I had assumed it without question. That was my role, one I was used to. But I was tired.

We had had three weeks of war and siege, and although we had suffered no casualties the strain was becoming untenable. And now our food was gone. I had hardly slept, for even though we had alternated our watches to guard the fire escape and deter the nightly attempt to tear down our barricades, the women taking a willing share in this, my sleep had been of a fitful kind. Worry was draining on my nerves, as indeed it was on the nerves of my comrades. Once Pip had attempted to slip through the enemy lines at night in order to set a few snares in the countryside, but this had been not only hazardous, but in the event quite futile. Our sole means of exit was by the fire escape, and they kept a constant watch on it. Pip had been lucky to return unharmed.

I could see him in the far corner, a dark bundle on the floor. He always slept in the foetal position, but tonight he was restless. Zo lay beside him, awake. I could see her eyes watching him in the fire glow. She was moving her hand gently over his head as if to soothe his sleep. Oona was also awake, sitting a few paces away, her knees drawn up to her chin and her arms wrapped around them. She, too, was watching Pip. It was too dark to determine any expression in her eyes. Barry was on the roof, on watch with Paul and Wani. I should have been sleeping, but I had to find an answer. Somehow I had to find an answer. The children were suffering, and the women would not last long without food.

Outside we could hear the sounds of the invaders, making merry as always, and tonight, because it was moonless, they were right inside our enclosure stripping the barricades. Already, after their efforts of preceding nights, a great deal of the masonry was gone. The warfare had adopted a pattern. As soon as it was dark they would attack the barricades and without vision there was nothing we could do to prevent it. On moonlit nights they were too exposed to our arrows to do much harm, and, after suffering some casualties in the early days, they had learned to leave rapidly as soon as it was light. There was no longer any fuel to light the evening fires within the enclosure, and although we had so far managed to repair much of the damage to the barricades during the daylight hours, material for this was becoming increasingly scarce. The savages made off with a lot of it in the dark, and we had to replace that with masonry purloined from the inner walls of the surrounding buildings. But our resources were limited and almost exhausted. I knew that tonight I had to make a decision. One or two more days and hunger, despair and weakness would defeat us.

I stood up. Lian rose quickly as well; she had not been asleep either. Her son lay quietly at her feet. At least he was not hungry. I shook my head at Lian, indicating that she should stay. She stood and watched me as I left the room. On the roof Barry and Paul were barely distinguishable, and Wani was hidden in the shadows of the parapet.

Paul saw me. 'Jeff, you must get some sleep,' he said.

'It's all right, Paul. It seems to be getting lighter.'

'Yes. It's nearly dawn. Did you sleep at all?'

'A little.'

He looked at me sternly but said no more. There was silence while we watched the dawn. It was not a spectacular sunrise, just an increasing lightening of the sky. Soon we could make out the savages below us. Barry began firing arrows into their midst and they quickly dispersed. Just to the north was the river, and not too far away the disintegrating hulks of once great ships. There were freighters there, too, red and dull in the hurrying sunrise, and tankers, some half sunk, and smaller boats, launches, tugs, naval vessels and barges; all just so much rusty junk. If only there was just one that would float, that was partially seaworthy with a motor that would turn over, I thought, not for the first time. But I realised that it was only a straw to clutch. Perhaps it was time to clutch at straws. And it was then, when the invaders would be at their least watchful, that I had to take the chance. I turned to the others. 'Keep me covered, I'm going down.'

They asked no questions, just looked at me worriedly and nodded as I began to descend the stairs. We had strengthened this vital structure and I scrambled down it quite rapidly, not fully conscious of my movements. I cannot recall what my thoughts were. I was probably too tired to think coherently anyway. The savages below hooted and let out weird shrieks designed to instil fear, but I was beyond that. I felt no emotion at all as I reached the ground. No fear. No hope, perhaps. There was an ache in my abdomen, which may have been the sheer need for food, and a tremendous pounding in my head. The enclosure was empty. The barricades were pitifully inadequate by then. If they had plucked up the courage for an all-out assault they would easily have overpowered us, but they were just ordinary mortals, no more and no less courageous in their savagery than men of our own time. I felt confident that they would not attack in daylight until the barriers were completely down and we had no cover for defence.

I reached the river, hidden there from the savages' view. Stripping to my bare skin, I lowered myself into the swirling murk. It was unbelievably cold. I had to hang on to the bank for several moments while my breathing became something more than frantic gasps. I could feel my limbs beginning to freeze. What was I doing anyway? I did not really know. Then I let go. I am a good swimmer, but my ankles had not fully recovered from their days of being bound as Oa's captive, and almost immediately I felt cramp begin to seize my feet. It should have been unendurable but I had learned to withstand cramp during those long hours as a captive and I continued to swim, concentrating upon moving my toes as I did so. Then pain gripped my right calf, paralysing the leg. I had been in the water less than three minutes.

Somehow I struggled on, using the current, swimming with only my arms for propulsion. I reached a barnacle-covered chain, the anchor cable of a freighter. It was so corroded the links were virtually cemented together with the barnacles. I clung on to it and rested. But not for long. Cramp and cold were winning the fight against my endurance. It was impossible to climb that chain with my crippled leg, and besides, it would have brought me within full view of the savages, but I could see a hole in the side of the ship where the metal of the hull had collapsed. The river swirled through the hole and I let myself go with it. Inside it was dark but I could make out the remnants of a steel ladder screwed to the bulkhead. It would lead directly to the deck if I were able to open the hatch above it. The ladder was pitted with corrosion and barnacles, but I hauled myself onto it, dragging my legs, and hung on, hands bleeding, legs in pain and shivering constantly, but out of that damned water.

I forced my limbs to climb. Exertion helped, producing an illusion of warmth and a lessening of cramp, but the shivering would not cease. My jaws were aching from the involuntary chattering of my teeth. If the hatch was locked or jammed I did not know what I would do. I could not go back into that water. I reached the hatch door and leaned against it. Something snapped, possibly the corroded latch, and the door moved fractionally. The hinges were welded with rust. I pushed with all the power of desperation and it moved a fraction more. Again and again I thrust at it. At length the hinge pins fell apart and the door suddenly gave way and crashed onto the deck behind. I stumbled out. Moving hurriedly for warmth, I searched every available crevice of that ship. I found a folded tarpaulin, decayed and with an appalling smell, but it served as a covering. There was nothing else of value.

From the ship it was not far to the opposite shore. There was no sign of the enemy; they were probably unaware of my whereabouts, but I could not risk a landing in daylight. I lay low for the rest of that day, slowly getting warm and conserving my dwindling strength. My friends would have watched my swim from the hotel roof so would have realised my position. I prayed that the North men would not decide to launch an all-out attack that day.

At last it was evening. I was dry then and not too cold wrapped in the tarpaulin. I returned to the water via the hole in the ship's hull, my legs wrapped in canvas and a lifebelt beneath my arms. It took less than five minutes to reach the harbour wall and some concrete steps, and I was soon ashore on the bank opposite the hotel. The shivering had started again. I wrapped myself as best I could in the tarpaulin, wet now but offering my only glimmer of warmth, and began to explore that section of the harbour. It was a hopeless quest. I suppose I knew that all along, but I remembered that the children had not eaten that day and the older ones hardly anything in two days. It was a miserable, dogged search. My feet had no feeling and were bleeding from the hated barnacles. I stumbled about, exhausted almost beyond caring. But I did care; I cannot explain why. Perhaps it was a resolve born of guilt, of conscience, or a resolve from the dictates of responsibility instilled in me by the ethos of another age. Three hours. Four hours. I do not know.

I was upstream from the hotel when I smelled the barge and decided to explore its decaying depths. It was putrefying, filled in some previous decade with vegetables for the markets of the inland towns, I suppose. I cannot describe my revulsion as I approached that reeking hulk, nor can I explain my reason for carrying on, forcing myself against the protestations of my senses. Perhaps there was some subconscious reasoning that in that centuries-old compost heap, organic vegetation might still thrive. There was light in there beneath the ragged remnants of the deck, huge torn holes letting in the starlight. And I stood there fighting hysteria. It was a sort of jubilation, a great laugh filling up the hollowness that was despair, and in smothering it I broke into uncontrollable sniggers. There I stood amid that rotting mulch, a grown man, a colonel, product of an advanced civilisation, highly educated, with twenty-five lives dependent on my calmness and continued sanity, sniggering away in the horrid caverns of that crumbling derelict.

It was full of pumpkins, hundreds of them, partly rotten after their summer ripening, but still with edible flesh, and in between the pumpkins, engorged upon the debris of their leaves, were mushrooms, packed clusters of them, certainly past the optimum time for picking, but such culinary considerations were far from my mind. They were large mushrooms, regenerating and spawning for endless decades unpicked on the constant compost heap. I ate some there and then, raw and unwashed, and they were delightful. I ate some pumpkin, too, relishing the feel of my teeth in its spongy flesh. Already I was feeling stronger. It was the strength of hope, a vitality born of new confidence.

There were several aluminium and fibreglass dinghies about the harbour, most of them little affected by the passage of time, and within half an hour I had brought one to the barge and loaded it with pumpkins and mushrooms. Then, squatting on top of the load, I allowed the current to carry me to within a few yards of the enclosure, steering with a piece of rusty steel plate. Further silence and patience were all that were needed then until dawn. With the coming of daylight the savages retreated from the compound and Pip, who had already spotted me from the roof, relayed a message to the others and scrambled down the fire escape to assist me with unloading.

Some hours later, with the whole group content for the moment with full bellies, and myself warm again and, having slept for three or four hours, feeling calm and refreshed, I outlined a new idea, formulated in the depths of the pumpkin barge. With a bit of debate and input from the others the plan was refined and accepted. It would be put into action that same evening. For the rest of that day all available hands were sent to scour the immediate accessible buildings for every conceivable scrap of fuel—anything that would burn—for it would be necessary to light a huge fire in the compound and maintain it for the first few hours of darkness. Two of us would remain at the barricades to defend the enclosure and the other two would cross the river in the dinghy, hopefully unobserved in the shadows of the river bank. It would be their task to collect three more dinghies and stock them with pumpkins and mushrooms, then to tie them together in tandem and drift back to the compound. We would then embark all the women and children in three of the boats and two of us would accompany them downstream. All this to be achieved without the knowledge of the invaders, which meant that the savages had to be kept occupied by the remaining two men. They would remain at the barricades until daylight or as long as prudence dictated, to give the women and children a good start. One boat would be left for the escape of the last two, who would have to rely on the power of their arms to propel them to safety. Barry and I were the clear choices for that. It was felt that strength of arm would also be the most useful attribute for the initial collection of the dinghies, so Barry and I were given that task. Pip and Paul would defend the barricades until we returned and then embark with the women to control the boats downstream.

It seemed a simple enough plan, but in the event the execution of it turned out to be anything but simple.

Everything went reasonably well until Barry and I were returning with the boats. It was then that the savages decided to launch the all-out assault we had been dreading. We had not reached the bank and had no way of giving assistance to our friends. I suspect that the unusual activity behind the barricades and the great fire had prompted their decision to attack when they did, or perhaps we had been seen and they were aware that the defences were undermanned at that time. The scene as we paddled frantically for the bank is etched in my memory. The walls of piled masonry that were the barricades, with many gaps by then; the fire leaping high, higher than the walls; dark transitory shapes that were the women, still calm, with armfuls of arrows to feed the archers. Pip on one side, Paul on the other; and the hordes of shrieking, fleece-clad warriors racing in from either side, seemingly certain of victory. How could two men hope to stop them?

Pip was superb. Several of the women had been trained in the use of the bow, and although not expert by any means, some had sufficient accuracy to be useful. The range was frighteningly close and, faced with perhaps thirty yelling warriors, it was not surprising that the courage of some of them failed. It was Pip who rallied them, leaping onto the barricade, shouting defiance, loosing arrows with deadly effect—for he had become the best shot of us all—exhorting the women and displaying an indifference to fear that was stimulating. A little man, a clown with a bald head and wild beard, a scientist from another culture, large then in his fearlessness. Zo stayed with him, and Oona was there, too, and Dua. Teena fled, though, screaming in panic, and it was Wani who knocked her down before the panic could spread. Close to Pip, Zo, fear large in her white, drawn face, continued to draw her bow. Oona fed them both with arrows. Dua stood, a huge spear in her hand, for she was useless with a bow, ready to fight to the death. A calm, stolid woman, whom I had known and could not like. Paul stood alone except for Wani who fed him arrows. So six of them stood defiant.

Barry and I churned the water in desperation. We could see that we were too late. The invaders were mere yards from the barriers. One hurled a spear as Pip shot him. The spear struck Zo, spinning her off her feet. She was struggling to rise. Paul stood at the opposite barricade. Several spears flew at him, but he did not appear to be hit. Fortunately that barricade was in a reasonable state of repair and the assault was less determined from that side. Still, Paul alone could not hope to defend it from several directions. We reached the shore and Barry rushed to help Pip, while I raced across to Paul. Zo had ceased trying to rise and was lying in the mud, hunched up and moaning. For a few more minutes the battle went on. I had reached Paul and, bow in hand, sent shaft after shaft into the attackers. There were maybe a dozen or so on that side, already many injured; two seemed to be dead. The two of us, with Wani handing us arrows, kept them at bay, but it meant a continual stream of arrows and I wondered how long it could go on.

Suddenly there came a shattering report from behind me. Everything stopped. For a minute all action was suspended and there was a tableau before me of savages poised as if petrified. I saw astonishment first, followed swiftly by panic, the fear of something unknown, something supernatural. And they fled. Very soon the field was clear. With Barry to take over, Pip had found time to fetch a contrivance he had prepared. It was a bomb, made of a gourd filled with some home-made gunpowder and tied off with a leather thong that was also supposed to act as a fuse. He had lit the thong and hurled it at the assailants. The bomb had landed among them but had promptly gone out. Pip had then shot at it with a burning arrow and had succeeded in setting it off on his second attempt. The resulting explosion had actually done very little harm in a physical sense, but undoubtedly the ensuing panic had saved us.

Victory was ours for the moment, but it had cost us dearly. Zo had bled to death in the mud. Dua had died by a spear thrust from one of the attackers who had penetrated the defence. He had been killed immediately by Oona, also with a spear. Pip was bleeding from a wound in his ribs which turned out to be very unpleasant but not serious. Paul attended to him straight away, but more hurt was done mentally to Philip Quincey-Jones from the death of Zo. It had a surprising effect upon the little man, one that quite astonished me for I had not been aware of the depth of his feelings for her, although the effect did not become apparent that night because we were far too busy to consider it. We had won a victory but the war was far from over. The siege would surely continue and we had to get away before the savages recovered their nerve.

Our plans were altered. We decided not to leave anyone behind, for it was unlikely the savages would attack for an hour or two. It would take them that long to reassemble and debate their future strategy. So we hurriedly collected all the women and children and what few possessions we wished to take, arranged them in the boats with one man to each unit and, keeping the vessels lashed stem to stern, set out into the night.

Chapter Twelve

We were not seamen. We had realised that on our voyage to land after leaving the spaceship. It was true that every one of us men had had some experience of sailing in former days, but that had been sport, for enjoyment. There was nothing enjoyable in being battered by demonic waves in a leaky boat less than thirty feet long.

We had found it on the dawn of our flight from Bordeaux, a motor launch with a mast and a fibreglass hull. It was lying askew on the bank, jammed in the rusted remnants of a steel slipway. During several hours ashore when Pip managed to snare some rabbits, the rest of us had freed the launch and allowed it to slide into the river. It had floated and appeared to be reasonably stable. We had transferred our stock of food and fashioned a sail of sorts from our sheepskins. It needed a new rudder which we carved rather crudely with an axe from the greenwood bough of a fir tree.

At the time it seemed to be a logical solution to our problems. It would enable us to shake off all pursuit, head for the open sea and land again somewhere to the north where, presumably, the country would be uninhabited until spring. The first twenty-four hours were encouraging. We found that we could steer the boat ably enough, and the outgoing tide assisted our passage to the sea. We had reached open sea before the tide turned and we hoisted sail. We fished with some success which bolstered our limited diet, and, apart from the women's pent-up fear—for to them the sea was as alien as the moon—the prospects looked better than at any time in the last three weeks.

The second twenty-four hours, though, were frightening. The boat leaked, which is undoubtedly why it had been on a slipway, and that meant continuous bailing. We worked in shifts, and it was hard, tedious work but bearable; the motion of the boat in the high seas, however, was unendurable. We were all ill, even the indomitable Barry, but the bailing had to continue, and the four men had to battle continuously to gain some measure of control over the unseaworthy craft. To make matters worse, Pip had become withdrawn and morose. Pip the eternal joker, the indefatigable lifter of spirits, a rock of humour in all our distress, had become a silent and hurting man. He did his share of the burden of work, but it was done without spirit, without that sense of cheer that we had depended upon so much without recognising it. Pip was actually a very plain man, ugly indeed, bald and close-eyed. His beard was black and untidy, and he had an absurd nose, bulbous and pitted with blackheads. I had never really noticed before how unattractive he was, since it was his personality that had made the greatest impression, but without his humour he seemed quite unpleasant. He pined for Zo. I sensed it, and Oona sensed it also. She watched him with a reflected pain in her own eyes. She attended him closely in those cheerless days. She made him eat, caressed him as Zo had done while he slept, and in some measure gave him comfort. That pleased me. And Barry, in his infinite love of Oona, saw, too, and was proud.

'She's a lovely girl,' he told me, referring to her compassion rather than her features. Oh Barry, Barry, your heart was great.

We had resolved to head for shore to escape the waves, but the limitations of our seamanship were becoming all too plain. The craft had been designed for pleasure-cruising in calm waters. It was overloaded and almost keelless, for most of the keel had been broken off unknown years before. Its single mast and crude sail were not intended for controlling the boat in a gale, and the makeshift rudder eventually collapsed. There seemed to be no way of moving that craft shorewards. We were sick and we suffered.

Day after day. I was revolted by the sight of pumpkin. The smell of vomit was on everyone's skin. Yet somehow, sunk in misery as we were, I never lost faith in an eventual successful outcome. It was as if I knew our present distress was only a temporary condition, merely a matter of enduring until it was over. Perhaps, having sunk to the limits of despair in the waters of the Gironde so recently, I was incapable of such desperation so soon after. Perhaps it was because Pip's melancholy left a void in our cohesion as well as our morale, so that I became sharply aware that I was the group's final source of strength, although Barry was *my* personal source of strength. He worked three times as hard as anyone else, bailing, constantly bailing; he seemed to need less sleep than the rest of us, and fought his sickness all the way, grimly refusing to succumb.

Yet it was to me that the questions were directed, not with voices, but with pleading eyes, with looks asking when, and why, and what. How could I tell them that the elements we fought, that were so completely foreign to them, were almost equally beyond our own experience? How could I tell them that this coastline, this bay, was one of the most fearful in the world? How could I tell them that I had no way of knowing whether we were within yards of being smashed to pieces against rocks or more than a hundred leagues off shore? So I told them to keep bailing, that the wind would ease soon, that everything was going to be all right. Oh, the faith of those people. They looked at me and bailed without question, and cooked the soggy pumpkins, and were sick and wet and cold and cramped. Young children, babies crying, pregnant women heavy and huddled and unable to stretch. No God. No sun. Just their faith in me, and hope, pitiful in their abject eyes.

It rained, and although this added immensely to our cold and discomfort, I was grateful because rain was our only source of fresh water.

Where were we? No one would hazard a guess. We did not even know whether we were north or south of the Gironde, just somewhere in the Bay of Biscay. Then one morning, several hours before the coming of daylight, alone on deck, I became aware that the motion of the boat was abating. As the hours before dawn slipped past, the sea grew steadily calmer. Later Lian came and sat with me. And the dawn spread across the world, promising peace and loveliness. A daybreak of gentle splendour, the sea just lapping playfully at the boat, the sky pale blue and pink, and the last of the clouds were golden and innocent. We were near a beach of gradually sloping sand and I knew we were safe. The sea was light green and scintillating in the creeping light. It was calm and soft and achingly lovely. I turned and smiled at Lian, and her eyes held an adoration such as I had never seen. She was giving me credit for the miracle. And indeed, perhaps because I was the one on deck when it happened, Lian's adoration was reflected in the faces of all the women. Their faith in me had been justified; I had led them to a haven of peace. It made me feel a bit like Moses. Even Pip, with a hint of his old jocularity, said: 'Well done, Captain.' And perhaps I, too, began to accept that I deserved the kudos, that I alone had been responsible for leading my people to a land of peace and plenty. Oh, how deceitful is our own vanity.

But it was no land of plenty. It was in the grip of an extremely severe winter. We survived. The handful of us made no great demands on the available resources. We could understand well enough why the North men made their annual trek south, but there were still winter fowl, and there were still rabbits and hares and fish. There were occasional horses, too, seemingly impervious to the cold, but we never managed to kill one.

'We must watch out for lions in this part of the world,' Barry told us.

'Lions? Why on earth would there be lions here?'

'Well, I don't know why, but what I do know is that the North men wore necklaces of teeth that would appear to have come from large carnivores.'

'Lions in France? How could that possibly be?'

'There used to be safari parks, remember. Perhaps those animals survived and their descendants still roam free. There's no reason why they shouldn't have. Most other animals appear to have managed well enough.'

Yet we saw no lions in that area.

We kept on the move. We had to do that. Our snares were never effective for more than a day or two. The pickings were slim, but we did not go hungry. The tribe was content. There were no other humans around, although evidence of a resident community was everywhere. It was obviously the country of the North men, and one day we confirmed our whereabouts when we saw Paris in the distance, some three or four weeks after our landfall. But the North men were south and we were safe until spring.

'Let's go there,' said Pip, gazing reflectively at the unmistakable configuration of the Paris skyline.

'What for?' I asked, although the idea had already occurred to me.

'Well, it seems so close and it would be a pity to pass it by. Besides, I'm curious.'

'I reckon it's further away than it looks.'

'Why are you being so bloody argumentative?' he protested. 'We've got no urgent appointments anywhere else.'

I laughed. 'All right, you've persuaded me. I expect the others will want to go anyway.'

We had all known Paris in days gone by and had been excited by it, by its gaiety and its music and its wonderful gastronomic delights, and we had all loved it, its living culture and its dead history. Now it is part of that dead history, a deserted and uninviting place, neglected by man it seemed, although its buildings had been pillaged extensively at some time over the centuries, and some of them burned to the ground. The indications were, though, that contemporary man did not visit the city. There were no signs at all of recent occupation. Undoubtedly, in summer the gardens and the parks were dense woodland, overgrown and the haunt of badgers and rabbits, but in winter they had the unfriendliness of desertion—entangled, matted places, inviolate and cheerless, defying intrusion, and we were not moved to intrude. The streets were decaying and cold; grass grew between the dislocated paving, and the smell of mouldering wood, of damp cellars, the slime and fungus of a subterranean habitat, clung to us unpleasantly as we wandered through the boulevards.

The streets were not strictly devoid of life; we saw dogs, a few solitary beasts, scrawny, slinking, noiseless creatures, shy and fleeting as the shadows of birds. And there were birds still. There were magpies and starlings and pigeons, and sparrows, too, without song in their relentless search for food. The city was an uncharitable place, frigid and unforgiving, and the women were afraid of it, afraid of its emptiness, so that they talked little and pressed close to us.

There were shattered windows on the pavements, rubble, charred shreds of wood, and pools of foetid water. There were the disintegrating remains of motor cars in the gutters, and the more durable statues in the squares, white with bird droppings, looking ponderous and comic amid the ashes of one-time glory.

Yet the river ran clean and astonishingly blue, and the Eiffel Tower still stood, an arrogant monument to another age, eaten with rust but sound, and so it will stand for perhaps another century or two before toppling to vanish forever from the history of men. We walked up to the Sacré Cœur and wondered, as we had done in the past, at the view of the city from that height. I took Lian to the top of Notre Dame. She was astonished and fearful. I tried to explain to her that Paris was built by people identical to her own in form and natural gifts, but of an advanced culture from which I originated. I do not think she understood, but her lack of speech made it difficult to be sure. She was relieved to return to the ground.

In the end we only spent one day in Paris. Its decay depressed us and there was nothing to eat there.

*　　*　　*

The weeks went by and the time for decision drew ever closer. 'We must leave this land before the spring arrives,' I told the others. 'I am not prepared to battle with the North men for ever.'

'Clearly,' agreed Pip. 'And we can't return to the south either, because we'd almost certainly have to cross their path.'

'I have a suggestion,' put in Barry.

'Well let's have it, you great ninny!' cried Pip, hopping out of range of retribution.

'The trouble with pipsqueaks is that they have no patience,' retorted the big man. 'I was going to propose that we go to England.'

'Well that's not a bad idea,' I said. 'But how would we get there?'

'No more boats, please,' begged Paul. That was certainly a sentiment that we all echoed. We had no intention of embarking on the sea again.

'You seem to forget there was a tunnel,' said Barry.

'So there was,' I nodded, 'but whether it's still trafficable or not is the question.'

'I don't see why it wouldn't be,' he persisted. 'We can give it a go anyway, can't we?'

'And what if the people there are just as hostile as the North men?' Paul asked.

'We don't even know if there's anybody there,' put in Pip. 'But there's only one way to find out.'

'All right, we'll try it,' I said. 'But how do we find the tunnel?'

'Oh, that should be simple enough. Just head north until we strike the coast, and then follow the coast road to the east. Sooner or later we'll come across the tunnel. We can hardly miss it.'

So it was decided. When the spring came and the North men returned to their homeland we would head for England, our own homeland. We began to move slowly northwards, meandering and roaming as our hunting led us, but making for the coast.

Despite the rigours of the season, I remember it as a happy time. Three babies were born that winter, fathered by men we had killed. Other women were heavy with pregnancy, including Lian and Wani. There were no serious illnesses, not even colds to contend with. There were no deaths, no crises. We all thrived. Pip had regained some of his old exuberance and was as outrageous as ever. It was near the north coast that we discovered the lions, and that meant that we often had fresh meat to eat since the lions hunted the horses that were too swift for us, and we sometimes located a fresh kill, half eaten it is true, but a horse provides a lot of meat, more than we could ever eat before it went bad. It was very strange to be living in lion country when there was frost on the ground and often snow, but the beasts were as noble and arrogant on the frozen landscape as they were on the overheated plains of Africa.

There was a certain risk attached in stealing a lion's kill, of course, but the rewards were worth it, and we never really had cause for alarm from the great carnivores. Except once.

It was a period of heavy snow. We were having difficulty

locating food animals of any sort. It was our habit to go about in pairs, two men hunting while the other two stayed with the tribe, usually in the ready protection of some rural village. The villages in the north were in a better state of repair than those we had found in the south; it seemed as if the North men actually used the cottages, and maintained them to some degree, with bark and mud. Paul would always remain in the camp, for some of the women were well advanced in pregnancy, so the other three of us took turns together. Barry and I had been out foraging for over two days, but on our way back we were feeling quite jubilant because we had found the carcass of a horse. We were struggling back with a great haunch apiece, as well as five rabbits and a pair of geese. We were about five miles from base when we stopped for rest at an old farmhouse. It was near evening and it looked as if another snowstorm was in the offing. We hoped to be in camp before either should happen.

It was with some astonishment that we heard the unmistakable sounds of human voices as we settled ourselves against the wall of a barn. There was the sound of a girl giggling. We looked at each other blankly and with some alarm. Had the North men returned already? Then, as we listened in earnest, I felt a sickening hollowness in the pit of my stomach. It would have been better if it had been the North men, for the voices we heard were those of Oona and Pip.

The giggles had subsided and the quickening gasps of approaching ecstasy had taken their place. My eyes were fixed on Barry. Pip was more than a friend to him. He loved the little man with a love far more profound than friendship, and Pip had betrayed him with the only person in the world that Barry may have loved more. I watched his soul crumble in unspeakable anguish. His great fat cheeks sagged visibly beneath his beard. His eyes were pitiful. I could find no words of comfort, I knew I could not even reach out to touch him. A whimper escaped his lips. He had forgotten my presence.

Then, as silence followed the cries of culmination, Barry lifted his head. A new, and to me surprising emotion had entered his heart. It was an aspect of the man that I had never suspected, a black and violent rage beyond reason, something to which he would never have given full rein in the world of his upbringing. But after months of bloodshed and a life of basic crudity, it was an emotion more fearful and uncontrolled than I had ever seen in a man. I remembered the one other time I had seen anger in him, when he had split the head of a rapist with an axe, and I was dreadfully afraid. He lurched to his feet and plunged for the door, and I knew that Pip was in great peril. The sounds had come from a barn similar to the one which we had chosen for shelter not very far away.

'Pip!' I called out. 'Pip! Run, for God's sake. Barry knows!'

There was the noise of scuffling as I sprang after the big man. I reached the door in time to see Pip race from the other barn clutching the remnants of his trousers to his chest. Barry halted and Pip turned to face him. There was perhaps twenty yards between them. Pip's face was at first merely conciliatory, but as he recognised the anger shuddering in the big fellow's frame, a desperate alarm entered his eyes—a strange reaction in so courageous a man, yet I understood it.

'Barry, listen to me,' he cried. 'Oona loves you, Barry. I tell you, she loves you. It's just fun between us, you see. It means nothing, Barry. It means nothing!' he repeated, frantic in his attempt to get through that implacable fury, to convey reason to the hulking figure before him.

'I'm going to smash you,' Barry uttered, his voice jerking and cracked as if still striving for a measure of control over his anger.

I could see Oona now in the shadow of the barn's interior. She was standing motionless and quiet, still naked, seemingly unaware of the freezing cold. Oona, the catalyst, was now only a spectator, as I was, of the drama before us. One could not blame her; she could only have been puzzled by this intrusion of a morality from another time, a morality she could never have understood. Pip was struggling with his trousers, not putting them on but getting something from the pocket. 'Be sensible, Barry,' he was begging, the fear palpable in his voice. 'You're a scientist, for God's sake, not a dumb brute. Keep back, keep back!' This last urgently as the big man strode two steps forward. Pip threw his trousers aside. He stood clothed only in a sheepskin coat, white and skinny legs, shoeless in the snow. In his right hand he held a revolver.

It was a different one from the one he had found in Bordeaux; I think he had collected it in Paris. It appeared to give him some command of the situation. He stomped his feet once or twice.

'All right, Barry, now calm down. Remember this is not our own society. You can't apply our moral standards here. Oona is a savage girl, a product of her age with natural cravings . . .'

'Damn you!' cried Barry in a strangled voice. And he charged.

Pip's face went suddenly pale in alarm. Fearful. A moment of terrible indecision. 'Stop!' It was a shriek. But Barry did not stop. There were three reports and the big man crashed headlong into the snow. Oona screamed and came rushing out of the barn. The wind howled, and whirling snowflakes swept about us. Nearby, very close, there was the snarl of a lion. I recalled the haunches of meat we had stolen. It was a momentary thought. There was blood on the snow. Pip was standing limp and stupefied. The light was nearly gone. Oona reached Barry before I did and threw herself upon him, keening shrilly. Barry rolled over and flung her off. I was beside him then. His anger was gone. He looked at Pip and his eyes were unutterably sad.

Pip bent down. 'Oh, God,' he said, 'what have I done?'

'I'm all right,' said the wounded man. 'It's only my legs. You got both of them.'

'I shot at the ground. I shot at the ground,' cried Pip. I believe that to be true, for I'm sure I saw him lower his arm before he fired, but the revolver was unlikely to have been an accurate weapon.

'Better fetch Paul,' I told Pip. 'Hurry now, there's going to be one hell of a blizzard shortly.'

Oona was sobbing miserably in the snow a few paces away, still unclothed and shivering for the snow was beginning to drive hard. 'Go and get your clothes on, Oona,' I said as gently as I could, 'before you freeze to death.' I left Barry for a minute and helped her to her feet. She strained towards Barry, her eyes beseeching, in total incomprehension of his rejection, as I led her towards the barn.

Then the snarl again, a few yards away. I turned. It stood

there: a lioness. She must have tracked her stolen kill, and she looked angry. There was little light left then, but she stood huge on the whiteness of the ground. We were puny against her might, and weaponless, too. I looked around desperately for a spear. I was too slow; far, far too slow. The beast was loping towards Barry. Its lope was almost leisurely. But Barry, strong and big as he was, was helpless. There was nothing I could do. I think I yelled. Perhaps I moved. Then Oona, young, naked, lovely girl, sprang over the injured man and threw herself onto the beast.

There was a distinct crunch of jaws closing on bone. No other sound, no growl, no scream from Oona as she died. The lioness held the girl easily in her jaws, a twitching white figure, small breasts inexplicably skywards, arms and feet limply resting in the snow. Reddening snow. Calm, yellow eyes contemplating us above the engulfed head of the victim.

Barry shrieked aloud as he vainly tried to reach her on his crippled legs, but his agony was of the mind, not of the body. I moved to help, so late, so very late. Oona was dead already; she probably died instantaneously, and the beast was trotting away carrying the girl with her. In a minute she was gone and only a trail of blood and huge footprints marked her passage. Barry was quiet then. Oona had loved him, had loved him beyond her own life. She had atoned for a sin she could not comprehend. I knelt beside him and gripped his shoulder. We did not speak. He looked at me and nodded. He had control over his grief then, and later, too, although I knew he did not sleep for many nights.

Pip still stood where he had been, shocked, stunned with his guilt. The storm was increasing rapidly to blizzard proportions. It was night already with an early dark. Pip moved to get his trousers. 'You can't send him to fetch Paul tonight,' Barry remarked. 'I'll be all right till morning. He can go then. Just get me inside out of this bloody snow.' He did not mention Oona then, and only ever mentioned her once again that I recall, except sometimes in his sleep.

His legs were shattered flesh and blood. There were bits of bone on the surface. But he was right, Pip could hardly find his way in such a storm. He was soon fully dressed and helped me drag Barry into the barn. We lit a fire. We did not eat. No one felt like eating.

The night was very long.

Chapter Thirteen

That was the first of several long nights. The blizzard blew for a whole week. I suppose we were well provided for, certainly better than our tribe as far as food was concerned, and there was plenty of wood for the fire. Yet it was one of the most harrowing weeks of my life up to that time. Barry suffered so much unbearable physical pain that many times I wished I had the courage to kill him. It would have been merciful. I am sure a mind less strong, a will less powerful than his, would have succumbed to insanity. As it was, even his iron self-control relaxed during his rare periods of semi-consciousness, and groans, almost muted shrieks, would escape his lips. Unfortunately he was conscious more often than otherwise, enduring his suffering with a grim and solid courage. Once, when he did actually sleep, he called aloud the name 'Carol'. Carol had been his daughter, four years old when we left Earth. Again he called her name: 'Carol, Carol, my love! Daddy's home.' And on another occasion: 'Oona! Oona!' in short, sharp gasps.

Meanwhile Pip suffered with him in a mental torment for which there could be no relief, and which was as horrendous to watch as the physical agony of his big friend. He did everything humanly possible for Barry. He bathed his forehead as he tossed in fever; he did what he could for the dreadful wounds; fed him like a baby, and became increasingly desperate at his own helplessness.

I did not sleep much during those seven dreadful days. I spent most of the night hours standing by the door of the barn, watching the driving snow and the dark and feeling utterly futile. The door of the barn was made of wooden slats screwed to a heavy timber frame, but the hinges were immobile and the base of the door had embedded itself into the ground; the slats there had rotted but the more durable wood of the frame, although cracked and split, appeared firm still, and the wind could not dislodge it. The door had jammed partly open and many of the slats were missing so that one could see well enough through it, as well as the blackness permitted, but the wind blew through the apertures bringing snow with it in spite of an extensive overhang. The barn itself was far from weatherproof and our own ravaging of its timbers for fuel did not improve matters. It rocked and creaked continually throughout the storm.

I recall the sounds most of all as I stood by the door, like the racking of a sailing ship in a high sea. And there were other sounds, the sound of the wind itself, sometimes like the toneless whistle of carefree boys, sometimes with the demented howl of banshees when the barn would groan under the strain. And while the barn groaned Barry would whimper and writhe under his own ordeal, and I would know that he was sleeping. I would see Pip's eyes glittering in the firelight, reflecting Barry's pain and his own torment. For neither of them did I have any means of comfort. There were the sounds of the fire, too, mostly muted, but often spluttering and muttering in irritation at the gusts of wind.

I remember that it was bitterly cold standing there by the door with the wind reaching through the gaps, while outside it was so dark the snow was grey, only visible for a few feet. I do not really understand why I chose to stand there, it would have been so much warmer by the fire, yet I was reluctant to move away. It was our way out, I suppose, our means of escape. But there was no way out while that storm blew so savagely. I pondered much standing there while my veins shivered. I thought about responsibility, I thought about England and felt a longing for home, and I thought about friendship. Most of all I thought about friendship, about my two friends and the sequence of events that had led them to the present predicament. Initially I had condemned Pip in my mind, but upon reflection I could feel no anger, no diminishing of my affection, only sadness.

One night, I think it was the third, he joined me at the doorway. He looked haggard from lack of sleep and the shredding of his soul by the claws of his guilt, but I could find no words to help him. His eyes were intense with decision

He said: 'I'm going to go for Paul in the morning. I can't bear to see him in pain any more.'

'No, you mustn't do that,' I said. 'We need you even more now with Barry out of commission. I can't let you take the risk of getting lost and freezing to death, and neither would I risk the possibility of Paul getting lost with you on the way back.'

'I don't care,' he cried. 'I will take the risk, any risk. Can't you see that? I must fetch Paul. I can't just sit and watch him suffer like that.'

'Would you risk Paul's life, too, to salve your conscience?'

That reached through the guilt that clouded his mind. He said: 'I don't care if I die, Jeff. Death would be welcome to me now.'

'The best way of easing your guilt is to look after Barry until he's well. Anything else would be running away. That would be unlike you.'

He said no more at that time but I watched him closely during the rest of our enforced internment. But he did nothing rash.

Barry's wounds had taken on a peculiar hue, and they were beginning to smell. The flesh around them was dead. It was about the fifth day when he said to me: 'You know, it doesn't hurt as much now. It's gangrene, of course. The smell is unmistakable.' He was quite calm, quite matter of fact. I was the one who was upset. I suppose that I had known the truth before but had refused to face it. Barry always faced facts. On the sixth day he talked to me of his family, of his home, for the first and last time during my knowledge of him.

I had known his wife. She had been a big, hearty woman, stout, but with a ready sense of the ridiculous. She laughed a great deal. Her name had been Martha, and I recall that she had a moustache on her upper lip, and very black hair; fat, grey eyes. I had liked her, she had been a popular woman. 'Martha was a very clever person, you know,' Barry told me. 'She had a mind equal to my own, really, but she was lazy with it, content to use it for entertainment, especially after Carol was born. She was a good wife, though. Her family was rich, of course, the Merediths. Did you know them? No, well just as well. I couldn't stand them myself, but their money was useful. Without it I would never have been able to push my projects through. Just think about that. If the Merediths hadn't been rich we wouldn't be alive now, not stuck in this dreadful barn, not imprisoned by a blizzard that must surely be the worst of the century, whatever century we're in, and my legs wouldn't be rotting away.

'Martha loved me, you know. She adored me, really. She was a very sensual woman, she had voracious appetites, but I never really loved her in the same way. Oh, I liked her well enough. Would you believe me if I told you that I married her for her money? It's true. I was ambitious then, you see, there was so much that I wanted to do, but I needed the finances. I thought I could live with her, with her intellect and her sense of fun. Well I did that all right. We got on well enough together, and I didn't need anyone else. But I never loved her, not like I loved Oona.' He paused there for a while, but he did not retreat into contemplation. I think he consciously avoided that. 'She was necessary to my physical and economical well-being,' he continued, 'and she served both purposes handsomely, and then of course, Carol came along, which made Martha essential in my life. I did love my little girl, though, Jeff. I worshipped that child. She was so pretty. Black hair like her mother, she was born with it, a great shock of it, and the most beautiful black eyes. Black eyes are rare, you know; very often you will find people with very dark eyes, but they are usually brown, intense brown but not black. Carol's eyes were truly black, and she had a mouth like a cupid's bow.' He paused again, and this time did get lost in reverie for a time.

Later on he said: 'I think that I've only ever loved her, and Oona.' I cannot be sure about the last name, it was murmured so low. I felt that he was crying then, but I would not look at him. And whether he wept for Carol or for Oona, I do not know.

The odour from Barry's legs was horrible. The flesh looked grey, a dark sort of grey. He seemed to sleep a lot more, from exhaustion, I suppose.

On the evening of the seventh day the storm finally eased. Outside the land was solid in its whiteness. The snow was up to three feet deep and, in places, no doubt, drifts of several times that depth lay undetectable. Pip had already fashioned a pair of snowshoes from boards and horsehide. Without a word to me and Barry, he fastened them to his feet with thongs and left. He would not be back before morning. Five miles would take several hours on that treacherous carpet. It would be dark before he reached Paul.

The following day was clear, the sky blue and fresh. Two hours after first light Pip appeared with Paul and two women who had come to transport the remainder of the meat. The tribe had had a lean time of it during the storm, with little to eat. Paul looked drawn and tired but he wasted no time in examining the wounded man.

'You know what it is, Barry?'

'Yes, it's gangrene. Brought on by the lack of circulation in the cold, I would say, and shattered arteries.'

Paul nodded. 'Plus the infection from these filthy sheepskins.'

'The sheepskins were necessary, Paul.'

'No doubt. I can't save your legs, Barry. Both of them will have to come off.'

'I've faced that fact for the last few days, my friend. Leave me some stumps, though, and I'll learn to walk again somehow.'

'Well, we can't do it here. We'll have to get you back to the village. I need pots of boiling water, sharp instruments and some of my witch's brews. Besides, there's not enough light here to operate.'

'And just how do you propose to transport me back? You couldn't possibly carry me across that snow.'

'We'll build a sled,' I put in. 'There's enough material here.'

'Well, build it good and strong,' said Paul. 'It's a rough road. It's going to be a painful trip, Barry.'

It did not take very long to fashion a sled from the palings of the barn. By that time we were reasonably adept at tying timbers together with hide thongs, and a sled hardly stretched our ingenuity. But moving Barry onto it was quite another matter; not only was he a very heavy man, the slightest movement caused him great pain. Actually there was no other choice but to lift him bodily onto the sled and even with his fortitude he was unable to suppress a cry of agony. We had constructed a handle at the rear of the sled so that one man could push from that end while the other two pulled from the front. The women had to carry the meat as best they could.

The snow was soft and Barry's weight made the runners sink into the surface. It would not slide easily. We had to almost lift the front of the vehicle to make it move at all. After about half an hour we had covered less than a mile. We had no proper gloves or shoes and, despite the sunshine, our hands were soon numb and our feet wet and cold and without feeling. Then the sled slid sideways into a particularly soft patch of snow and Barry fell off. His muted scream hung like an organ note in the unmoving air. We ploughed across to him. His face was deathly white with the effort to hold back his pain.

'Stay with it, old son,' I said. 'We've got to get you back on the sled.'

He nodded. 'Get the women to go on ahead,' I told Paul. 'They can send some of the boys back. We'll need all the help we can get.'

Paul saw to that while Pip and I struggled with the weight of Barry. We rolled him back onto the sled. He seemed to be gasping for breath, and he was covered in sweat in spite of the cold. We tied him on. Soon after, we came to a rather more solid surface where the towing was slightly easier, but the sled twisted and tilted continuously. Barry suffered relentlessly, every jolt and lurch, and there was a jolt every yard. There was nothing we could do to help him; our own efforts were concentrated on just moving that sled, and it was muscle-tearing work.

Later we were met by four of the older boys and their strength was some help. It took us more than three hours to complete that dreadful journey. In the village there was a fire burning and already the smell of roasting meat.

We gathered around the fire to dry out and to restore some life to our hands. We were shivering, not only from the cold but also from utter exhaustion. 'We can't waste too much time,' said Paul quietly. 'I must operate almost immediately if we are going to save at least some stumps for him. Every hour more flesh dies.'

We built a table for Paul to operate on. The women were

set to boiling water and also boiling every bandage and cloth that we had left. Paul concentrated on making some complex infusions from his stock of dried herbs, attempting to devise an anaesthetic of some sort. I will not dwell on the operation itself; the anaesthetic was not very successful. Pip and I assisted by holding Barry still. It was torture for all of us; echoes of bitten-off screams stay with me still. But at last it was done. Barry had only stumps for legs but he was alive.

That blizzard must have been the last flurry of winter viciousness. The snow carpet melted very quickly in the early spring sunshine. The winter was over. Soon the North men would be coming home.

Chapter Fourteen

We located the Channel tunnel. That was no problem for the roads leading to it were exceptionally wide and still in good condition. The surrounding terrain was sandy, with little destructive vegetation to obscure the route. Once we had discovered the entrance we explored some distance into it to make sure that it was still trafficable. It appeared just like most other road tunnels, with a gentle gradient leading down below the sea and the opposing lanes of traffic separated, at least as far as we explored, by a central strip. But it was a dark place and the roof dripped constantly. The air was so still that Paul suggested there was likely to be a blockage somewhere. It smelled stale and had a strong odour of bat excreta. There were bats in there in their thousands and the women were afraid of them. They really did not want to go into the place.

We laid in a stock of birch twig torches. We prepared bundles of dried meat, bags of vegetables and hide bags of drinking water. We had already made a cart for Barry, and we strengthened it to carry some of the load. Then we waited and enjoyed the spring.

For a while, several weeks in fact, life was very good. Food was abundant as the herds returned. The sun shone benignly and living was as effortless as we had had it in our new existence. As the spring progressed, with birds chirruping and nesting frantically and the meadows pregnant with surging life, the earth everywhere was jubilant with colour: the delicate yellow of primroses and the demanding yellow of daffodils; a roaming infinity of bluebells, the floors of the woods carpeted with them and the air full of incessant bees. Who could blame us for forgetting the violence of earlier months? We even began to hope that we might be too far north for the North men, but that was hard to sustain since evidence of their occupation was everywhere. It was inevitable that they would foray into our area and detect our tracks. We took the precaution of having lookouts posted, a task undertaken by the women and older children. It was imperative that we knew of their presence before they knew of ours. Then came the day when a lookout reported a group of hunters stalking a herd in a valley to the east. It was time to go.

We left at daybreak. Each adult, apart from the more heavily pregnant women, carried a pack, mostly of bundles of birch twigs and bags of water. The children carried small loads of vegetables. The men had heavier burdens of meat and our weapons, and as well we loaded up Barry's cart with more supplies, making it heavy and cumbersome to wheel. It was fabricated from wood and hide and it had no springing. With just Barry in it the cart rolled fairly well, but loaded with provisions it required two men to keep it moving. We took turns at it. Still, it was sturdy and unlikely to fall apart and, importantly, it could float if required.

Barry himself was over the worst of his pain and was amazingly cheerful. He was beginning to fill his days with talking to the children, introducing them to the rudiments of education in the form of stories, rehashing the fairy stories of our own days to suit their views of the world and to stimulate their virgin minds to think in terms other than those relevant to immediate existence. He tried to encourage them to use other media than their restricted vocabulary to express and record their ideas, suggesting paint, wood carving and the working of stone. He hoped to sow powerful seeds. Apart from that, he passed his time whittling away at two hunks of timber that were to be wooden legs.

The first day in the tunnel was not too bad; we had already explored much of the route and so were aware of the obstacles over which we had to manoeuvre the cart. We kept closely together so that just one torch would serve for light. The cart governed our rate of progress. Possibly we covered ten miles that first day, although it was impossible to gauge distance, and indeed difficult to gauge the passage of time. Strangely, our acquired skill in divining the time of day, almost instinctive above ground, left us completely in the tunnel. Still, by mutual consent we declared a day had passed by and paused for our evening meal of previously cooked mutton and fruit. We rested. Some slept for an hour or two. Then we carried on.

The next few miles were difficult and took perhaps twice as long. There were many roof falls. The tunnel had been designed to take four lanes of traffic and generally it was wide enough for us to clear a passage for the cart by shifting the debris from the least blocked area. But it was hard, limb-wrenching work in the limited light and the foul air. The floor of the tunnel was wet and there was no draught at all. Barry voiced the possibility that the blocked portion we knew must lie ahead might actually be a drowned section, but we had no choice but to push on and find out. One of the roof falls was so large there was no way of clearing even a part of it. We had to manhandle the cart over the top, unloading everything but its passenger and making an extra trip to transport the cargo. That was a bad time. We were gritty with dust that clung to our damp clothes and skin. The air was frightful to breathe, even the torches burned uncertainly; we used two or three then in case one went out. But after some two hours it was done and we took a second rest.

The women were admirable. There was not a single complaint. Was it just unwavering faith that made them so uncomplaining, so confident, when we took them into the bowels of the earth? They were scared, we knew that. Indeed, so were we. Scared of the damp walls, the damp floor, the absolute, impenetrable darkness. They were people of open spaces and free, fresh air. Their claustrophobia was reflected in their frightened eyes in the torchlight, in the whimpers of the terrified children, in the way they huddled together, never letting go of each other's hands. Yet they followed where we led them; we were their men. And assuredly more than men to them. Certainly men unlike any they had ever known. The inbred ideas of our own time made us protest at their submissiveness, but to expect any other attitude from women of their background would have been unrealistic.

That second rest lasted several hours. We were weary and needed it. The supplies were lasting well and only the drinking water was rationed. At last we set off again and for a while the way was clear, although there was more water on the road surface. The tunnel sloped always downwards, and the lower we went the more water there was. It was as if the tunnel was slowly filling up. Then we reached the lake.

The tunnel there was flooded for its full width. The question was, for how far? Did the roof slope down and down until it met the lake's surface? We could not know. From where we stood at the edge the torchlight revealed only darkness a few yards away and the water still and black, evoking irrational thoughts of lurking creatures from the world of fantasy. The wheels of Barry's cart were in the water. 'Come on, Pip, let's go and have a look,' he said. Pip, who was pushing him at the time, nodded his agreement. I handed Barry a new torch and Pip pushed the cart further into the water. At knee depth it would float. Pip climbed in with the big man and, using it as a boat, the two of them propelled it with flat pieces of wood removed from the side of the cart itself. We watched their torchlight diminish and the sounds of splashing water came back to us. Later there was silence and the light vanished. We waited.

Drip. Drip. Constant and magnified like beats of a drum. Wordless faces about me. Fear as palpable as the clinging darkness. They looked at me in their faith, their desperate faith. I could not see their eyes, they were just shadowed pits. Drip. Drip. Echoing and re-echoing from wall to wall. Heartbeats. Fear beating. The torch was cold and white, a flame cringing before the limitless dark. I began to whistle; a toneless, ineffective sound. It emphasised the stillness. Then Paul, too, began to whistle. We kept it up in a pitiable imitation of confidence. But I did hear a baby suckling and saw that a child near me had fallen asleep. A woman began to hum. That was all. Then an hour later—it could not have been longer—the light reappeared, first as a speck in the blackness, then increasing in size until at length Pip came into sight on the cart, alone and dripping wet. Soon he jumped out and pulled the cart behind him. The torch was tied to it.

'Where's Barry?' I cried, running into the water and helping him.

Pip nodded. 'It's okay. He's waiting on the other side. We can get across all right. I've checked the depth. It's wadeable most of the way except for a few yards in the middle. We can swim that. We thought the cart would be needed to ferry the supplies and the kids. So Barry elected to wait over there.' For a moment I pictured the big man waiting totally alone and in utter darkness on the far side of the lake, helpless, with only his faith to sustain him. That was the second time we left him alone. But I had no time to indulge in fanciful thoughts. We quickly loaded supplies and several children onto the cart. Pip was shivering. 'We need more buoyancy,' he chattered. 'We don't want any accidents on the way across. Tie some of those empty skin bags under the cart.'

This was soon done and Pip took off again, with Paul and most of the women wading and holding on to the cart. It took three trips to ferry everyone over. Paul returned on the second trip and I went over then and came back for the last few. We all got wet and the water was icy cold. It was hard work in the middle trying to control that clumsy craft on that currentless pond. The ceiling came down very close for part of the way so that if one reached up from the cart one could touch it. We knew then that we must be at the lowest point of the tunnel: half-way, perhaps. I wondered where the lake drained to for it seemed as if water was continually pouring into it. Later Barry told me that tunnels such as the Channel tunnel had subsidiary arteries below them designed to carry away exhaust gases from traffic, and it was likely that the lake drained through an air shaft in the floor.

'But surely the other tunnels would fill up as well,' I pointed out.

'Oh yes, certainly, but the leak is probably no more than a pressure drip or this lake would not have formed.'

'But even a drip would eventually fill another tunnel.'

'Of course, eventually, but thankfully not yet, eh?'

Once everybody was safely ashore on the far side of the lake we took stock of our supplies. There were still plenty of birch boughs, so we lit a fire and dried ourselves, also using some of the planks from the cart. We rested for a time, but as the fire began to fade we forced ourselves to our feet once more and pushed on. The tunnel was beginning to get on our nerves. We had lost all sense of time and distance. We did not know whether it was daytime or night. Every couple of hours we rested. It was uphill all the way and the cart needed two men to push it. Hard, grinding labour. Stale air. Women shuffling along. The loads should have been lighter but they felt very heavy. Several of the women were thrustingly pregnant, some carried small babies. Lian was limping, her own pregnancy obvious beneath her breasts. We were all dirty, caked with the grime of fallen masonry. We trudged on. The cart creaked. No one spoke. There were grunts, an occasional cough, laboured breathing. On and on and on.

Then the blockage.

I took a torch and climbed to the top of it alone. After some fifty yards or so I reached the roof. I searched right across the width of the blockage but already knew there was no opening since there was no flow of air; my torch burned undisturbed by vagaries of draught. The rockfall seemed to be composed of natural debris, nothing man-made, no concrete or bricks that I could see. It must have been part of the bed of the English Channel. I became suddenly very conscious of the millions of tons of water at some unknown height above our heads, and I felt a little awed, not so much at our own temerity, but that the mind of man, members of the same species as the savages on the plains of France, had conceived and built this submarine road. The descendants of those engineers had not even managed to invent a bow, and a cart was a machine of staggering ingenuity.

Would mankind ever attain such heights of technological genius again? I wondered. Probably not, but perhaps it was not really desirable for him to do so. Putting aside such imponderables I faced the immediate question: could we get through the barrier? The alternative was to return to France and endeavour to outwit the North men, to commit ourselves to a life of constant peril and harassment, or to defeat them. Neither prospect filled me with pleasant anticipation, but the fact that I considered them reveals something of my desperation. Was I so close to admitting defeat? It was the effect of that damned tunnel, of no sunlight and days of dampness, of spirit-sapping claustrophobia. How dense was the barrier anyway? Did it extend from here to Dover? If we dislodged some of the rocks, would we cause a further downfall? Perhaps exacerbate the initial fault and bring the sea crashing in upon us? I doubted the last possibility for the debris was dry and fairly loose. Clearly it was at the top, near the ceiling, that we had to work, where the thickness would be at its minimum.

Returning to the others I asked them to retreat back down the tunnel for some distance in case we started a rockslide, and with Pip to help me and a ten-year-old lad to hold a torch, climbed back to a point near the roof where I had determined to make a start. There was a large boulder there that, if dislodged, should create quite a cavern behind it. It turned out to be a much simpler exercise than I had supposed. We freed it easily and allowed it to roll down the slope, booming alarmingly within the confines of the tunnel, the sound echoing on and on as it bounded down the road. Beyond the space we had created was another boulder of similar size. Pip said: 'This one is very loose. Look, I can rock it.' The very next moment, as he heaved against it, the boulder fell away down the farther slope. A draught of cool air came through. The torch flickered casting strange shadows. Fresh air! Our lungs soaked it up. We were through so easily and we felt exhilarated.

Quickly we enlarged the opening to enable us to get through one by one. We would not be able to pull the cart through. From here on, Barry would have to be carried. I went down for the others. It took two hours to get the big fellow up and through the blockage. We hauled him up the incline with leather ropes. Once he screamed involuntarily as one of his stumps bumped against a rock. Immediately he called out: 'I'm all right, I'm all right! Carry on.' But Paul scurried down to help him. He told me later that Barry's face was grey and distorted with strain, his eyes closed with the effort of endurance. But at last we got him through. The descent on the far side was quite steep. By good fortune we had chosen the only spot on the rockfall where an easy access would have been possible. Elsewhere it was yards thick. This sheer luck was attributed to my wisdom once again, and added to my increasing stature in the eyes of the tribe. That effect did not become evident till later, though. Our immediate attention was concentrated on making some kind of sled as transport for Barry.

Cheered by the flow of air we plodded on, dragging Barry on a kind of litter fabricated from pieces of the cart and rawhide ropes. We did not want to rest although all our muscles shrieked for it. We just wanted to get out of that dark and chilly place.

Eventually, many shambling, mind-benumbed leagues farther, someone croaked: 'Light, I see light!' The exit. Ahead of us the exit. Pip shuffled on in a sort of half-run, unbalanced and tittering. Paul, too, though with more control. I was dragging the litter. I stopped and walked back to Barry.

'We've made it, old son,' I said, and grinned stupidly. Wonderful, formidable man, with greater fortitude than anyone I have ever known. There had been no complaint, no whimper during all those pain-wrapped hours, all those jolting miles.

'Of course,' he nodded. 'I knew you'd bring us through.'

'Didn't you have any doubts?'

He looked at me oddly before saying: 'Now, Captain, why do you think that you're our undisputed leader? Because of some rank given to you by a bygone age?' He shrugged. 'Not at all, such ranks are meaningless now. That whole institution is meaningless. No, you are our leader because you are most fitted to lead. You are not the strongest of us, and both Pip and I are more erudite, but those aren't the traits of leadership. That quality is much more abstract, but positive for all that. It's a combination of guts, example and moral determination. Above all it's the ability to make people have faith in you. And these poor people do have that faith, Jeff. I have it. No, I never doubted you would do it.'

'How do you feel?' I felt an immense affection for him, lying there helpless.

'I feel marvellous now. Come on, Jeff. On to England. Let's go home.'

I took up the thongs again and began to drag him towards the light.

*　　*　　*

The countryside was empty. Green. Cold. But the sun shone on gossamer-dotted grass. It was early morning and the dew was liquid silver. At my feet were primroses. I stood tall and breathed as a god breathes. We were in England and there was a feeling of peace. I had led them here. I had led them here and their eyes expressed their awe. I turned slowly and possessively to survey my kingdom. This was our homeland.

It seemed a very quiet place.

BOOK TWO

The Intruders

Chapter Fifteen

What deep conceit for a man to liken himself to a god. It ranks with man's former conceit in believing that a god would choose to become a man. But I suppose mankind has always selected a god to suit his own peculiar vanity. If age gives man wisdom, my own years have convinced me no creature could be less godlike than man. Yet, how can I say that, seeing my son standing there, so tall and straight and beautiful? He turns his head towards me and the simple movement of it, relaxed, unafraid with the confident arrogance of his youth, stirs in me a reluctant faith, a faith in my kind, so far from being gods, but perhaps nearer that debatable apex than I will accept from the scarred retreat of my withdrawn soul. Could this boy, looking at me now with those grave eyes, so calm, asking nothing of his society, of me, of any man, so undoubting of his strength, so unaware of his grace, could he be somewhere near that apex? Is the pinnacle of godhood anything other than the attributes of this youth, not yet a man, but already with the capacity to control the exigencies of his environment? Always excepting situations created by his fellow beings.

This age does not suit philosophy, though. It has not yet produced any gods at all. Present humanity does not think beyond the immediate demands of survival. I find myself lately tending to drift into philosophical byways that are totally irrelevant, rooted as they are in the indoctrinated concepts of my own youth, my education, an education so far removed from the needs of survival in the current age I wonder sometimes at the utter uselessness of it. What point in knowing about the squares on the sides of right-angled triangles? What use to know the distance to the sun? How pointless to understand Schroeder's theory of the flattened curve of light.

And why search so intently for the causes of the present state of man? The causes do not matter, only the effect should have occupied our concern. Even if we have discerned a cause, and all we can say with certainty is that we have produced a theory to fit the evidence as we have understood it, what value is that to our descendants? And theory is not truth. Yet truth or wild guess, it will not affect the remainder of history. Does mankind survive elsewhere in the world with greater heritage of technology? I have never been satisfied that he does not. But now I do not care. I have known contemporary European man, and I have known contemporary English man. In essence they are little different from each other, and really little different from men of past times. Man has always been a cruel animal. He has always been a greedy animal. Yet he has also been cleverer than other creatures, and he is clever still, as clever as he needs to be, but he has always been conservative, too. So conservative now that it must be tens of thousands of years, as in the dawn of the age of man, before he becomes a man of dreams again, a man who reaches for the stars, and for understanding, and control of the infinite.

There is a city. London. How uninspiring to a man with a spear. It will not last as long as the spear. It has so much less relevance.

We went to London often in later days, but Canterbury was our first home. We stayed there all that first spring following our arrival in England. It was a good time, a good land. Kent, and indeed all of the south-east of England, we were to discover, was heavily wooded country, dense, uncontrolled deciduous woods with abundant fruit trees and carpets of untouched woodland flowers. The game animals were shy creatures of more solitary habits than those of the French plains, and hunting them required the learning of new techniques. Sheep were few, limited in our early experience to the coastal grasslands where they were extremely difficult to capture, but in the woodlands there were cattle, horses, too, and deer, and pigs in large numbers. We relied heavily upon pits and traps. Gone were the days of stalking herds in the open. We began to depend less and less upon our weapons and more and more upon our ingenuity. We feasted well.

It was peaceful that spring. The only unhappy note was the

death of a small boy who had contracted pneumonia in the tunnel, our sole casualty from that trek. His mother was a woman called Lee, a sublimely uncomplicated and cheerful person who was gifted with a superb singing voice that she took great delight in using. Lee was not tall but attractively formed if with a tendency to become overweight—a tendency that bothered them little—with raven-black hair, dark and deliberately sensuous eyes. She had a capacity for instant ardour and was capable of shattering intensities of passion. But she was not a demanding woman. I took her to wife that spring following the death of her child. Lian gave birth soon after to a son. My first son. I named him Kerry.

For several months we saw none of the local inhabitants, although we knew they were about. We were cautious and it appeared that they were shy and unaggressive. Once we came upon a village of about ten dwellings, small dirty hovels built of sticks and mud and repulsive with the smell of human faeces. They did not use the still habitable buildings of an earlier age, and one could only suppose there was some superstition attaching to them. We found fashioned pots of clay, thick-walled and shallow; still, although amazingly crude, they did indicate that some vestige of culture existed amongst them. We learned, too, that there were other sophistications to their technology. They had discovered the advantages of twisting multiple strands of leather together to achieve a stronger and more durable rope than mere strips of rawhide. We also found carvings of wood and necklaces of teeth, dog's teeth and pig's teeth mostly; no lion's teeth to my personal relief.

'Distinctly a Magdalenian culture,' remarked Barry, breathing heavily on his crutches. He was learning to walk admirably on his wooden legs.

'Oh no, hardly as advanced as that,' disagreed Pip, thus beginning one of their interminable but amiable arguments.

The summer came in, hot and slumberous for endless weeks. We were still unsophisticated with our traps then, and the local game had learned to avoid them. We did not go hungry, but obtaining sufficient meat for our needs entailed considerable effort.

'I think we should go somewhere else,' suggested Pip. 'We

shall have to learn to follow game as our ancestors used to.'
He had restless feet and an eagerness to discover.

'You bloody gypsies are all the same,' muttered Barry. It
was really quite an accurate description of the little man. 'No
sooner do we get settled in one spot than you want to go
gallivanting all over the countryside.' But his eyes gave the lie
to his protestation. He was perfectly happy to move on to
new pastures.

Pip ignored him and turned his back. He winked at me. 'I'd
just like to be a bit closer to London. I'd like to see how the
city has fared. Of course other people with no sense of
adventure prefer to vegetate.'

'Oh, dear. Well, if you're determined to go I'd better go
with you,' sighed Barry wearily. 'Can't trust pipsqueaks like
you in a big city on your own.'

So we decided to move on. But not directly for London.
The land was new and the climate kind, not at all conducive
to urgency. We followed the roadways since they were still
the easiest way to travel, although overgrown with thistles
and brambles and waist-high grass. We roamed leisurely as
the whims of the moment and the fortunes of hunting dictated,
heading ever west towards Maidstone. There were sometimes
stretches of open countryside where the air was redolent with
the soporific fragrance of wild poppies in their thousands.
There were foxgloves and cornflowers by the armful, straw-
berries lush for the picking, early apples on the trees. The
land was alive with the calls of birds, aflutter with colour, a
dreamy, abundant land. The women were convinced that we
had led them to an earthly paradise although they had no
concept of such an explicit term. I was adored. I strode tall
and strong, yet I was humble, too, humble within and afraid.

Yes, I was afraid. Life then was good. But winter would
come. No, I was not afraid of winter. I would cope with that.
It was a fear more profound, more indefinite, a fear of the
failure of arrogance, perhaps, and the vestiges of youthful
teachings still in the dusty attics of my mind, stories of the
serpent in the Garden, of the defilement of Eden. Or it may
have been the realisation that we did not fit. Then we were
supreme. We appeared to have adapted. But we were inescap-
ably men of a different culture, governed by different ethics,

products of a technological society as exemplified by Pip's compulsive inventiveness with snares and traps, and Barry's preoccupation with the children in the patient processes of education. We were men out of our niche, but in those early days I felt it as no more than a background anxiety, a shadowy, unvocalised thought that I had neither the time nor the inclination to dwell upon. More than anything my fears were concerned with the nature of man, naked man unclothed with the *mores* that were an integral part of our own social cloak. We had yet to confront the men of England.

And there was yet another sentiment that lingered on the surface of my soul. This was, after all, my country. I was a child of Kent, and no rational argument, could dampen that sentiment. I did attempt to suppress it, for Keston, home of my schooldays, was some distance away and in our first days in England we were unsure of our reception by the locals. The others talked casually of visiting their homes at some undefined future time, although those places were even further away. Barry came from Cambridge and Paul from Harrogate in Yorkshire. Pip had never had a home as we understood it. He had been the victim, or as he preferred to term it, the beneficiary, of an inherent vagrancy within the family, going back for generations, he told us proudly, so that as a child he had rarely lived in any one place for more than a few months. How such an itinerant education ever produced such an outstanding brain was beyond my understanding, but it had also given him his ebullience and his versatility.

We settled in Maidstone and, in that old town of hills and orchards on the clean, green stream of the Medway, made our home. As the autumn came in with winds and fitful rain we learned to trap cattle alive and pen them. We harvested the hay for winter feed, and although too wild then for milking, we hoped to rear milk cows in the years ahead. They thrived in our pens and soon became remarkably passive. We only kept cows. We would not go hungry that winter. There was a local indigenous group in the Maidstone district. We learned of two villages, one quite substantial settlement at Aylesford which seemed to be more or less permanently occupied, and one in the region of West Malling which was clearly only a summer encampment. We avoided both places.

There were other large villages further west at Sevenoaks and at Swanley and a big settlement at Orpington. We explored no further that first year.

I had developed an enthusiasm for fishing, a pastime I had always enjoyed, but which in my advancing years I increasingly preferred to the more strenuous activity of hunting. The Medway actually yielded plenty of freshwater fish right in the heart of town, but we had a preference for salt-water varieties and I would make frequent trips to Chatham and sometimes to the Thames mouth where the fishing was excellent. The first few times Paul came with me as we had a rule not to venture too far afield unaccompanied, but later, as it became clear the indigenous people posed no threat, I would go with only Lian and the eldest youth of the group, a lad called Kip, then about twelve years old. His mother was one of Barry's two wives.

One day I went on an expedition to Milton Regis, more for my personal diversion than for any needs of our larder. Kip accompanied me, with Lian and John, Oa's son, then two years old and named after Major Clark, the second of us to die. I expected to be away for three or four days. It was a cold day on the coast and Lian sat near me as I fished, wrapped in deerskins and crooning peacefully over her new baby. Kip and John played some distance away. I was content, with a gradual realisation of the depth of my contentment, as a fish jerked strongly at my line. There was a cool wind off the sea funnelling up the Shale, and the smell of seaweed was pungent in my nostrils. I pulled the line in hand over hand, but allowed it to run when the resistance was too strong. There was a marvellous satisfaction in playing the fish, and I must have smiled, for Lian was smiling back at me, appreciating my contentment as her own satisfaction. She often smiled in those days. The good living had erased the signs of ordeal from her body and from her mind. She lived for the present, for me and her two children. For her the past was dead. Her horizons were small, perhaps, but for her they were enough.

She was lovelier then than ever and I adored her with a sort of wonder that men feel on examining the unalloyed loveliness of a butterfly or the fragile beauty of a flower, as if such things were the product of the sunshine, and somehow one felt endowed with a special insight because of one's own deeply personal appreciation, one's singularly human recognition of the wonder of beauty. But Lian was not a butterfly and my love for her was no sublime sense of the aesthetic, it was a powerfully physical and profound emotion, carnal but more than lust, an emotion without reservation or doubt or insecurity, wrapping the mind and the soul and the seat of all pain. That I was still to understand.

The fish was kicking on the surface, its fight at an end. Evening was drawing near and it was becoming uncomfortably cold. We intended to camp that night in the town and return to Maidstone the following day. I had enough fish. I called for Kip; he would come and help me clean them. But looking around I could not see him. 'Kip,' I called again, more loudly and with some irritation. I had come to expect almost instant responses to my commands. Still I was not anxious in this land of tranquillity.

'You had better start cleaning the fish,' I said to Lian. 'I'll go and find the boys.'

It was some distance before I discovered them, led by the sounds of high delight and the groans of a person in anguish. Kip and the infant were tormenting another lad whom they had ensnared in one of Pip's devilish traps. It consisted of a loop of rope concealed on a pathway beneath fallen leaves, the other end of which was tied to the strained limb of a tree held in place at ground level by a stick braced against the trunk. Any animal stepping into the loop and jerking the rope would release the prop and the strained bough would fly upwards, thus tightening the loop about the leg of the unfortunate captive and hoisting it aloft. In this instance the captive was a young boy, no older than Kip himself, now swinging upside down and quite helpless against the proddings and pokings of his captors. It was pointless to berate them. I cut the lad down and treated his swollen ankle to the best of my ability. I was astonished that he spoke in reasonably comprehensible English, if somewhat distorted from my own familiar tongue. 'That's a good trap,' he said, still looking at it with interest. Then: 'Are you going to kill me?'

I smiled at that. 'No, why should we?'

'Because I've been following you.'

I did not reveal that we had not known that. 'That's no reason to kill you,' I said.

'Then why capture me?'

I refrained from answering directly, instead I asked Kip in French if he had deliberately set out to ensnare the boy. Kip denied this. He said that he had been merely experimenting with the snare and had gone into concealment to await developments. The captive had come along apparently to examine the reason for Kip's preoccupation and had triggered the trap.

Sending Kip back to fetch Lian and to carry the fish, I picked up the captive, for so cruelly had the rope cut into his ankle that he was unable to stand unaided, and carried him back into the town to spend the night with us. John toddled happily behind. That evening I questioned the lad closely. His name was Hal, a good English name, I thought. He had been detailed to follow my little band to the coast; it seemed all the expeditions of our tribe were watched and reported upon. By the lad's naïve candour in answering my questions, it was revealed that the suspicions of his people were tempered with a certain degree of awe. We had come mysteriously out of the sea—I had no idea that our arrival on English soil had been observed—killed beasts from afar with magic weapons, had axes and knives of some wondrous material clearly superior to their own blades of stone and bone, and we devised amazing ways to trap animals and pen them up alive, a concept completely alien to them. Plainly we were a race of beings to be watched closely and yet to be feared.

I learned that the peoples of the south-east, although separate tribes, still considered themselves to be more or less a single clan, unlike the fiercely territorial men of the French plains. Yet Hal told me of the savage western people, who appeared to correspond with the dreaded North men of France, although I gathered this aspect of their folklore was probably due more to an undefined fear of the unknown than any recorded instances of savagery by the westerners. Hal certainly did not accuse them of being cannibals. The various tribes of the south-east clan were in constant communication with each other and indulged in various forms of intercourse, trade, ceremonial and marriage. Hal was very communicative.

He seemed to hold me in some sort of special reverence as the leader of the strange and awful band that had come to dwell in their midst, and he answered my questions as if some calamity would befall him if he refused. I tried to assure him that we were a peaceful folk, and meant no harm either to him or to any of his people. We fed him, but I suspect he had never eaten fish before and I was not sure that he liked it. In the morning he was gone.

That was our first encounter with the local inhabitants, an unremarkable and comparatively anticlimatic confrontation. Its one notable effect was their adoption of Pip's ingenious animal trap. We discovered them at times on our own forays and soon learned to watch out for them. We congratulated ourselves that our superior technology was having an impact, and that gave impetus to our dreams.

Only now I wish that we had never had that impact at all. Oh, God, I wish we never had!

Chapter Sixteen

They visited us in winter. We found them one morning on awakening: twenty-eight miserable creatures, thin and dirty and offensive to the nose. They presented quite a contrast to the admirable men of France. Hal was among them but he turned his head away and would not be acknowledged. Ten women, unattractive in their filthy skins, odorous and unkempt, nine men and nine children, excluding any infants carried beneath almost every woman's stinking hide.

'What do you want?' It was Paul who spoke.

'Food.' The spokesman was an old man and he came forward a few steps. 'You have plenty here, and hunting is hard in winter.' That was true. Naked trees and a scarcity of pasture had forced the game to the marshlands of the east coast or westwards to the downs where, in both cases, snares and traps were far less effective. Animals could be stalked and killed but it took a great deal of effort and meant endless hours of exposure in the bitter cold. We had abandoned hunting ourselves many weeks since, for we had plenty of live beasts and fodder for them, enough to last the whole season. 'My people are hungry,' continued the old man, 'there is no fruit on the trees and the dogs eat the rabbits. Give us a cow to fill our bellies.' It was a simple speech, not exactly a demand, but delivered in such a surly and unfriendly manner that one's immediate response was to tell him to clear off. I thought then of Oa and could not help comparing his arrogance to this surly beggar; it was difficult to imagine Oa begging from anyone. I hoped that he was still alive. Yet these people were fellow human beings, apparently in some distress even if that condition was due to their own sloth. We gave them a cow and they took it less than a hundred yards away and slaughtered it. They cut it up immediately and carried it away, viscera and head as well as the meat itself, already chewing raw pieces of liver as they departed.

'Not one word of thanks,' commented Pip.

'Gratitude is an emotion of some sophistication,' explained his fellow scientist.

'Not at all,' disagreed the other. I left them to their argument, but wondered about the lack of gratitude none the less, and a warning note of anxiety registered in my mind. Were we setting a precedent of more insidious implications than we could know? The peace of England had not completely erased the scars of French violence from my memory.

It was not bad that winter. Snow came later, presumably about January, although we had not adopted any formal classification for the passage of time. It seemed to have no relevance, really. We hibernated during the snow time, withdrawing into our little wooded world of Maidstone. There the vegetation, stark in those months but living still, had overgrown the town. The houses were concealed beneath veritable jungles of vines, ivy and honeysuckle. The streets were wooded, trees rooted in the very macadam of the roads. Even the roofs were covered in grass, and in other seasons were decorated with random patches of flowers, a kind of elevated tribute to the soft blue sky. Beneath that piled undergrowth were many ruins providing an inexhaustible world of adventure for the children and a haven of quiet for the adults. We had our cave, built by the hands of our ancestors, refashioned by time and nature and the elements; a cave that was shelter, a cave that was sanctuary, a cave that in that bitter winter was home. We were inviolable and happy. Although those winter days were sometimes long we found enjoyment in simple crafts and conversations of great complexity. We carved wood, discovering the rewards in acquired skills and the sense of achievement when craft bordered on art. None of us really had the talents of an artist, but there were some works that we felt came close and we hoped that from emulation might spring a new culture in this artless land, and perhaps somewhere, at some time, a great talent might emerge from our stumbling beginnings.

We had many such strong hopes for the future. It gave us a feeling of purpose to believe that we could be the source of all future art. How naïve we were. Or how conceited. We made pottery, too. And told the children stories to which the women listened with as much eagerness as their offspring. But mostly we just talked. Endless discourses, inconclusive discussions about what had happened, and why had it happened. Where was mankind going now? Should we attempt to influence a new evolution? Was the present way in lots of aspects more desirable than the way of our own time? Were people happier now? Was there a destiny? Was there a God? And we were noddingly wise; unseeingly foolish. The hours were cosy and very pleasurable. Life was good. There was plenty of food, there was laughter and song, there were the warm and eager bodies of the women. There was adoration, security, an absence of pretence and pretensions, no anger that I recall, no tensions. Perfect peace for a while, too short to become dull.

When it snowed, the indigenes came again. Thirty-seven of them the second time, and they did not bother to ask. They had observed our technique for roping a beast from the throng of milling cattle and they simply came and took a heifer for themselves. We berated them strongly but permitted them to keep the animal. They came once more that winter, during the hours of darkness, and stole two more head. But soon afterwards spring crept over the land in a gradually greening blush. The trees threw off the starkness of winter and bloomed rampantly. The birds returned with frantic energy, hysterical with their seasonal loving, and the woods were filled with song and fresh green grass and bluebells stretching forever. Lee was pregnant. Barry, who then had four wives, was presented with his first child that spring. It was a boy, I think. There was a total of six new babies altogether before summer, but before the advent of that season we had undertaken an expedition the four of us had planned over the slow winter fires. We took the tribe to London. On the way we made a diversion to Keston. I had succumbed to my nostalgic impulses. The others understood and raised no objections. Besides, there was no real purpose in visiting London, and certainly no urgency. Our sole reason was curiosity.

It took us four weeks to get there, for we ambled, enjoying the awakening surge of the land, the uninhibited sensuality of growing things, hunting leisurely and exploring villages and towns en route as the fancy took us. Keston itself was a difficult place to reach, surrounded as it had become with heavy woodland and dense thickets. There were acres and acres of brambles on what had once been commons, laden with unripe fruit but much too daunting to penetrate. In the end we skirted such terrain, but even the roads in the area were overgrown with creepers and uncontrolled shrubbery so that not only were they almost impassable, they were often indistinguishable. I began to despair of ever locating my home. I could not even find my way in territory that had been as familiar to me as the classrooms of my school. We found the ponds. They were choked with water weed and stagnant. The growth about them was especially lush. It seemed like a strange country. Many were the hours I had spent on the banks of those ponds fishing with home-made tackle; I had spent countless weekends and evenings playing Cowboys and Indians in the copses around them, but there was nothing there now that struck a single chord of recognition in my mind. It was as if we had found a new and different land imposed upon the one of my childhood.

I knew that north from the ponds lay an area we had called the 'Quarry'. While the tribe set up camp near the ponds— for the children thought it a wonderful place and there were plenty of small animals to hunt thereabouts, wild turkeys and geese, too, even deer if one was quiet and patient—I went off with Lian, baby Kerry and young Kip to try to locate the 'Quarry', because I was sure I could find my home from there. In the end Pip decided to come with us as well. He said it was for the fun of it, but I suspect he was also being cautious. He brought his weapons with him.

It is easy to find north in an English woodland. I remembered the trick from my boy scout days. The moss on trees always grows more thickly on the north side of a tree. We followed game trails for the most part, cutting overhead foliage as we went to suit the passage of a man as well as to indicate our return route, wandering as the paths led us but ensuring we went generally north. After about an hour we came out into some open country. We never found the 'Quarry', but we did find a roadway that I thought I recognised. There was the crumbling structure of a large house on top of a hill that I felt sure was one I had known in childhood as the 'Mansion'.

'I used to live about twenty minutes' bike ride from here,' I told Pip.

'Which way?'

'Oh, straight ahead. I can find my way from here all right.'

But it was easier said than done. The road soon led into woodland again and promptly vanished beneath ferns and brambles. There were no landmarks to guide me. My memory of the locale was so utterly different. Yet the nostalgia was too strong in my veins then to give up. The environment was unfamiliar but the ground I trod on seemed to have an affinity with my feet, as if I could feel my roots through the very sod. Surprisingly enough, Pip, who could not have understood my feelings, gave me cheerful encouragement. 'Having come all this bloody way, we ain't going to give up now,' he said.

Beyond that stretch of woodland were more fields, once farmland, now dense with tall grass, much of it wild wheat, and there were poppies there and stinging nettles. It was easier going then, though not by any means a country stroll, and Kip and Lian had something of a struggle through the grass, but Pip and I went ahead and made a track. We came to a slight rise. 'Beyond that rise is a valley,' I told them. 'In that valley there is a village. It is my home.'

'Come on, then,' cried Pip, 'let's see the place that brought you into the world. I might be able to remove the curse.'

'Wait a minute,' I said. I had a very odd feeling. I knew my voice was unsteady. For some moments I felt reluctant to go over the rise. I felt like turning and going back. But John ran ahead and soon disappeared over the other side.

'Come on,' said Pip, and we went forward. The houses in the valley were falling down. We could see that as we approached from the hillside. There was evidence further on of human occupation in recent times. The houses had been pulled apart for firewood and to build a strange monolith of bricks. I thought at first that the monolith might indicate some spiritual beginnings among the local people. Perhaps the despoilers of the houses had some religious understanding.

'It's nothing but a phallic symbol,' scorned Pip. 'Just the

ultimate expression of male vanity, as if possession of genitals made him godlike. There you see it, the arrogance of man, his stupidity and his pride, expressed in one pointless edifice.'

'It doesn't look so different from many monuments of our own time,' I pointed out.

'Exactly. That facet of our species hasn't changed, anyway. Now, where's your house?'

I led them through the village. But the affinity had gone. The reality of what was there had no relevance to my memories. It was a dead place. Without the traffic and tended gardens and the sounds of people chatting, there was nothing. It might as well have been a village in France for all that it moved me. I stopped and looked at the church. It was built of stone and had a spire. It seemed the least damaged by the centuries. There was a gravestone in the churchyard with my father's name on it. I did not want to find it. I moved on.

There was really no feature to distinguish my old home from the ruins of all the other houses in the street. I am not even sure that where I led the others was indeed the site of my home, only somewhere close to it. Perhaps some deep inner knowledge, some ingrained instinct, directed my footsteps to the right place. I had no sense of it and I shall never know. There were no houses as such, no walls other than a few jagged projections through the thickets of thistle and thorn. There were only fragments of the street itself visible through the tangles of grass and weeds. I felt nothing then, not even disappointment at the meaninglessness of the whole expedition. It had always been an indulgence. The earlier excitement, the nervous anticipation, had gone and had been replaced by a sort of indifference. I had no links with this place, this throttled residue of settlement. My boyhood, the intensity of my adolescence and the foundation of my being was here in the thickets, in this wilderness, but smothered beneath it, lost now, irretrievable. It was as if that boyhood had never been. There was nothing to be found of it here. I bent down and picked up a housebrick.

'Is this where you lived?' asked Pip. Lian stood by him, watching me silently, and Kip, too, probably wondering why we had struggled so hard to reach this unprepossessing spot.

'I think so,' I told him, and dropped the brick. 'Let's get back to the others now.'

Pip was quiet. He nodded, looking at me as if he sensed some sentiment within me that was not there. All I felt was a sense of futility, a foolishness. 'How we were doesn't matter much now, does it?' I said, and, turning, I began to make my way back.

From Keston we went on into London.

* * *

London was as empty as Paris had been, but the pathos it generated was heightened for all of us by our familiarity with this city of our own land. Some birds survived there, and rats, too, although not as many as in Bordeaux, so far as we could tell, for without human debris rats would have had a struggle to survive in the streets. I think London has suffered more than Paris from the ravages of the years. Trees grew in Trafalgar Square; Hyde Park and St James's Park were thick woods which we did not bother to penetrate. Where once had been lawns was now shoulder-high grass. Many of the bridges had gone, and we could not understand why. Barry suggested there might have been a flood. It seemed the only explanation. But most of the buildings still stood, more derelict and crumbling than we would have expected from the condition of other towns, but that may have been due partly to the quite extraordinary luxuriance of growth there, to the assaults of creepers and the roots of trees. Perhaps underground water encouraged such growth, or perhaps it was due to the abundance of parks. The Thames ran clean and it abounded with fish. We swam in its cool waters and caught huge carp from its wharves.

We spent our first night there in one of the once great hotels and spent most of the next day exploring. As we had a tendency to disperse in our eagerness, we established the hotel as a base in case we became too separated. That pattern continued for a few days, except that I grew sad at the desolation of a city that once held many ties for me, and I tended to restrict my wanderings to the area around the hotel. I was happier simply fishing, and I would do that with just

Lian and Kerry for company. But even fishing made me pensive and depressed. The state of the city weighed upon me. I had lived in London for many years in my early adulthood and it still had the power to affect me. I felt an affinity with it as if its decay reflected the erosion of civilised standards within my own personality. On the third afternoon, leaving Lian at the hotel, I ventured alone down the once familiar streets. I went back to Trafalgar Square and stood there, allowing nostalgia to seep from the flagstones until I felt cold. I looked at the large buildings all around me, pathetic and meaningless in their emptiness, crumbling slowly, inevitably, into gravel and dust. And I remembered the Square as it was: the crowds and the traffic and the continual noise; the industry and the energy and the sheer force of human beings striving amid the congestion of their structures. And I wondered. Even standing amidst the hollowness and the awful silence it was hardly credible. It was this city that I had known, this very Square where I had stood so often in the past, feeling that I was part of the heartbeat of commerce, part of the limitless ambitions of my kind. I shut my eyes and the sounds came to me, of people, crowds, children crying, laughter. And always the traffic.

The shadows lengthened as I stood there with my memories, and those shadows were more than the falling sun: they were the shadows of the failed aspirations of mankind, greed and vanity, ambition and lofty ideals condensed into moving darkness; and they filed by, the hordes that were no more, silent and without substance as the evening possessed me. I walked around the Square with illusions for company, and the shuffle of my footsteps was the only interruption of the quiet. I walked with ghosts and I could not communicate. The pavement was alien. The dirt and the smell and the hush were alien. And I was left with the ashes of my memories like vomit in my gut.

I went back to my companions.

We left the following day. On the whole the city held little to attract us, but Pip had found something of inestimable value. In one of the office buildings he had discovered a vault, shut, but with the key still in the lock. Inside were shelves full of stationery, pencils, rulers and all the paraphernalia of an office. He had removed a fair amount, and had resealed the vault for future use. Writing paper and pencils! It is difficult to express just how much that meant to us. For many days we indulged in an orgy of writing and scribbling. But Barry welcomed it most of all. He was determined to introduce the rudiments of education to our children and he had great hopes for the potential of that paper.

* * *

My daughter Jenny was born on the way back to Maidstone. It was then high summer. The weeks merge in my memory. Languorous days. Was that the summer of the horses? It was early during our time in Maidstone that we had captured two young foals, and as they grew older we broke them to a saddle and learned to ride them. That was claimed to be a major achievement by the women, one more indication of our omniscience, but for practical purposes it turned out to be of much less advantage than we had imagined and seemed hardly worth the effort involved.

Kip was the only lad who attempted to master the skill, and indeed he learned to ride quite well, probably better than we did. Actually hunting from horseback, which was one of the advantages we had envisaged, required the acquisition of new techniques which none of us men were young enough or proficient enough riders to develop. Besides, obtaining meat by other means presented few difficulties by that time. I remember Barry remarking in his unconsciously pompous fashion: 'Inventiveness will only develop when the need is there. Ingenuity needs incentive. This is not a land that requires more then the barest modicum of inventive skill. Without the impetus of hardship man is fundamentally an apathetic creature. But it will not always be so.'

One morning Kip advised us that he was going off for a ride, and he rode away at a gallop. He was inclined to be a show-off, for he was at that age, probably fourteen years, when his awakening ego and his surging adolescence dominated his common sense; there was absolutely no reason for galloping other than youthful swagger, and very effective it was, too. But he did have a great deal of common sense and his ability was such that we were not unduly concerned. Except that he did not return.

By midday we were anxious enough to send out some of the other lads to try to find him. We thought that he might have had a fall and could be lying injured somewhere. That was quite a possibility because he had no real saddle, just a sheepskin blanket strapped to the horse's back with some leather stirrups attached. That, plus a bridle, a bit and some reins was all the equipment we used. The search party came back just before sunset, without him. They were good trackers and, although unshod hooves leave only a faint trail, they had been able to follow it until they came to a bitumen road. Kip must have ridden along the road for some way and they were unable to pick up his trail again, although they searched for several miles in both directions.

We determined to organise a more extensive search in the morning if he did not show up that night, but there was heavy rain during the evening so that even the more obvious traces of his passage would have been obliterated. Yet we did search. We searched over the next few days, systematically exploring every acre of the surrounding countryside, all to no avail. Kip had vanished.

He was the eldest of our youths and his disappearance affected the tribe profoundly. He was a popular boy and his mother, although a sharp-tongued woman, had adored him. She cried for days. Such open grief was rare in these women and Barry could do little to comfort her. But I, too, was saddened, more than I could show. Kip had become a close companion to me; he would always accompany me on my own expeditions and a strong affection had grown up between us. He was very willing to learn and eager to participate in all our activities, even though some of them must have seemed strange to him. He was not especially clever, nor did he have the arrogance and ambition needed to be a leader, but he was confident in himself, finely built and strong. In my maturity it seemed that sadness was sharper somehow, less readily dismissed. It was not exactly grief, but there was pain.

The summer seemed longer that year than usual, and the autumn was particularly windy. I remember the landscape as brown, for the wind encouraged the fall of leaves and scattered them, some of them green still. The wild apples fell off the trees before they were ready, and the fields were yellow with early hay. We gathered the hay and prepared for winter. That was the summer that we began to train the dogs. The children had killed a wild bitch and found her litter. The puppies were old enough to survive and we raised them. They became remarkably docile as they grew up and by wintertime we had four watchdogs, still too young and exuberant for discipline, but the locals would no longer be able to steal our cattle unnoticed.

Yet they came. It appeared that because of our presence and the ready availability of meat, they had become somewhat lazy. It was not a hard winter and game was easily available. They had managed to survive before our arrival and at first we refused to part with any of our stock. 'It is bad policy,' stated Barry. 'We are just encouraging their indolence. I don't want to see us as an influence against motivation. Let them go and hunt.'

So we sent them away. Two days later they returned. They had Kip with them. He had a rope around his neck like a leash. His hands and feet were free. He looked very dirty but unharmed and well fed. 'They want to exchange me for some cows,' he said.

We gave them two cows and they released Kip. That was a night of some celebration. His mother clung to him all night, crying in her happiness almost as much as she had cried in her grief. Kip came to me as soon as he was released and I hugged him, I would have kissed him but he would not have understood. Then I left him to his mother. After the homecoming celebration, he told us his story. We learned a lot from him about our neighbours.

Upon leaving us Kip had galloped away, allowing the horse to have its head for a while. They had covered a few miles and he found himself on heathland. He knew the area well enough, but as it was on the fringes of our normal range, he decided to turn back. The horse was tired and he reined it to a standstill without much trouble. At that moment a hare darted in front of them. The horse reared up, almost unseating its rider, but Kip managed to hold on. All might have been well, but a fox, no doubt pursuing the hare, raced boldly beneath the horse's legs. Again the animal reared, and then it began to run. Kip having hardly recovered from the first surprise and losing his foothold in the stirrups, could only cling on to the horse's mane with one hand while groping for the reins with the other. He did not know how far the animal ran. They were off the heath and into wooded country. The inevitable happened. He struck a branch and was swept from the horse's back. The horse ran on. He recalled the shock and a sense of falling but he could not remember actually landing on the ground.

His next recollection was of an awareness of hurt. 'I felt as if my left shoulder was being separated from my neck and my arm was just one mass of pain.' He was lying in bracken. Above him was the canopy of the trees and far beyond that little fragments of cloud like apple blossom. Then a face, a strange face, bearded and unsmiling; a filthy face, but the eyes were concerned and not unfriendly. Kip tried to sit up, but he hurt too much. The man above him helped him and said something, although Kip could not understand him.

'I think my arm is broken,' the boy said in his own tongue, but there was only a puzzled frown in reply. There were two other men standing close by, younger men, one barely older than Kip himself. They looked at him curiously but with no hint of hostility. 'Will you help me get back to my own people?' Kip continued, not realising that they could not understand a single word he said.

As the only response he could elicit was silence, he tried to stand up. They came forward to help him, surprisingly gentle as if recognising his hurt. Once on his feet, Kip found that he could walk all right, although he had to hold his painful arm with the uninjured one. They beckoned him to follow them and led the way through the trees. Kip could only wonder if they were taking him back to our settlement, and at first he was quite happy to follow them.

They walked many miles, in and out of woodland, sometimes through villages, but heading generally due west. Realising then that they were certainly not taking him home, Kip protested, but they seemed not to understand him even though Kip was adamant that he had made himself very plain. He wanted to go the other way. By then he had no idea where he was at all and felt too ill to turn back on his own. At least he was encouraged by their concern for his obvious suffering. They rested often, and later, when he nearly fainted, the youngest boy, with evident shyness, placed his arm about Kip's waist and supported him. He continued to do so for the remainder of the journey. Kip felt very ill indeed. Not only did his arm and shoulder throb continually, but he had developed a severe headache. He told us he felt quite dizzy and could not always see well. We thought he must have had some concussion.

He remembered arriving at their encampment, although, by his description of it, the place was more a settlement than an encampment. There were many huts built of sticks and mud, all reasonably similar in size, with only bare earth between them, packed hard by the perpetual traffic of naked feet. The men and women all wore skin coverings, mainly deerskin or cowhide, and they smelled abominable. The village was incredibly filthy, so that even in his sickness, Kip recoiled from the odour. There was the smell of human faeces, urine, bad meat, animal skins and decay. Yet the villagers seemed impervious to it. Still, Kip could travel no more. He was already nauseous and that odour made him vomit. They were kind to him. They led him to a hut and made him lie down on a pile of sheepskins. They were foetid and dirty, but his vomiting had defeated him. He lost consciousness for a short time—how long, he did not know, but when he came to it was still daylight. The young man who had assisted him on the journey was sitting beside him. Kip felt so stiff and sore he had trouble even moving himself on the pile of skins. He could not focus properly. The youth gave him some water from a hide bag, holding it for him while he drank.

So far as we could determine, Kip slept quite a lot for a day or two. He recalled a woman coming into the hut and wrenching at his shoulder so that he screamed, but after that it hurt much less. His arm turned out not to be broken, just bruised, and with that wonderful resilience of the young, he was on his feet and investigating his surroundings with his normal vigour after just a few days, accompanied by his new friend, whose name as far as he could tell was Ari.

The two of them never learned to communicate, at least not with speech, but they seemed to understand each other well enough. Kip was anxious to go home, of course, but for some reason that was one idea that he could not get across. He realised very soon that, in spite of all their kindness, he was actually a captive. Not only did he not know the route home, but whenever he wandered far from the village, Ari always turned up beside him, smiling and not at all hostile. Kip recognised that he was under constant surveillance, although he never understood why. Perhaps that was just as well, since he would almost certainly have become totally lost, and at least with Ari's people he was being looked after. In the end Kip accepted his lot with resignation, simply deciding to await an opportunity to return to us. He was not unhappy in spite of the problem of communication. He ate well and very much enjoyed the company of Ari. He had even become used to the smell.

One can only wonder at the tribe's reason for restraining him. It is doubtful if they immediately envisaged using him as a bargaining factor for winter cattle. They may genuinely have liked him, or they may have enjoyed the presence of one of those extraordinary people who had come into their lands from nowhere, whose ways were so different from their own. It may have been that they were a little in awe of Kip. Perhaps having him in their midst gave them some kudos in the local tribal community. Whatever the reason, they treated him kindly and he learned much of their way of life. They also learned from him. He taught Ari our ways of trapping animals, including refinements of Pip's snare which, although already adopted by them, was used with less sophistication than it might have been, thus reducing its rate of success. Their method of making fire was different from the French way which was to strike flints together to make a spark and, by blowing assiduously onto dry leaves, eventually cause a flame. It was very arduous, but less so than the English method which meant continuous rubbing with a dry stick in a groove of a log, with dried grass as the combustible material. This was actually done fairly infrequently, for fire was carefully conserved and even carried from place to place, but rain and long journeys sometimes meant that a fresh blaze had to be made. Kip was quite adept at making fire and his captors were eager to adopt the new technique.

Once Barry and Pip learned of this, it provided them with material for a new debate on the interaction of cultures. Pip enthused about the idea of one culture learning from another. 'You see,' he said, 'if they can see the benefits they will adopt new techniques. It opens up a whole range of possibilities.' He was quite excited and spoke so rapidly that one had to listen very carefully to take in all that he said. He normally spoke unusually fast, but sometimes ideas flowed from his brain in such a stream it was as if his tongue had difficulty keeping up with them. 'Just think of it. If we could make long-term contact, a continuing intercourse, we could pass on all sorts of technology. The wheel. The cultivation of crops. Pottery, real pottery that is, not that crude burnt clay they produce. And art. We could teach them to paint and mould and carve. We could show them how to smelt iron. We could . . .'

'Steady on there, Pipsqueak,' smiled Barry. He was much calmer, tending to weigh things up in his mind before uttering so that he often spoke ponderously. 'They won't learn such things and we would be wrong to try to impose them on them. They have no need, you see. All right, they might adopt some trapping methods or an improved method of firemaking, but those things only help them at their existing level of culture. They are hardly an advance. Such adoptions do not indicate any propensity to enter a new iron age. Neither do they mean that there is a potential Leonardo da Vinci among them. They are a lazy people, and they are lazy because their environment is bountiful. It does not stimulate any motivation for advancement as we understand the term. Even the winters here can be easily withstood until the spring so long as they have fire and sheepskins.'

So they argued in their amicable fashion. I sometimes suspected that they deliberately contradicted each other and that the views they maintained in their debates did not necessarily reflect their true thoughts. Their conversations with Paul and me were usually much more laboured and probably more sincere.

Still, we learned something of our neighbours from Kip's

sojourn with them. We learned, for instance, that they were basically not aggressive, and even kind, if Kip's treatment truly reflected their nature. We put the surliness that we had encountered down to shyness, perhaps fear. As Pip frequently stated, we could not presume that our sensibilities were the same as theirs, or that our reactions in any way corresponded with those of an alien culture. We learned, too, that they did actually have some spiritual concept. Kip told us that on nights of full moon they would sit in a circle and chant strange incantations. Unfortunately, as he did not understand what they were saying, the significance of this practice was hard to gauge. Kip also said that they buried their dead, although without a great deal of ceremony. Two people had died while he was with them, both old people in their terms, and they had been interred in the woods beneath oak trees and covered with rocks to prevent attack by dogs. This task seemed to have devolved upon the children, and the only rite attached to it, if it could be described as such, was that the close relatives each touched the body before interment.

Kip had endeavoured to persuade Ari to capture a horse so that he could teach him how to ride one. Ari had understood well enough, but he had laughed at the suggestion, indicating to Kip that there seemed to be few advantages and much danger attached to such an exercise. He patted Kip's shoulder and arm to demonstrate his point. That was certainly one skill that was unlikely to be adopted in a hurry. Upon his return Kip himself only rode once or twice; he appeared to have lost confidence and did not enjoy it any more. The practice soon fell into neglect. We did discuss the idea of using horses as beasts of burden, and even as the motive power for Barry's cart, but the pace of our life was too leisurely. The syndrome that Barry averred afflicted the indigenes, that of motivation for inventiveness, seemed to have afflicted us. We simply did not have the stimulus or the need to pursue the domestication of horses. Perhaps if we had, the outcome of later events might have been different. Mobility then would have helped.

Chapter Seventeen

Years passed. Smudge, my last child, was born, and Lian his mother remained as lovely as ever, more rounded in her complacency, her face serene and gentle with the crowsfeet of many smiles around her eyes. My love for her had not diminished, although it was surely less openly intense in those years, but strong and settled in my bones and my flesh. I must have neglected Lee a great deal, for although I felt compassion for that uncomplaining woman, I could not love her. I liked her and it seemed as if that was enough for her. Their ideas of love were quite different from our own.

It was during those years that the legends began. They started with stories told to the children. Stories of the men who had come from the sea and whose might was invincible. Men who had taken the tribe of the Mekans and that of Oa, destroying those warriors in desperate battles in which deeds of heroism were exaggerated to superhuman proportions. Many were the tales told of that saga, of the might of Barry the Legless, and the arts of Pip, and also the magic in the hands of Paul, but above all was the awe they placed undeservedly on my own wisdom amid all that mayhem. It was I who had saved them from the dreadful North men, huge people with horns and tails and goodness knows what else, who ate children alive for their dinner—and the listening children's eyes would be large and timid. Yet I had defied those terrible men and had taken the tribe onto the waters without end, and the North men had made the sea a wild place; but I had controlled the sea and brought the tribe to safety. Great was my battle with the forces of evil; alone on the deck I had pursued a personal struggle with the storm; I had wrestled with the wind, throwing it back onto the waves, again and again and again, until finally the wind was subdued and I had brought the boat to a gentle land. It did seem as if it was always I who was the controlling figure in their stories. The tales they told of the tunnel trek were quite horrifying, and only then did I fully appreciate the terrors that I had inflicted on their souls. But always I brought them through. I had led them to this land of peace and plenty, and then the children would look at me in wonder not without a touch of dread, and I did not like that. I did not want to be aloof from them. Barry and Pip they loved with the joy and the laughter of healthy children. Paul, with his quieter ways and his insistence on regular baths, they respected and disobeyed discreetly, but went to unafraid with their juvenile injuries. But I was held in some sort of awe, rather like a headmaster or a priest, and neither role sat well on my shoulders.

There was a winter when our fire exploded for some inexplicable reason while we slept. Our house caught alight and we were utterly unprepared. There were no casualties but I recall standing forlorn and helpless under a scornful moon and uncaring stars as our settlement burned to the ground. There was a lot of snow and it did not spread beyond our immediate area. We took up residence somewhere else. All our books had gone and we would have to go to London again. There was another time, also in winter although there was no snow, when a horse panicked in its corral. They were very wild things and it broke loose. A young boy tried to stop it in spite of our shouts to let it go. He was only eight, and I remember my overwhelming sadness at the sight of his trampled little body. Yes, there were some very sad moments among the tranquil years. No other deaths, though, not even in childbirth, thanks to Paul's unstinting attention.

There was one small but noteworthy incident that I recall well. The children had discovered a row of what had once been shops in the heart of Maidstone, or was it Bromley? They found bottles and jars and plastic containers which they considered highly intriguing, and although Paul gave strict orders that they should not play there because of a high incidence of lacerations from broken glass, in the excitement of play the children often forgot his injunctions. They played much the same games as we did in childhood and 'hide and seek' was a particular favourite, one in which Barry and Pip would join; Barry would hobble along on his crutches roaring fearfully like some Danish troll, while the children, showing their delight with shrieks of alarm, would run before him to disappear into the mazes of tunnels they had created in the undergrowth, beneath which were the buildings of a bygone age.

So it was that Pip found himself creeping around the gloomy, worm-eaten counters of a chemist's shop, when he was halted by the sight of a plastic bottle with the brand name embossed on its surface. He was interested enough to bring it out with him and he showed it to Barry that evening. As usual we were seated around a fire. It was in the open so it must have been summer then.

'Read the name,' Pip insisted.

'I think it's Biocinetrin,' said Barry.

Something stirred in my memory, tugging me from a drowsiness to a full consciousness of what they were saying. 'That's what I thought,' muttered Pip. 'It opens up quite a provocative field of enquiry, doesn't it?'

'Let me see that,' I said. Barry passed me the bottle. It was about the size of an inkwell and much the same shape, and the plastic of its manufacture was brittle and colourless after so long. The embossed letters were indefinite; the 'B' was indecipherable and the last three letters were too worn to be certain at all, but I did know that word. Why should I? I stared at it, struggling for recall; the recollection was on the tip of my mind.

'What would they have used it for?' puzzled Barry.

'As a cosmetic,' I answered him, almost unconsciously.

'Why do you suggest that?'

'Because . . . well I don't know. Something in my mind. Something I should remember.'

'But you wouldn't know about Biocinetrin,' Pip put in. 'Even in scientific circles it was very much a classified drug.'

'You mentioned it once in Bordeaux,' I pointed out. 'You found an article about it in a magazine.'

'Yes, I remember that. Did you read it?'

'Good Lord, no. Not the sort of light reading I would choose.'

'No. But the fact that there was something in published

184

material about it does indicate it was no longer so strictly classified.'

'Why was it so secret?'

'Because I insisted that it be so. Look, I led the research team examining the drug. It had enormous potential for the human race, but I had reservations. It may have been due to my absence that the drug was released.' He looked very worried, as if he had been responsible for the demise of mankind on Earth.

Just then I happened to look up and see Lian approaching me from across the flames. In that instant there was a vision of a tatter of newsprint, vivid then, and the picture was clear. I saw a mouse's nest with living mice being suckled close to my eyes, and I read again the advertisement for a new miracle drug, clearly Bio . . . something or other, and immediately I knew it had to be Biocinetrin. I had not known the word then, having probably only heard it once before in my life, but knowing of it, the masticated jumble of print read plainly.

I told them about the nest. Barry shook his head. 'You're putting the word into that scrap of memory because it fits. You couldn't possibly be absolutely sure that the word was Biocinetrin.'

'I can and I do,' I stated emphatically. But I did not add that those hours were painted like a reviewable album on my mind. The vision was vivid and indelible and as accurate as if it were the present. I can still see that nest as clearly as during those days of suffering.

Pip and Barry were silent, looking at me pensively. I looked at the fire and the geometry of the embers. I reached out and dropped the bottle in.

'There is no proof, well not enough,' said Barry. Pip was almost withdrawn.

'No, you're right. It is inconceivable.' They were on a wave-length that I could not comprehend. But they said no more that night.

I recall another summer, in London this time. It must have been our fifth summer in England for my son Kerry was four years old. Smudge would have been only a few months old. As a tribe we were living in Bromley then, mainly because Pip and Barry were still attracted to the city, and they would make periodic excursions there, Pip wheeling Barry exuberantly in a barrow-like cart and usually accompanied by several of the older boys. They had explored the British Museum, the Natural History Museum, the Victoria and Albert Museum, and had discovered treasures of a varied but esoteric kind in the ruins of these once majestic edifices. But this particular summer we all spent some weeks together in the city, despatching the new generation of adolescents, led by Kip who was becoming more and more independent of us as each month went by, into the surrounding countryside to hunt. It was a task they welcomed, and one that we encouraged. We were perhaps a little saddened to watch the lads we had seen grow from childhood to eager manhood becoming increasingly estranged from us, but we recognised it as inevitable if not desirable; they were, after all, the future leaders of the tribe. As yet there was no hint of defiance, and their respect was still clear, their own legends a powerful influence upon them; but they did not need us, did not seek us out for advice or direction. Still, they were just boys; Kip himself could have been barely sixteen. Young John, by then a sturdy six-year-old, always accompanied Kip on his expeditions. The two had formed an odd friendship in spite of the disparity in their years. John was a sharp and bold young fellow; already he had the look of Oa, his father, the same courage and arrogance were plain enough even then, if undeveloped and unrealised at that age. John was clearly a future leader of men.

I went one day to the bank of the Thames with my son Kerry. It was a perfect day, the sky a deep, unsullied blue for the most part, with here and there a few fragments of cloud drifting like dandelion seeds without cohesion or purpose. We were alone. We had swum in the river and lay side by side in the deep green grass of the embankment. Yet we were in the heart of the city and beneath the grass and the underlying mat of roots was a gravel road. Lying on my back I wondered at the blueness of the sky. It was a blueness that only temperate skies can achieve, and the sun behind me did not intrude into that blueness. There was no wind. Despite the sun I realised that I was shivering in occasional tremors as the cold water evaporated from my skin. Kerry did not lie still for long. A four-year-old is too eager for discovery to waste time lying on his back on such a perfect day. He soon sat up, then stood on my stomach with shrieks of laughter, striving for balance as I writhed, then he leaped off and wandered away. I closed my eyes. I had no fears for him, far less than I had had for my two daughters at his age in that world of so long ago. I think I slept.

The sound of Pip calling urgently disturbed me. There was a note of alarm in his voice that caused long-dormant anxieties to well up within me. Tranquillity had vanished with an awful suddenness. I sat up collecting my thoughts. Why was Pip here? Where was Barry? The two of them had set out in the morning to explore the tunnels of the underground railway system for some obscure reasons of their own. The tunnels were cold and windy places, haunts of spiders and bats, and in many instances sealed by rockfalls. But something had inspired the two scientists to investigate them while I had preferred the company of my son and the summer day. It was early for them to be showing themselves, and the feelings of dread were impossible to control as Pip came stumbling up, his hair and clothes covered in dust, his fingernails bleeding.

'What is it?' I cried.

He mouthed something, gasping too hard to be intelligible.

'Come on, man! What is it?' I was on my feet by then and he was holding on to me, struggling to speak.

'It's Barry,' he forced out at last. 'There was a ceiling collapse. He's trapped! I can't get him out!'

'Is he buried?'

'I don't know. He was further up the tunnel than I was and he had found something that excited him . . .' We headed for Kerry, playing blithely not very far away, as Pip told me what had happened.

'He yelled something that I didn't catch. The echoes reverberated through the tunnel. No doubt the ceiling was poised to collapse anyway.' Pip had gained control of himself once more. We had reached Kerry and I picked him up, nodding to Pip to lead the way. 'The whole tunnel is built of bricks, you know, and trees roots have grown down through them. There was a sudden rumbling sound and before I could get to him the tunnel had filled with rubble. I tried to break through it but it was hopeless.' He finished on a note of desperation, almost of panic. He felt a great responsibility for Barry. It was the third time we had left him on his own.

'We'll get him out,' I said. But we did not know if he was still alive. My own heart was unsteady with anxiety, yet I refused to consider that the big man might be dead. Barry was not so easy to kill. Or perhaps I simply refused to face the idea of losing him. He had always been my own source of strength and I needed that.

The access to the tunnel was no great distance from the river and we reached it soon enough, a tube station off a main London street, the entrance overgrown with stinging nettles and thistles, whose bursting growth had literally lifted or shattered the paving slabs. We descended by means of a frozen escalator, collected Pip's torch from where he had left it, a contraption of waxed twigs set in a protective haft, and, relighting it, proceeded up the tunnel along the corroded tracks with Kerry clinging to my neck. He did not like this dark place of cobwebs and fluttering silences, of dark smells and gritty air.

At first glance the roof fall looked formidable, but it was of loose bricks and could be shifted. It would need a team of people and many hours of effort. 'What about the other end? Can we get at him from the next station up the line?' I asked.

'No. We went there first. It's blocked by an old fall, packed solid, I'm afraid. Much more dense than this one.'

'How far along?'

'No more than a hundred yards, I suppose. It's hard to say, I've only come across it from the other direction but the stations aren't far apart.'

'So Barry could actually be trapped between the two falls?'

Hope quickened in his eyes. 'Yes. Yes, he could.'

'All right. Now take Kerry back to camp for me. I'll stay here and have a look round. Bring back every able-bodied person in the camp except nursing mothers. They can prepare food for us. And bring torches, too. Plenty of them. This is going to take a long time.'

'What about tools?'

'Some steel bars would be useful, perhaps some old railings, or strong sticks will do. And the axes, bring the axes. Quickly, now.' But there was no need to stress the urgency. He left without light for I retained the torch. I climbed the heap of rubble and started work near the top.

We worked all the rest of that day, that night and most of the following day. Nails broken, fingers raw and bleeding, lungs hoarse, dust in our hair and eyes and our noses and mouths. We ached. Boys collapsing, stumbling strengthless in the debris. The torches flickering. Everything white, shadows of people seen through a curtain of mobile air. And the continual passing of bricks, arms swinging, dead arms, smarting eyes wiped with grimy hands, dead hands, grey blood, grit and coughs, and somewhere in the choking crevices of the mind, hope, just a little hope. Then the roof shifted again and all our work had gained us nothing.

We stood and looked at it in despair. No one had been hurt. No one had complained. But we stood in a grey, shapeless bunch, drooping with the fatigue of futility, and silent. Pip began to cry, soundless tears tearing wet grooves down his layered face. And he threw himself upon that pile of bricks and began to hurl them aside in a frenzy as if he meant to tear his way through in sheer fury. I went up to him and touched him on the shoulder. Then he stopped and crumpled onto the rubble, sobbing. I climbed back onto the heap and began to work once more. And Paul was right behind me. Once again the swinging arms, the closing mind, the small hope, so very, very small.

Late on the second day we heard Barry's voice. It came to us without clarity, any emotion deadened by the masonry. But he was alive. Within an hour we could hear him plainly. He sounded cheerful and said that he was unhurt. Finally, by nightfall, we had broken through and found him sitting on some fallen bricks, seemingly unconcerned.

'You took your time,' he said, yawning.

'Couldn't see any reason to hurry, really,' grunted Pip, his face beaming in the flare of the torches. Mighty little man. He had worked non-stop for the whole period and must have been on the verge of collapse. Still he found a joke.

For the first time I asked the question: 'What the hell are you doing down here, anyway?'

'We were looking for advertisements,' Barry said.

'What?'

'I found something,' he added. 'Bring a torch over here, Pip.' He took a torch from the little man and held it up. We were standing below what must have been a platform. Behind us piles of debris blocked the exits. An extensive collapse led away from us to a point where it blocked the whole tunnel, less than a hundred yards away. But before us the tunnel wall had escaped damage. 'Look there,' said Barry.

We looked. On the wall was a still legible poster advertising a brand of cosmetics proclaiming: '. . . contains Biocinetrin.' There it was again, the mysterious wonder drug that I had first read of in some obscure factory in a French country town. Biocinetrin. What was it? And what did it mean to these scientists? Pip was reading the complete advertisement aloud, his fatigue momentarily forgotten. It was like a scene from the discovery of Altamira in reverse. Here we were looking at the art of some long-dead commercial artist of an advanced culture from a state of being representing some twenty thousand years before his time. Barry stood unconsciously sagging on his crutches, his grey face lined with a strain that his spirit refused to acknowledge, but his eyes bright with the excitement of his discovery. He had sat for two days trapped in this dark and lifeless chamber without food and without water, waiting, just waiting for rescue, with total confidence in his friends. How long and lonely and claustrophobic were those hours, how grimly dry, nerve eroding and insanely empty? He showed no signs of it, only the grey face, and later the secret smiles of relief. He said that he never doubted that we would get to him. He had stayed still, sitting on his pile of bricks while his torch burned away. His greatest concern was the lack of water in that dusty atmosphere. He had heard us working but had not called out till he was certain we would hear.

'. . . removes wrinkles in tired faces,' Pip was reading, too intense to recognise any irony, perhaps, 'see grey hair vanish in a few days. Feel your flesh grow youthful and firm again. Biocinetrin, the elixir of youth, now combined with our exclusive formula, Stericimen, in an easy-to-apply lotion that guarantees you a new youthfulness sooner than you would believe possible. Available at all chemists and supermarkets in individual and family sizes. Ask for NuYuth by name.'

Pip finished reading and looked at Barry unsmilingly. 'The fools!' he said. 'The bloody fools!'

'Well, that seems to clinch it,' was Barry's response. There was a great weariness in his voice.

'Let's get out of here,' I said, 'this place is giving me the creeps.' And I led the way out.

So to another fire more than a day later. The grime was gone, and sleep had worked its habitual miracle. We were aching still, for we were ageing men and our muscles would not recover as quickly as those of the young men, but we were content and serene again. We were in Battersea Park, and trees loomed about us, eerie and whispering in the gradually glooming night. Barry, with children draped sleepily all over him, sat beside me and Pip sat alone across the fire, peering into the heart of the blaze with some deep reflection of his own. Paul came up later and sat with him. For a long while there was silence, as was often the case about our fires early in the evening. We poked the fire and meditated. My thoughts were seldom of the world past, mainly of the years to come, of the assertion of youth and the values we should give them as they took over the reins of authority. We had planned a celebration, a night of song and dance for the next full moon, not so much in remembrance of a particular event, but as a conscious effort to establish the idea of festival, of tradition, of a planned event on the calendar. They were without festivals, and although there was often singing and dancing as a spontaneous expression of success such as in a hunt or following a particularly lavish feast, the idea of a special occasion, occurring over and over again on a regular schedule, was not within their experience. My thoughts on this particular night were concerned with that. Lee disturbed me. She had brought Jenny to me as the little girl preferred to go to sleep in my arms. Lee smiled hesitatingly as I took the child from her. Her eyes were gentle and anxious, pleading for some small attention. I had been neglecting her, I knew that and felt tender towards her. Perhaps tonight I would share her bed. I did not love her, not as I loved Lian, for with Lian I had found a peace and contentment of a degree that I had never obtained before in my life. Soon Lian came, and Kerry snuggled into my other armpit. Jenny was already asleep.

My thoughts broken, I felt the need for conversation. 'Tell me about Biocinetrin,' I asked, disturbing the quiet.

'We think it's the drug that brought about the demise of our culture,' stated Barry softly.

Minutes of evening silence, crackles of erupting flames, thoughts detaching slowly and heavily. 'You mean the elixir of youth was the elixir of death?'

'Well, in a way. It was probably worthy of that silly name. It was a sort of youth drug. Pipsqueak here probably knows more about it than anyone, even his contemporary researchers. He was connected with its discovery and led the research team that examined it.'

'It should never have been released for public use,' said Pip. He was quite intense. I am sure he really did believe that he had some responsibility for mankind's regression.

'What were your reservations?' I asked.

A wind was blowing and the fire responded with little aggressive flares. It was a very dark night and the flames were bold and strong. Pip must have had smoke in his face for he moved to our side. Paul lay back with his arms behind his head. There were women about us, suckling infants and crooning lullabies. It was a peaceful, perfect time. There were few perils and the bounty of the land was excessive, surely as close to paradise as man could achieve.

'The original compound from which Biocinetrin was distilled was an experimental contraceptive,' Pip explained. His voice was slow, which was unusual for him, deliberately controlled. It was as if his normal exuberance and free flow of speech were constrained by an uncertainty, as if he was as yet unsure of his conclusions. 'It was observed that the women who used the drug, the original one, that is, began to look younger. Now the women were all volunteers, you understand, for the drug was never released into the market. It was clear that although the drug might not be as effective a contraceptive as we had hoped, it had some apparently beneficial properties that were worth further investigation. Eventually we produced Biocinetrin, which seemed to have lost its contraceptive qualities but retained a youth-producing property. Some of my colleagues even went so far as to call it the elixir of youth. Naturally we were greatly excited by the drug. It held some quite astonishing prospects for our species. Yet I was more cautious than my staff and I imposed the strictest confidentiality upon our research.' He paused. He was toying with a lighted stick, poking at the embers of the fire, his face dark and brooding in the unreal light.

Then he began to talk again, almost coldly, defensively perhaps. 'You see, I was always aware that Biocinetrin had been produced from a contraceptive. I was never convinced that that factor had been totally eradicated. For the next eighteen months prior to our departure from Earth I made it my policy to keep a close eye on the further experiments, even though my commitment to Barry's venture did not allow me direct involvement. Up until that time there had been no further testing on humans, although records were kept of the continuing effects of the original drug on that group of women.'

'Did any of them become pregnant?'

'No they didn't.'

'But you said that the original drug was ineffective as a contraceptive.' It was Paul who was probing. He murmured his comments so that one could detect little emotion in them other than the queries of logic. He might almost have been disinterested, except we knew he was not. Paul's manner of speech was sometimes deceptive, as if disguising his real feelings.

'I didn't say that exactly. We didn't consider it as reliable as necessary. Some of our experimental animals did become pregnant. But what worried me more was that those who didn't never did again, even when taken off the drug.' He kept poking the fire with his stick. 'Biocinetrin was only ever tested on animals while I was in charge, but having made that point, I must add that in my opinion the observed results could be directly translated to the human metabolism.'

'What were the observed results?' I asked.

'All that could be determined with assurance was that Biocinetrin could certainly assist people to retain their youthfulness to a degree, even to recapture it, although it would not increase their life-span for one single day. Their bodies would not last longer because they looked younger. The ageing of the heart and other organs would proceed as it had always done. The benefits were not entirely cosmetic, though, since it did seem that reproductive capacity continued for a much longer period. I must make the distinction between capacity and actual fertility here. They are not synonymous. Capacity and with it virility or sexual drive were the obvious benefits other than the cosmetic one.'

'One can see that it would have been a popular drug,' I commented.

'Yes,' Pip said drily. 'It seemed to most of my colleagues that there were no detrimental effects of any significance. I was pressurised to make our findings public, but it seemed to me that we still had insufficient evidence that there were no hidden side-effects. In fact I had some reports from old Dr Lisle. You remember him? A very pedantic man, very careful. Used to drive everybody nuts. Well he was convinced that there was a loss of fertility generally among the laboratory animals, not to a sufficient extent that would tempt him to draw any conclusions. He was not a man who would draw conclusions readily. But his records did indicate a decline in the birth rate. That may have been due to any number of factors, of course, and I remember the old sod saying that his job was to provide data, not to produce theories. Still, his reports coupled with my own reservations made me insist that several more years of experimentation be conducted before Biocinetrin was released. My colleagues considered my caution just the foible of an eccentric biochemist. Well, that eccentric biochemist left upon one of his eccentric expeditions with his even more eccentric companions and perhaps that caution went with him.' One could barely hear his last words. He was being savage with his stick, really jabbing it into the fire.

'Are you telling us,' asked Paul in his quiet, controlled fashion, 'that Biocinetrin was released despite your warnings and that the whole population of the world became infertile?'

'Something like that,' said Pip, and threw the stick into the flames. He lay back on the ground with his arms behind his head.

'I had some very strong reasons for my reservations,' he went on. 'Biocinetrin was an effective youth drug because it impacted directly on the amino acids that form the proteins of which we are made, and also of which our genetic structure consists. That in itself is not alarming, for everything we eat has some effect on our body chemistry, but as Biocinetrin had the potential to affect the genes in ways that we could not know and would not be able to control unless we knew, the need for caution appeared obvious. The benefits of Biocinetrin were splendid, but the risk involved might have been genetic interference whose effects would not be apparent possibly for generations. If, as I suspected, Biocinetrin lowered fertility by an effect on the genetic structure, eventual wholesale infertility would have been almost inevitable.'

The night was suddenly very big, and hushed. The trees rustling gently around us were part of that hush; the fire's playful chatter at our feet was part of that hush; Lian suckling little Smudge was part of that hush; small sounds within an immense silence. Silence and a single thought—genetic sterility, fertility zero, oblivion. How big was the night? I could hear Smudge gulping. The moon was a huge, unclear glimmer far away. The trees were black shapes creaking about us. Props to our thoughts, but just the one thought and the ramifications from that thought. No one spoke for a long, long time. I think it was Paul who finally broke the silence.

'It would have had to be used universally. That seems most improbable. Besides, the various governments would surely have banned its use once its effects were realised.'

'Once they realised it, it would have been too late, that's the sadness of it,' Barry responded.

'And they may never have realised it at all,' added Pip.

'Just consider genetic sterility,' intoned Barry, leaning forward and adopting his best lecturing voice. A black Santa Claus in the unsure flicker of the fire, all beard and hair and twinkling eyes. 'The parents show no obvious effects, they have children just as before, since Biocinetrin had no apparent contraceptive properties, yet their children are carrying a new genetic message. The first point that arises from this is that no effect, no recognition of the syndrome will occur for a minimum of twenty years, and possibly thirty or forty years. The second point is that although an affected child may marry an unaffected partner, if the genetic message is dominant no offspring will be produced within that marriage.'

'If the partners remain strictly faithful, that is,' muttered Paul. 'Fidelity was not a widely practised aspect of married life as I recall.'

'Yes, yes,' said Barry impatiently, 'but extra-marital affairs were unlikely to result in children, such liaisons deliberately avoided such a result. But there is a third point that needs to be mentioned: genetic sterility could not be detected by normal physical examination. It may have been that mankind never recognised the cause of reduced fertility at all, and until it was recognised the pervasive nature of it would continue uncontrolled. Even a period of thirty years would have done untold damage.'

I had to interrupt there. 'I understand what you're saying,' I said, 'but surely sterility that was genetically founded could not be passed on beyond one generation. That syndrome has to be self-defeating.'

'Unfortunately not. There are recessive genes, you see, and dominant ones. Recessive genes do not always take effect, but the genetic message is still passed on. It may be that two or three generations would eventuate before a particular combination of genes produced sterility. That is the insidious nature of such a syndrome. Think of it as a mutation if you like, acting exactly as evolution works, spreading undetected throughout humanity, irreversible and eventually universal.'

'I'm sorry,' I said, 'I find that hard to accept. Everybody in the world sterile! No, I can't see it. Biocinetrin was a cosmetic as far as we can tell. Are you telling me that vanity destroyed our species?'

Pip sat up. 'Look, we only know that it was used as a cosmetic, but it may have been used in other ways. The retention of virility and sexual drives into old age would have been a powerful motive, but the reproductive functions also continuing into old age would have become increasingly important once the declining birth rate was realised. It may have been that people were using Biocinetrin to try to counter-act the very syndrome that it was causing.' He sighed. 'Besides, there were other potential benefits.'

'What other benefits?' The smoke from the fire had subsided with the logs almost embers. We had talked for a long time. Many of the women had gone to their beds. Smudge was fast asleep in Lian's arms, and she appeared to be sleeping, too. Only the four of us were sitting up, dark shapes, probably indistinguishable in our sheepskins from a few yards away.

'Oh, medical benefits, mostly. The indications were that the illnesses that we generally associate with age were held at bay with the external evidence of it—you know, arthritis, deafness, loss of vision, that sort of thing. The economic implications were extraordinary. People active until they died. No old people's homes or geriatric hospitals. Huge amounts of money becoming available for other social schemes, research or whatever. One can readily imagine governments actually making the use of the stuff compulsory, much as they did with fluoride, and that was just to give people stronger teeth. Just think what they would have done if they believed they could raise the whole standard of health by such a simple method.'

'You think they may have placed it in the water supply?'

'That would certainly be a very effective way.'

'But if they were doing that, why advertise the stuff as a cosmetic? Surely there would have been no need of supplements.'

'I would imagine the amount introduced into a water supply system would not have had such instantaneous effects as cosmetics, say. They would have been cautious about such an action. Mind you, with no recognised detrimental effects, they probably met less resistance from the masses than they did with fluoride.'

'All the same,' Paul murmured, 'it's hard to accept universal use, and even harder to accept worldwide sterility.'

'All right. Look, it's only a theory and we could well be wrong. I believe it would have reached every corner of the world in some form within the time frame we are talking about; maybe as soap, or some soft drink made with treated water, Coca Cola or something, even as a tonic deliberately distributed. Who knows? Sure, some parts of the world may have taken longer than others to use it, but if even one member of a remote community used it in one way or another, its genetic effect may well have caused increasing sterility in the community's succeeding generations. But of course the likelihood is that the drug was widespread enough for very few not to have some contact with it.'

The moon had pulled back its curtain. It was a huge, yellow thing, ugly that night with only a handful of stars daring to compete with it. My brain had become tired. The impact of the converse was becoming difficult to register. I don't remember falling asleep.

The following day, as I recall, I went fishing. I needed some moments of solitude. Thoughts about Biocinetrin and human sterility were plodding through my mind without cohesion or sequence. I wanted some hours alone to sort them out. I sat on the river bank and thought about my wife, something I had not done for many years. I rarely think about her now, actually, for her image has faded in my memory; that is part of my ageing, I suppose. Now I am clear. The memory of my thoughts on that day by the river bank are clear, at least. Her name was Stella. She was very beautiful when I first met her and we became lovers. She was surely still beautiful when I left her for my explorations in space, but I see the lines around her eyes in my unfocused image of her now. She had brown eyes, soft and rather sad, for she was very much a sad person, a compliant person. Her face occurs to my mind as it was in the last months before our separation. I see it as old and tired although that cannot be the truth. She had brown hair, but it is greying in my remembrance, a fine figure for she had been a model. Perhaps if our return to Earth had been as expected, Biocinetrin would have made her appear as young as I would have been. I think about that, and I think about my two daughters, Mary and Beth. I remember Beth crying when I left to embark on the spaceship. She was the younger of the two and had always been very emotional, as her mother might have been had the discipline of her upbringing not constrained her. I think that is what made Stella so melancholy. I had been intolerant of it in the end, not understanding it within the bounty of her life. We had a nice home and our children were not particularly difficult. A marriage that had always seemed to me to be a happy one. She was a kind woman with many friends, eager to please. Why do I only remember her melancholy?

The face I see is perhaps the face she showed on the day of

my departure. She had already said, oh so many times: 'I wonder if we'll ever see each other again,' for which I had no response that was adequate. But that morning she said very little, except that her face was spiritless, and the moment that should have been so sentimental and so affectionate was for me a moment of impatience. I wanted brightness and optimism. I did not want that mournful look, and Beth was crying, only Mary had a smile. Mary had been my favourite, even though Beth was the prettiest and I loved her very much. I think Mary was more like me, she was bright and confident and few things depressed her, although I suspect her smile that morning was forced. But the images of my children are not clear at all.

I was disturbed in my ponderings by Pip who came and sat beside me. He had brought some arrow shafts and bone tips and he began to fasten the tips carefully onto the shafts with horsehair. 'It's very nice here,' he said. 'Caught anything yet?'

'No. I've probably lost my bait. I've been thinking, you see.'

'Oh. What about, may I ask?'

'The thought occurred to me that if we had returned to Earth as we originally expected, our wives and children might not have been as old as we thought if they had had access to Biocinetrin.'

'That is a possibility, I suppose. It depends a bit on the timing. We don't really know when the world began to use the stuff widely.'

'I remember you telling Barry that the article you found on it was dated only a few years after our departure.' I pulled in my line. There was indeed no bait on it. I rebaited it and threw it out again.

'Yes, but it didn't suggest that there was any intention of releasing it for use. It was just a report on a debate in the World Science Council. That certainly indicates a wider distribution of the results of the research, more than I would have liked, but on the whole the Council was a very responsible body. Still, when you think about it, it meant that there were at least forty-nine countries with an understanding of it. That might help explain how easy it would have been to have universal use of the stuff.'

'But what made you explore the Underground for advertisements?'

Pip looked at me with a hint of mockery beneath his monstrous beard. 'Oh, you did,' he said.

Fish were tugging at my line but my attention was distracted and they were in little peril. 'How on earth did I have anything to do with it?'

'Look, you told us that Biocinetrin was used as a cosmetic. You see, we had already come to the conclusion that the present level of culture had come about through a complete abandonment of technology, art, religion and social structure as we knew it. We asked ourselves why. There seemed only one acceptable explanation. The old culture had died out and a brand new one had commenced, and that could only have occurred by the death of every adult, in fact the death of every person, say, over the age of about eight. Picture a world peopled only with children. Untaught. Unskilled. Very little conceptual base at all. But what was the explanation for such an unlikely set of circumstances? We didn't really consider Biocinetrin until we found that bottle in the chemist's shop and you suggested that it had been used as a cosmetic.

'Well, that set my mind thinking along the lines we discussed last night, but Barry considered the evidence too slender. After all, we only found that single plastic bottle and the only other indication was some half-remembered experience of yours.'

'The memory is plain enough,' I said.

'I'm sure it is. But we had to seek confirmation, my dear fellow. It was Barry who pointed out that if Biocinetrin had been used as a cosmetic it would have been widely advertised, and the one place where advertising was likely to remain little damaged by the years was in a sheltered environment such as an underground tunnel, particularly a blocked tunnel where the air remained static and the rain didn't reach, much as the best cave paintings of our early ancestors were to be found in the most inaccessible caverns. So we began a search of the underground railway system where such advertising would probably have been displayed and where its chances of being still legible were the greatest.'

A fish pulled at my line but it was only small. It had hooked itself and I pulled it in and freed it, then threw it back. 'So you might never have formed your theory if I hadn't been taken prisoner by Oa.'

'Perhaps not. We would never have dreamt that mankind could have been so unthinking as to use a genetically loaded drug for the purposes of his own vanity.'

I was silent for a long time, baiting up another hook and casting again. 'Do you really believe that is what happened?' I asked.

'Don't you?'

'I'm not sure. It's one theory, that's all.'

'But it fits, doesn't it?'

'Yes, it fits. But at one time, the theory that the sun revolved around the Earth also fitted.'

'True. Look, I agree that the state of our knowledge and its clear limitations are insufficient for any conclusive statement. But any theory that fits the known facts is preferable to no theory at all. I doubt if we shall ever know the whole truth.'

'We can't even be sure that the condition of England and France is worldwide,' I commented.

'Oh, I'm sure about that,' Pip declared. 'Not to face that makes our whole life here fairly meaningless. No, I'm absolutely convinced of that. If I entertained any doubts in France, when we found England in a similar condition all those doubts evaporated. They are such accessible countries.'

'What about isolated continents, Australia for example?'

'You think that they would not have used Biocinetrin?'

'Of course they would have used it, but that is presupposing the correctness of your theory. If there was another cause . . .'

'Then there is no way we shall ever know,' Pip said shortly.

* * *

I had not been the only one musing about Biocinetrin. Paul had obviously given it much thought, too, and a few evenings later, as we conversed by the fire, he asked much the same questions that I had done of Pip that morning in Battersea, and Pip gave him much the same answers. There was a drizzle that evening so that it was unpleasant out of doors, and we had lit our fire in the great fireplace of our latest chosen residence. We had moved out of London again, back towards Bromley, and had found an old manor house on a country estate. It stood alone, isolated in the woods, but the gardens that had once encompassed it were still clear of high growth, just shrubbery and thickets of fern, and a little distance away an orchard. At that time of year the trees were abundant with apples, sweet, red apples, and the windfalls attracted wild pigs so that we had meat and fruit aplenty.

'There are two clear problems with your proposition,' said Paul in his quiet, unhurried way. 'The first is that although the whole concept hinges on this universal sterility of yours, the new culture, if I may call it that, depends on there being children around too young to have learned anything of significance. And as well as that, there has to be a sudden worldwide extinction of all old people, which you define as over the age of eight. I'm afraid you haven't explained that satisfactorily.'

'They are valid points,' agreed Barry, in his best debating manner. He tucked his thumbs into the armholes of his vest. It was a skin vest; we were not wearing sheepskins that night for it was a mild evening and the fire held some heat. It had only been lit for the sake of cooking, but we had eaten by then and Barry was in the mood for discourse. 'But you see that age of eight just represents an arbitrary line. Beyond that age children of our own time had usually acquired some technical skills. We would expect that any survivors above that age were too few to have had an impact on the new direction of our species. But there must have been a vast gap between any children that were born and the parents, possibly sixty years or more.'

'But what children?' I put in. 'There weren't supposed to be any.'

'Clearly there were,' Barry said shortly. He had always been impatient with interruptions when he was lecturing. 'If there hadn't been there would have been no humanity at all. We know, or at least we surmise, that there were no children born at all for many years. If the situation as we see it did occur, that time must have been in the region of three generations. Generations that weren't, you might say.' He smiled hugely, pleased with his joke. We stared blankly back at him. Serious again, he continued. 'The last generation, the one from which the parents came, would already have been much fewer in number than we could ever imagine from the teeming millions of our own time, just a fraction of it actually, and they were growing old. Still sexually active, mind you, and still physically capable of reproduction owing to the supposed beneficial effects of Biocinetrin. But the human race was literally dying out.

'So consider this: a genetically sterile race, virile to death, valiantly attempting to repopulate the world. And possibly, just possibly, right at the very last the miracle happened and children were born. Just to some. Not many. Perhaps at that stage there weren't many potential parents left anyway. But some conceived. Think about that. Think about those parents with just a few years of life left. So it was possible that some of them lived on beyond their children's eighth birthday, but in general terms surely the scene would have been much as we have suggested.'

'It still seems a bit far-fetched to me,' I said. 'Why would children suddenly be born again?'

'Yes, there's the rub,' admitted Barry with a scowl. 'We don't know. Let's say the genetic imprint did revert in time or was the subject of a further mutation, although both proposals are doubtful to say the least, not possible, really. What was more likely was that some assiduous scientist, by that time recognising the basic cause of the sterility, found a compound that countered the effect, even a derivative of Biocinetrin itself.'

'That's quite likely, actually,' agreed Pip. 'But there is another possibility. Look, it is conceivable that with the state of the world as Barry has described it, governments would have instituted a programme of mate circulation in an endeavour to ensure that possibly fertile women would at some point mate with a still fertile male. It may have been just possible that even with the universal distribution of Biocinetrin, there were a few people still unaffected by it. I am not really convinced that that was possible, but genes are in many ways unpredictable in spite of all the supposed laws governing their behaviour. Such a programme would have been extraordinarily long-term, of course, for couples would have had to stay together for a year or two to prove anything. It may well have taken decades for a successful genetic mix to have been found.'

'That strikes me as even more improbable than Barry' theory of a diligent scientist,' muttered Paul. 'And I suppos you are going to tell us that this geriatric miracle was universa as well.'

• 'That we can never know,' answered Barry, rather sadly thought, but he may have been just pensive.

'Look, we only know about Europe,' added Pip. 'Jus France and England, really, and even those tribes may all hav sprung from a single stock. America may still be totally devoi of humanity for all we know, and other places, too.'

'Do you really think that?'

'What does it matter? Eventually mankind will develop again, eventually humanity will spread across the face of th Earth once more. I don't know that that is for the best, bu whatever my judgement may be, the process is inevitable.'

We spoke for many hours after that, that evening and fo many evenings in the weeks and months that followed. W spoke of children without parents in a world designed for th use and convenience of technological man. Sooner or late the last of any preserved food would have been eaten or gon bad. The youngsters would have had to hunt. One suppose hunting rabbits would not have been too difficult for them Pip maintained that the old people would have passed on suc simple skills as their priority for education; the techniques o survival would have been paramount. Barry did not full agree with this point of view. He postulated that childre on their own would have developed their own cunning their own priorities. Whichever argument was correct, the agreed that the outcome would have been the same. Th hunter—gatherer culture had to evolve. There was n other way.

Pip began to express the view that it was the best thing tha could have happened to our race. 'It was time,' he averred 'to wipe the slate clean, to return humankind to a natural life In many ways we are privileged to be part of a cultur corresponding to the Magdalenian culture of our ancestors and perhaps even to help direct it onto a new path in som small way. One also appreciates the insights we have obtained into many of the controversies that were so hotly debated among anthropologists.'

'The guesses of the anthropologists were amazingly accurate as far as I can make out,' stated Paul.

But Barry did not agree with that at all. He declared it a futile exercise to make any comparison between contemporary man and a prehistoric culture. 'The present state of man is only superficially similar to Magdalenian culture,' he said emphatically, 'but it is the differences rather than the similarities that are really significant. Apart from the lions of northern France, modern man seems to have no large predators to contend with, although in other countries it may be different if men exist there. It is that lack of challenge, of any real competition in the fight for survival that is the relevant factor in the indolence and complacency of the present race. And no doubt it is the root cause of their lack of any metaphysical awareness of note. All right, there have been one or two indications that that unawareness may not be total, but compared to Magdalenian man they are barren. Look at the glorious works of art produced by the Cro-Magnon people. These people have nothing to compare with that. Current man is peculiar to his own time and to his own brief evolution, that is all one can say.'

Pip could not accept that unchallenged, of course, and one of their interminable arguments developed, without heat, just pleasant disagreement, sometimes too esoteric for Paul and myself, sometimes not too sincere, but really quite useless contributions to our own awareness of our neighbours.

Chapter Eighteen

The warm weather lingered on. It was certainly a beautiful summer, one of the best I had experienced in England in any age. Pip made the prediction that it would be followed by a severe winter and so we took the precaution of enlarging our resident herd and accumulating an enormous stock of feed. As winter grew closer and evening fires became the established ritual once more, our discussions became more and more our main source of mental stimulation, something we found quite vital to our well-being, but which was far less important to the women or the younger members of the tribal group. They had never known formal education and so had never acquired investigative minds or anything approaching a profound philosophy. Their minds were inquiring to a degree, but surprisingly accepting and placid in comparison with the fashioned intellects of the twentieth century. Incredible as it may seem, our serenity and unchallenging life was beginning to seem drab and tasteless. Even peace, full bellies and constant adoration can grow dull to men of exercised minds.

* * *

That winter was harsh. Pip's prediction was all too correct. For the first time in our sojourn in England the game moved away, presumably in search of fodder in another corner of the land. This was of no great concern to us due to our foresight in fencing in our herds and laying in large stores of hay. Surely, we believed, the benefits of this agricultural lesson would be demonstrated quite clearly to the indigenes. Our own tribe gave us credit for uncanny prediction rather than common sense, so perhaps the impact of the demonstration was not as far-reaching as we might have hoped.

The winter dragged on, week after week of bitter cold, with hail and ice and fearful winds. We snuggled around our fires and under our furs. Within our edifices of concrete and brick we were sheltered and snug. The cattle and the sheep were cosy, too, in prepared barns, once domestic homes, and they were completely amenable as if appreciating our efforts on their behalf. Feeding them was arduous work, but we devised a roster and we had some strapping adolescents to assist us. Otherwise our time was filled with carving and craftwork, perhaps an indicator of how man's artistic talent had evolved to such a high degree in earlier generations. With the darkness of a long winter, without radio, television or reading matter, the stimulus of creativity in the media of wood and flint, of pigment and clay, absorbed the endless hours. The women preferred to scrape hides and fashion clothes. We had taught them the simple benefits of the needle where before they had only used a sharp flint and thongs to fasten hides together, and that was one technique they willingly adopted. They sang often and they laughed much, and they grew big in their perpetual pregnancies. For them life was good. They were provided for and they were safe. Their men were good and kind and clever. They held little care for the interminable winter.

Then the locals came. At first they were unobtrusive, a few women and children, gaunt-ribbed and clearly in distress. No one Kip knew, probably from a different group from his captors. We fed them and they stayed, uncommunicative and ungrateful. Then more. Then the men. Kip knew some of them, but Ari was not among them. He made one or two attempts to re-establish communication with them but for some reason they turned away from him. It seemed that the affinity had gone. Of course the language barrier did not help, but neither would they respond to our questions on Kip's behalf. Soon we had a hundred to feed, camped in the streets about us. Well, we fed them all. It was simple enough and we had plenty. Twice a week we would lead out a live beast and they would slaughter it themselves, dividing it up with an astonishing fairness. They made no attempt to fraternise which pleased us at first, although we found it difficult to appreciate their seeming resentment. Pip did try on one occasion to make friends with them, but they remained silent and wary, even hostile.

'To hell with them!' he exploded. 'Why should we feed the ungrateful bastards? Let them go and find their own food.'

'There is none,' was Paul's quiet comment.

'Let them starve, then. There's not a grain of gratitude among them.'

'Is gratitude so important, then, Pip? Can't we do something for our fellow men without expecting something in return, even if that expectation is just recognition of our benevolence?' There was a hint of ridicule in Paul's voice.

'Oh, for Heaven's sake don't preach, Paul! I'm not asking them for anything, just civility, that's all.'

'Civility is an advanced idea, Pip. There are women and children there and we have a moral duty to prevent them from dying when we have food available. We do have plenty, after all.'

They were with us for six weeks. Then within three days they had all gone. Finally the weather had broken. The timid sun had encouraged buds onto the trees, and there was game returning to the woodlands. Living resumed its habitual rhythm. It was three more years to the next bad winter.

Once again we had herded numbers of sheep and cattle and fenced them in, and we prepared shelters for them. That winter may have been even more severe than the earlier one. We were snug and smug and complacent in our preparations. We anticipated the arrival of the local people, and they did arrive and settle as before. In retrospect it is easy to see that we were foolish in not posting any sentries, but it was cold and seemed unnecessary, although that was not our reason. It was simply that the idea of doing so never occurred to us. After all we had our dogs, and they were loudly territorial beasts.

Then came the morning after a particularly stormy night, one of utter darkness and howling wind packing the blackness around us, and sleet that was malevolent in such a wind, when we were stirred from our beds by a lad who had been sent to milk a cow, another art they had learned. He came back quite bewildered. He was only eight years old—little Dan, son of Bartholomew Mann. 'There's no cows,' he said. 'They're all gone!'

At first we could not believe it. There was no way the cattle could have broken out of the fences even if any had been inclined to venture away from the shelters on such a night. Pip went to see what it was all about. He came back. 'It's true,' he confirmed. 'There are no cows and no sheep and none of our local friends.'

'They must have driven the cattle off under cover of the storm. The fools! How will they feed them?'

'It wasn't the locals,' said Pip solemnly. 'Their tracks head due south. I would say they ran in panic. The cattle were taken westwards.'

We did not doubt Pip's words, he was the finest reader of a trail among us; but we went to look for ourselves anyway. There was no real question about Pip's assessment. The tracks were plain enough even for me. The dogs were dead. It appeared that somehow the men of the west had learned of our stockyards. We would never know how that happened; perhaps they had captured a local woman, or there may have been greater intercourse between the tribes than we had assumed, although the evident signs of flight portrayed clearly in the mud indicated that the western men were greatly feared. With a sinking heart, memories of the North men of France cast a shadow over my soul. 'Not again,' cried my spirit. 'Please, not again.' But I refrained from spreading my disquiet. I simply said: 'We had better hold a conference,' and led the way back inside.

Our situation was grim indeed. We were without provisions, just a few stored apples, some potatoes, little else; we had depended almost totally upon our herds. Nevertheless the general feeling was that we should try to last out the rest of the winter rather than risk a battle with the westerners. We had all had enough of violence. So we went out with our bows and arrows and our snares and our fishing lines. Our success was minimal. Three scrawny rabbits, themselves emaciated from hunger, a hedgehog or two dug from hibernation, and five little fish. A useless offering for a community of over fifty souls. Three days later our original decision had to be revised. We were desperate and desperate measures were needed.

'We'll head west,' I said. 'We'll follow the tracks of the cattle. It may be necessary to fight, but we must retrieve some of the herd.'

'Fighting will be necessary, there's no doubt about that,' commented Paul.

'We'll try to negotiate first,' I replied. 'They can keep most of the cattle, but will have to return some. They may see sense.'

'How many of us will go?'

'All of us. We are going to need all the able men we have and the women could hardly fend for themselves here alone. It will be a hell of a trek in this weather, but the cattle won't move far without fodder. We should catch up with them in a couple of days.' I looked around them all. They just stared at me. I could see their despair, their eyes echoing my own sentiments '. . . not again, oh, God.' But no voice was raised in dissent. 'We had better repair Barry's cart,' I said.

The big man heaved himself off the floor and braced himself determinedly on his crutches. 'I'll start right away,' he uttered, and his voice could not conceal his dejection. Dear Barry, please don't let me down. He clumped out heavily and Pip followed on his wooden heels. No quip from the little man, no joviality, just grim silence. Paul walked up and gripped my shoulder. I looked into his grey eyes, at the weary lines and tired skin around them, at his thin, now quite white hair, and I felt very close to him. And I am sad because of it.

Chapter Nineteen

It was a trudge. Every step of the way. We moved slowly, though hopefully not as slowly as those we followed, for they were necessarily kept to the pace of unwilling sheep being herded across frozen slush by inexpert shepherds. Pip led the way, a misshapen bundle of shaggy furs, his feet and lower legs wrapped in tattered hides; hunched, a strange short-limbed object, top-heavy and headless, plodding into the frozen landscape. Behind him came Barry, wheeled along in his wooden cart, usually sitting up and motionless, a huge heap of hueless fleece, pushed along by two of our strongest youths, Kip and another, equally shapeless beside him. In that cart were our weapons, far too awkward to carry about our swaddled persons, our hands buried deep in our furs. Following the cart were the women carrying children indiscernible upon their bundled forms, hunched figure after hunched figure shuffling along. Paul and I brought up the rear pushing a second cart in turns, smaller than Barry's and loaded with the last of our provisions and dry fuel.

The wind was cruel, keening around us. It was a continual fight to maintain direction, and so bitterly cold when one exposed one's face to it that the moisture froze in one's nose and breath would not come. There was snow all about us, very light, like swansdown in the air, kept adrift by the wind and hardly settling on us. The ground was rugged with the iced tracks of the cattle and sheep following the Great West Road through the centre of London. We knew that the people of the west avoided the city as a rule, but could recognise the sense of their route. On streets lined with buildings it would be a relatively simple matter to control the waywardness of the herds compared with the difficulties they would have encountered in open country, and the road surfaces offered more reliable and more tolerable conditions, and undoubtedly speedier progress. Indeed, we were astonished at the speed at which they had travelled. We had found evidence of their first camp some twenty miles from Victoria, an amazing distance under such conditions. No doubt the animals were docile enough in the cold and only too willing to move quickly. We could appreciate the savages' need for haste for there had been no indication that they had brought any feed with them, making it vital for them to drive the beasts with all urgency to their destination. We were hopeful from this that it would not be too far.

Night came, and a blizzard. We camped in the Victoria and Albert Museum, tearing off massive pieces of its beautiful woodwork to feed our fires. We stayed there all that night and the next day. The storm eased that evening, and the following morning we trudged on. It was harder then. There was a hand's depth of snow on the roads and the tracks were no longer visible. Still, it was a reasonable guess that they had kept to the Great West Road.

Every mile or so, Pip would clear the surface of the road to check that we were indeed on the right track. On and on we plodded. Ever west. We made about twenty miles that day and finally dragged ourselves, exhausted, into the crumbling ruins of Heathrow Airport. There had been no signs of man, only the frozen tracks beneath the surface of the snow. The countryside was dead. There was not a single beast or bird to be seen. It is possible that there were rabbits but we had no time to set snares and they had left no visible traces. But inside the most substantial of the buildings we found evidence that the western people had taken refuge there; it was an ideal place to corral the herd. It was also clear that they had had the foresight to store some hay there, an indication that the expedition had been carefully planned. We found some discarded hunks of head and bone from a cow and cooked ourselves a meagre meal with that and the last of our potatoes. At least it was hot and filled our bellies.

That was a cold night, but clear. There was a huge moon. A moon of ice, frozen cheerless in an eternity of blackness. But the morning revealed a flawless sky, an uncluttered sun, no warmth but still some hope. Then again out into the snow, crackling now beneath our feet. Swaddled feet. The cart creaking. Breath solid and alive in the air. A dark cavalcade visible for miles around. That could not be helped. The people of the west would know they were being pursued. I still hoped it would be possible to negotiate with them. All we wanted was a share of the cattle, not confrontation. A few miles and the tracks turned off.

'They're on the Windsor road,' remarked Pip. We looked at each other as a mutual thought occurred to us. 'Not Windsor Castle,' he said, and almost chuckled aloud. 'Not the home of the monarch, a refuge for weary cows!'

'It would be an ideal place for their purposes,' I pointed out. 'Just drive them through the Main Gate and shut it. No way out and plenty of shelter for them.'

'It's also a wonderful place to defend from invaders,' commented Barry. Barry was very familiar with Windsor Castle, having been a guest there on two occasions.

'Yes. Well, let's keep moving.'

By midday we knew we had guessed right. There was no doubt that the cattle thieves had holed up in Windsor Castle. The tracks could actually be seen again on the rising ground leading up the curving gradient towards the Main Gate of the castle. There was also no doubt that they knew of our presence, for we could see figures on the rim of the crenellated walls gesticulating with spears and pointing at us derisively.

We went into the town, amazingly overgrown with quite dense vegetation so that the buildings were concealed and access through it was far from easy. In case of an assault, we realised that this would put us at considerable risk, so we made our way round to the river frontage where there was some open land. The tribe waited there while I clambered up the road leading to the castle on my own. When within hailing distance I called out. I had no wish to go within range of their spears. I called for several minutes before they deigned to respond. Then a figure, quite indistinguishable from the others at that distance, appeared at the top of the wall. 'Go home!' he shouted.

'I just want to talk,' I called.

'Go home!'

So I talked anyway, if yelling at the top of my voice can be so described. I told him that we were willing to go home on condition that he returned ten of the cattle and an equal number of sheep, which would certainly last us for the rest of that winter.

All the response I could get was: 'Go home!'

I told him that we would teach them how to entrap and feed animals for themselves, and if necessary could supply them with livestock every winter. They need never know hunger again. There could be intercourse and trade, and even friendship between our two groups.

The reply came: 'Go home. Go home!' I was still outside accurate spear range when the gate opened and an enormous boulder was rolled through to be sent crashing towards me. It missed me by several yards and I was never in danger, but it was a clear warning. Yet if they were aggressive, why wouldn't they attack? We knew they did not lack courage. Their whole exploit was one of daring and endurance. Were we held in some sort of awe? But looking back down the hill and seeing our group huddled around a fire, in plain view from the castle walls, I realised that what the westerners could see were fifty odd figures clothed in furs giving no clue to sex or size, and presenting a potentially formidable foe. Besides, safely ensconced in the castle grounds, they had no reason to risk unnecessary conflict. So that was that. Reconciled to the futility of negotiation, I returned to my companions. It seemed there was no alternative: we needed cattle, so we had to take them; it had to be warfare. My soul was weary beyond measure as I made my report.

We devised several plans. There was no bridge across the river close to where we had camped, so we erected one under cover of darkness to facilitate any retreat. We had ropes made from twisted leather with us in one of the carts and it was a simple matter to suspend four of them between trees on either bank. One of the lads braved the freezing water to secure the initial transverse rope, and the others fastened cross-pieces of wood to the two lower ropes. It took some time, but it had the one great advantage of being easily cut down to prevent pursuit. While Barry supervised this work, Pip and I went up to the castle to reconnoitre. This was not at all difficult for although the Main Gate was under surveillance, there was so much vegetation on the road that approaching undetected was simple enough. The night was bright with moonlight reflected and emphasised by the silver landscape, and the trees were so still that moving objects would immediately catch the eye. But our skill was sufficient to overcome that. We passed the Main Gate unobserved and followed the wall along towards the Royal Apartments, then continued right round to the far end. We entered the grounds by means of a small opening partly blocked by stones, really quite a pathetic attempt to bar access to anyone with determination. One could only assume that they had not anticipated any approach from that quarter. They could not possibly have known that we had previous knowledge of the castle's layout.

The castle grounds at that point were deserted. The palace loomed black-eyed and unwelcome on our right. It was silent, uninviting and deathly cold. An aloof place, conscious even in its ravaged desolation of past majesty. There were no guards in the area at all. The westerners were clearly not accustomed to the discipline of sentry duty, and it seemed as if their attempt at it was something less than half-hearted. We could see their fires flickering beyond the wall separating what had been the private grounds from the area occupied by the Keep and the Chapel. We crept to the arched gateway, no longer with a gate, and looked directly into their encampment. The great rising mass of the tower obscured much of our vision, but what we could see was sufficient for our purposes.

The cattle had been herded at the base of the tower, confined within a limited area by means of small fires burning between the Chapel and the outer wall. Beyond them, in the open space before the Main Gate, was the camp. We were unable to distinguish any sleeping forms, but assumed by the light emanating from the Chapel that they were using that as their dormitory. Its spaciousness would have appealed to these people of the open fields far more than the confines of the palace itself and, besides, the pews made excellent firewood. So, if that was where they slept, then the few men we could see around the fires and on the walls were only a portion of the total manpower available. A plan began to form in my mind as I surveyed the scene. Between us and the raiders was a herd of almost wild cattle and sheep, and beyond them the only way out. Pip must have reached a conclusion similar to my own, for he breathed in my ear: 'Just like a cowboy movie, eh?'

'All right, I've seen enough,' I said. 'Let's go.'

Ten minutes later we were back with our companions. The older lads were still tying pieces of wood to the deck of the bridge.

'Looks shaky,' I commented.

'It'll do,' declared Barry. 'It swings about a bit, though. Mind you, once those ropes get wet they'll tighten up all right. Paul has already been across to check the fastenings at the other end, but I'm damned if I know how I'll cross the bloody thing.'

'Well, it may not come to that. If it does I'll carry you on my back. Just get them to hurry it up. We're going to be busy tonight.'

It was still before midnight. We had ample time if we left soon. The ideal moment would be in the small hours of the morning when watchfulness would be at its most lax. The bridge was quickly finished and I gathered my band together. Everyone would have to be involved to give the impression of numbers. I explained what we intended to do and impressed upon them all the need for silence. Silence was the key. The biggest problem was the transportation of Barry, for we could not risk the creaking of the cart, and we had no grease to put on the wheels. So we had to carry him. We improvised a four-man litter and headed once more for the castle.

It was quite a tense operation getting everyone past the Main Gate without detection, but really the anxiety was uncalled for. These were women and children born to the plains, reared as hunters, and they had an instinct for shadows where our own skill was of a more conscious kind. Moreover, the moon clouded over, which was certainly welcome. Pip made several trips guiding the women in small groups. Then Paul and I, managing Barry's litter between us, completed the first phase of the operation. From then on it was an easier matter. With the aid of Pip's home-made gunpowder and with everyone positioned strategically, we awoke the night, and the cattle and the drowsing tribesmen with enough startling noise to ensure that panic was the inevitable consequence.

And panic there was. The cattle stampeded just as we had anticipated, away from the noise towards the gate. The line of fires, by that time burnt low, could never have stopped them. The sheep milled around at first, bleating and desperate, then followed the cattle in a wild, raucous bolt for escape. The tribesmen were equally quick to react. There was a terrified exodus from the Chapel. Those in the open had already fled from the stampede. Meanwhile Pip raced along the top of the outer wall unnoticed in the frantic terror that had seized the wild beasts and the wild men, all fleeing headlong into the open.

As it happened, some of the more courageous of the tribesmen tried to turn the stampede, and did actually succeed in diverting it from the gate itself, enabling the women and children to reach the roadway beyond. Then these brave ones fled, too, seeing our own apparent horde on the heels of the stampede. The beasts were also streaming through the gate by that time, but another explosion well placed ahead of them by Pip from the wall, caused the panic to reverse and most of the animals flooded back in.

We spent the rest of that night blockading the several entrances and assessing the casualties. I will not speak of them. Guilt still tortures my mind at the memory of the few mangled bodies, little limbs like those of Kerry . . . Enough. We had achieved our objective. Windsor Castle was ours.

Chapter Twenty

They camped all around the castle walls. Once again we were under siege, but this time without much real concern. We had plenty of food and water, and the westerners had stockpiled firewood and hay in the Keep. We would sit it out till spring or until they went away. Many times during the first few days the besiegers tried to climb over the walls, but such attempts were quickly thwarted. Fortunately the nights remained clear and visibility was always adequate. We prepared fires at strategic points around the walls in case of an overcast period, so that if the moon failed us we could provide our own illumination. Still, our safety depended on constant vigilance, and this was especially wearing on our nerves, and then after a time, physically wearying, too.

Then came a spell of bad weather. Heavy snowfalls. Unlighted days. And, when the snow stopped, gusting, ice-cold winds. We were forced to patrol the walls continuously. There was little sleep for the adult males during those harrowing days. Twice we repulsed attacks under cover of snow and darkness. They were dreadful patrols. So cold even our numerous coverings of fleece could not keep us warm. And we were tired. So tired our eyes burned from the constant strain. Then, worst of all, the snow and the winds ceased. Within hours a fog closed in. All the vigilance in the world was futile.

We made frantic preparations. That was when they would come, we were sure of that, and we decided unanimously that we would move out as they did so. There was no cart for Barry; he would have to be carried again, for although he was quite mobile on his wooden legs, it was a limited mobility, and far too slow for an operation that would depend upon utmost speed for its success. Unfortunately it was the invaders who held the aces and would dictate the timing. They would make the first move, and when and where from were two vital questions, unanswerable and imponderable. So we worked. Paul and Pip supervised the slaughter of four beasts, and cut them up into reasonable loads for the women and older children to carry. I took Kip and three other youths, and we piled masonry into every single crack in the walls, while Barry busied himself with two more lads erecting a sort of baffle wall at the gate separating the palace grounds from the Chapel area, so as to limit any access through that gate to one person.

While we worked I tried to assess from what point the assault would come. I had nothing to guide me but intuition. I considered what I would do in their situation. If they attacked from the rear as we had done, the cattle would be between them and us and that would reduce the aspects of surprise to a large extent when the cattle became nervous. Also cattle would make hand-to-hand fighting almost impossible in the fog. So the probability was that they would make a frontal assault from the Main Gate end. Of course, it was always possible they would attack from both ends at once, but I reasoned that as they were unaware of our actual numbers and probably believed our fighting strength to be far greater than it was, they would be unlikely to split their forces. What if I was wrong? I dared not think too much about that. I expressed my thoughts to the others and they offered their suggestions, but the truth was they were no wiser than I, and the final decision had to be mine.

We rounded up all the tribe and made them pass one by one through the gate dividing the palace grounds from the Main Gate area, counting every head. Once satisfied that they were all on the palace side of the wall, I grouped them in the centre of the area and sent two lads to free the barrier of stones we had erected at the same break in the wall whereby we had made our own invasion. That was to be our exit. Then we had nothing to do but wait, and we did that in silence. There was a temptation to lead them out by that rear exit in any case and so avoid the possibility of bloodshed, but the thought was there that if I was mistaken we might walk right into their arms.

I suppose our wait was not so long, really, probably less than an hour. But standing there together, visionless, voiceless and utterly cold, it seemed that we were doomed to an eternity of hushed and shrouded immobility. As the minutes passed my doubts grew, shrank, ebbed and flowed, ever stronger, argued away, to return and return again, until my mind was screaming: 'What if you are wrong?'

And I was wrong. Utterly and stupidly wrong. They came from the loosened break in the wall that I had fortified and then opened again. And suddenly they were in amongst us. It was hopeless in that fog. But everyone had been given directions in case of such an eventuality. Thank God for that precaution! 'Retreat!' I cried aloud in French. 'Retreat to the Main Gate. Get behind the cattle!'

I was with Barry. 'Hang on to me, old son. Where the hell is your stretcher?'

'Tag and Ian have it. Don't worry about it now. Just get me to the gate as fast as you can.'

All the time we were moving. My people were running, but orderly still as far as I could make out. There was no way of checking their numbers. Paul and Pip were behind us throwing hand bombs. These were not very effective, but they did give us precious minutes of time. Soon they were out of them. We had not brought much of the gunpowder with us. They came running up to assist me. 'I'll be all right,' I said. Barry was making good progress with a single crutch and one hand on my shoulder. 'Just go on. Get everybody out of this damned place. Get them out of the Main Gate and down the road.'

They nodded and sped on. We were fifty yards from the arched gate. The assailants were behind us, still confused at the explosions but recovering rapidly. They were no more than dim shapes in the murk, but I could see that they were closing on us.

We reached the arched gate and Barry's baffle wall. 'Okay, leave me here,' said Barry.

'Good heavens, man! What are you talking about?'

'Go!' he said. 'I won't make it to the Main Gate in time, that's obvious.'

'Don't be ridiculous,' I snapped. 'I'll carry you on my back before I'd leave you.'

We had to turn then for the foe were within a few yards of our position. I had my bow, arrows and a spear. Barry had just his axe. I had to loose two shafts quickly and without accuracy. A spear was thrown at us, but it struck the pile of debris that Barry had had piled up earlier. It was an effective shelter. They could not approach us straight on. They would have to fight at close quarters.

'My life is only one.' Barry spoke quietly as I fitted another arrow. There was no immediate target. The figures had vanished in the fog. 'Your responsibility is fifty lives and those include my children, Jeff. You must save them for me. I promise that I will give you time. They won't pass me at this gate easily.' He swung his axe. 'It's as good a way to die as I can conceive.'

Two figures loomed up out of the fog. We were ready. Barry's axe flashed and I released an arrow at two yards' range. But behind them rose two more. 'Go now,' cried Barry. 'I am dead anyway.'

And I left him. I looked back once before I rounded the Keep. I could just make out his shape in the murk. He stood huge on his wooden legs, braced against the rubble, but undefined in the shroud. Just a swinging axe and a hulk of fur as they came at him. That was the last time we left Barry alone and I was crying as I ran for the Main Gate.

Pip was there, and Paul. 'Hurry, Captain. Where's Barry?' I did not answer. There was no need to with such sensitive men. They saw my face. Pip hesitated for an instant as I swept past them, my jaw trembling as I tried vainly to control an emotion that was uncontrollable. Then he followed on my heels and those of Paul who was already running.

We kept the tribe moving till dawn, a driving and exhausting pace. At the first hint of daylight, with the fog lifting and our circle of vision growing, we stopped. The women collapsed. Many of them were sobbing but they had not abandoned their loads of meat. And we, too, were just about done in, but our physical weariness was of no significance compared with the emptiness of our souls. I felt so drained, so dead inside with a grief that clawed at my nerves, that at first I did not even look for Lian. She would come up to me soon, she would offer her silent comfort. 'Better check that we're all here,' I heard myself croak, but I walked away from them. Barry, Barry, where are you? Barry, I have no strength without you. I looked out over a white and naked landscape and suffered my agony. A little hand stole into mine. Not Lian's. It was Kerry.

'Mummy isn't here,' he said.

Lian. Where was Lian? 'Your mother,' I cried. Kerry shook his head. I left him and ran to the huddled group of women. I looked. She was not there. I began to tremble. My whole body began to shake. Not Lian, too. Not Barry *and* Lian. A scream filled me, filled my chest, my throat, my head. I made no sound and my body screamed. It screamed. I could hear it. I could hear nothing else. But reason was struggling for a shred of control. I can remember looking at my hand, stretching my fingers so that all the sinews and veins stood out, seeing the broken fingernails and trying to stop the fingers trembling. But it was not coherent thought. Then it was that I died, my emotions frozen into my being forever. There were some moments to come when I would live again, momentarily, but I know now that it was then, on that frozen road in the lightening winter dawn, that my soul withered within me and I was never the same man again. One episode still remains to be described, and although it is agony to relive that event, I must do so, if only because in some measure it is my excuse for my conduct in all the time that followed.

Some time later—I have no idea how long it was—I became conscious of Paul shaking my arm. 'Jeff. Jeff. Listen to me!' I looked at him. 'Jeff,' he said, 'Wani is missing.'

'Wani, too?'

'I'm going back for her, Jeff,' he stated, and his courage and quiet resolution shamed me.

I found words. 'You think she's still alive?'

'I can make sure. I love that woman, Jeff.'

'We'll both go.'

'No. You are needed here, Jeff. They will manage without a doctor in their own crude fashion, but they must have their leader.'

'But you see, Paul, Lian is also missing.'

He looked at me then, perhaps for the first time conscious of my pain in the oblivion of his own. 'Oh, I see,' was his only comment.

'Wait here,' I said, and I walked across to where Pip was

standing watching us. His eyes were dark and dull with an agony of his own. If Barry had had legs he would not have died. His thoughts were not hard to gauge. There was guilt, an emotion of long standing, never really suppressed, and there was an intense grieving now, a loneliness that he would have to endure until he died.

'What are you going to do?' he asked. His voice was colourless. I saw his face very clearly even through the weariness and pain of my own heart. It was lined and grimy. A dirty, ugly face. He was very tired.

'You take the tribe on to Heathrow and wait for us there. Rest here for a few hours, I don't think there is any danger. Paul and I are going back to Windsor. Give us three days and then go home.'

There was no argument in his sagging frame. He was not defeated, he would never be defeated, but he understood. He nodded, whispered: 'Good luck, Captain,' and turned back to the tribe.

I walked wearily back to where Paul waited and we simply headed off in silence. There was no parting. But as we walked, the thought of action, that Lian might yet be alive, stirred the dregs of hope and cleared my mind, restoring strength to my muscles and courage to my heart. Ephemeral courage.

Yet it was with tired and heavy limbs that we reached the town. We spent a few minutes inspecting Barry's rope bridge, for that was an essential element in our rather nebulous plan, but the bridge was as we had left it. Then up that arduous hill to the castle. Not on the road, for it was still day; a day of muffled sky, but not one of imminent snow. We must have been physically exhausted. How else could it be? We were not young men, indeed old men by the axioms of our own time. Neither of us had slept for more than thirty-six hours, and the flight from the castle had been ordeal enough for the fittest constitution. Then the cold had taken its toll of our reserves and that, combined with the state of our minds and the return trip to the castle, was pushing our endurance beyond any man's normal limits. But strangely enough, aware though we were of our physical state in the aches and the irresolution of our muscles, neither of us was aware of exhaustion other than subconsciously. Consciously we were keyed up to a condition of anticipation overriding any physical factors.

It was mid-afternoon when we finally arrived at the castle walls. They had posted watchers in spite of the sounds of high revelry from within, but they were easily evaded, especially as our approach had been calculated expecting such vigilance, and no doubt they were expecting a force of some fifty persons. Once past the Main Gate we crept round to the rear as before, and discovered no sentries there, even at the break in the wall. Still, it was almost certain that they would be watching it, so we proceeded to a point further on and scaled the wall at a position behind the palace where it would have been impossible to be seen from the Chapel area. Soon we were within the Royal Apartments. They were unoccupied as we had expected, and I doubt whether any living person had been in the building for centuries. Our own people had avoided it. We climbed to the roof from where we were able to view the savages' activities. They appeared to be having a celebration of some sort, and were dancing and feasting around a huge fire in a state of great excitement. We could not see Lian or Wani anywhere, either alive or dead, but as our vision was partly obscured by trees and by the mass of the Keep, this was not really surprising. We could see Barry's body, though, still lying by the arched gate, still clutching his gory axe. They had not mutilated him at all. From where we viewed the corpse he could have been asleep. Around him were the bodies of his assailants showing how dearly he had sold his life, and how long he had endured to give us precious time. We could not see what had finally brought him down for they would have retrieved their spears.

'We must get to the tower,' Paul said.

I nodded. That would present no great difficulty, and there was no reason for them to be guarding its entry. We climbed up inside until we achieved an excellent view of the area before the Chapel. Immediately we spotted the two women, still alive, it seemed. The relief was agonising, so powerful that I was trembling. I saw that Paul was shaking, too, his face white and his hands clenched in the intensity of the emotion. We could not speak for some time. They were trussed up in two separate bundles, apparently unharmed, although that was hard to determine, but clearly the focal point of some ceremony to come. They were lying on large bundles of faggots some ten yards from the actual fire located at the central point of the arena formed by the prancing savages.

The dancing consisted mainly of unrhythmic leaps, raising and lowering of spears, yellings reminiscent of wild dogs and sundry urinations over the trussed captives. The women as well as the men took part, the women performing hysterically, occasionally going on all fours and openly exposing their genitals. This would cause some posturing male to prance about the swivelling posterior in an elaborate preliminary to a crude mating. It was basic and primitive, not far removed from the animal state. Were these people the legacy of British culture? Was my judgement of such crudity nothing but the false perspective of indoctrinated inhibition? I ponder those questions now, but then my concern was concentrated on those two figures lying on that pile of sticks. Their intended fate could not be mistaken. When would it be? I looked up at the sky. Were they waiting for darkness and the rising of the moon? It would hardly be visible in such curtained skies. But it had to be that. Our already half-formed plan began to be more clearly defined in my mind. But we would need the cart. It was still down there in the town.

I whispered some instructions to Paul. He nodded and left quietly. I waited with loaded bow. Of necessity Paul could not be back before dark if he was to bring the cart close enough for our purpose. Even unloaded it was liable to squeak, but a lot less than with Barry's weight upon it. He should be able to get it close enough. So my arrows were ready, poised in the direction of our women. If things did not happen as we expected then an arrow would bring a speedier death than flames. The range was too far but I had plenty of arrows.

I should have rested. My body cried for rest, but I was far too tense. Yet perhaps those hours of sheer inactivity did do some good and that surely was some help in what was to come. Paul would be resting, too, somewhere in the town. He was older than me and must be feeling the strain that much more. Should I have gone for the cart? No. If we had guessed incorrectly and I had to use my bow, it meant certain death for me. I did not think that I wanted to live without Lian anyway, not then. But it was not for me to condemn Paul. His skill might yet save lives, and those lives could be of Kerry, or Smudge, or Jenny, or of Barry's children. My thoughts were morbid and empty, born of weariness and despair and the still unreleased grief. They were hardly rational. The time in the Keep was endless. There were moments when my mind seemed totally detached from my physical being. My legs were objects to be observed but not part of me. The scene before me retreated into the distance; the drab, shrieking humanity, the fire blazing as the only colour in the dreariness, vanishing into a detail in the infinity of inactive space. I knew my mind was wandering, but did not have the will to retrieve it. Then Paul returned and I realised it was dark. He told me where he had concealed the cart. He had done very well. I saw his total fatigue and wondered if his desperation was strong enough for what we had to do.

'Let's go before the moonlight gets too strong,' I said, and led the way down to the ground.

We crept from the tower and on all fours crawled in amongst the sheep. We hoped that with our sheepskin robes we would be indistinguishable amongst them. The sheep remained placid, settling themselves to sleep. We crawled to the limits of the flock. Ahead of us, just a few yards away, were the small barrier fires defining the cattle area. It was not then quite dark enough for our purpose. For perhaps half an hour we waited. The darkness gradually became absolute apart from the glowing of the fires. We inched our way past them. No tribesman glanced our way. We were close to the Chapel walls. There it was almost totally black. Standing up we crept along in the gloom of the wall until we were as close as we dared approach in secret to the trussed women. Paul looked at me for command; still I was his leader. 'Yes,' I said.

And we walked out into the firelight.

We could have been one of them. They were certainly not expecting enemies to walk into their midst. In any case, they were quite preoccupied with their cavorting. It was only twenty yards to the pile of faggots. I swept in and picked up Lian in one lunging movement. Then I was running. I was ahead of Paul, but I could hear his footsteps right behind me. We reached the Main Gate before pursuit began. It was a very dark night; too dark, thankfully, for the use of spears. But the gate was heavy and awkward to open one-handed. Paul came up beside me then and it was open enough for him to lurch through. Right behind him I slipped on the road and went sprawling. Paul had not heard and he ran on clumsily under the weight of Wani. Lian was whimpering. The fall must have hurt her. No time to check. I was on my feet. Somehow I scooped her up. Paul had reached the cart and dumped Wani in. He was actually moving it when I reached him and tumbled Lian alongside Wani.

'Push! For God's sake, push!' I cried, and turned round to loose arrows at the pursuers, now crowding through the gate. It was not possible to distinguish individuals in the gloom so I aimed generally at them. We were among trees on a clearly defined path. I could hear the cart creaking frantically as Paul raced away from me. Have strength, Paul. Have strength now. There was not enough time. I had to give him more time. I stopped again at a bend in the road and held them for a moment or two with three well-directed shafts. I was using up my arrows too quickly. There were not many left then. I must not waste them. I turned and raced on.

Paul was in the town. An open stretch to the right, a few trees only, then the river and the bridge. He would have to cross twice to get both women across. He still needed more time. I realised suddenly that I could see much better, the sky was lightening. The moon had risen. I stopped yet again as Paul turned a corner. Ahead of him would be the last stretch before the bridge. The pursuers could see me quite clearly. Had they seen Paul's change of direction? I shot off some more ineffectual shafts, holding my position. Anything to delay them. Then there were no more arrows. I let them approach to within spear range, deliberately exposing myself. I had to divert them. I raced up a side street leading uphill. They had to follow me. Please, God, let them follow me.

They never followed me. I came out into an open area well beyond the bridge. There were groves of trees there. If I sprinted down the hill I could still head them off. I could see Paul at the bridge. He had reached it. I still had some time.

Then suddenly I was jerked off my feet. I thought my back was going to break. The world spun round, and I was hanging upside down, my head some ten feet from the ground. I had stepped into one of Pip's animal traps. He had not set any here so one could only assume that the westerners had adopted the device. Clearly they had known a lot more about us than we had ever realised. It was hanging upside down that I watched the ensuing events. And I watched them in utter helplessness, and also in agony although that was but a fringe discomfort compared to the anguish of my heart.

Paul had stopped. The pursuers were only fifty yards from him. He had time to cross the river, but he could only take one of the women. Was there a faint moment of hesitation then? For years I did not think so, but now that memory is less clouded with emotion I do believe that there was a momentary look of indecision on his face. But perhaps I have just decided that from the view of a conscience still ridden with guilt. For him there could have been no decision to make. He scooped up Wani and ran.

I cried aloud: 'No! No! No!' but my voice was strangled and only I heard. The tribesmen did not bother to follow him. There were eleven of them. I counted them later, one by one. They halted by the cart. I saw Paul cut the bridge down from the other side. He stood looking back across the river, his eyes searching for me. He must have seen me.

The savages pulled Lian off the cart. She was unable to cry out. I watched. I watched every horrible moment, my view inverted and wavering as I swung erratically on the tether. They untied her. Tore off her furs so that she was white and naked in that frightful cold. I could see her eyes. I could see the terror. Then they bent her over, knees forced up against her breasts and on the ground. Her head thrust down and held there with a foot crushed against the side of her throat. Eleven of them. Savage indeed. Incredible in their cruelty.

And I watched them.

Then finally the spear. The final rape. And they left her. They left the spear, sticking out still, stiff and phallic. She toppled over slowly, still crouched like a frightened animal, and the spear pointed at me.

They never looked for me. It is possible they would not

have seen me anyway against the darkness of the trees, and they would have assumed that I had escaped. I hung there. Swinging. Waiting to die. Wanting to die.

For hours Lian jerked as life refused to leave her, her fingers moving feebly in the slush. It took her a long time to die, and I watched every pitiful moment. And I prayed to die with her. Please, please let me die. At dawn the dogs came. She had stopped moving then. I could not tell if she had finally died. The dogs ripped her to pieces, snarling and hideous, greedy from their winter hunger. Blood and scraps of flesh on the thawing snow. They were still there, gorged and vile, when Paul returned with Pip and cut me down.

Chapter Twenty-one

At first I was physically sick. At least the physical sickness was most obvious. Paul treated me, of course. I hated him then. He knew that but said nothing. My left ankle, the one I had hung by, was almost severed and the foot was useless for many months. Shock and mental exhaustion, plus the complete lack of will to live, undoubtedly retarded my recovery. I became an unspeaking man, morose and withdrawn.

The winter ended. The meat we had brought from the castle lasted well enough. Spring must have been as lovely as ever, but it mattered little to me. Lee endeavoured to establish a new relationship with me; she tried hard to fill the void left by Lian's absence. She meant well and was tender and patient with my bitterness. I abused her and could not find any love for her at all. Only with Kerry was I kind, and with Smudge whom I spoiled, and Jenny, too, though I saw little of her in those days.

It took my body six months to recover, although I retain a marked limp to the present day. But in my mind I was more profoundly ill. Paul had specialised in psychiatry as a young man, but how could he treat a man who hated him? One day he said to me: 'Jeff, if our positions had been reversed, which girl would you have taken?' But I would not volunteer a reply. Of course, he was right. Even at the time I knew it. But rationalising would not help me forget, and it would not help me forgive. The tribe was fully aware of my illness of mind. I was a bitter and unkind man. More and more they leaned on the decisions of Paul and Pip, and even then on the surgent independence of the young men. Somehow, inevitably, in the years that followed, they lost their faith in me.

Was it three years? Four perhaps, even five. Although that time is comparatively recent, my recall of it is elusive. Some of the children we had brought from France became men and mothers. I knew there was no more hunger. These young men were strong and arrogant. Fine hunters. Far superior to the local people. The environment of their early years had conditioned them more subtly than we could have imagined. Soon they would be usurping the leadership of us older men. Not yet, though. Soon. Pip and Paul, for all their erudition, were not strong leaders. They never were leaders of men. I cared not. I cared for nothing other than my children and a little for young John, son of Oa. There was no more attempt at education. Hunting was enough. And the winters were supplied by trapped cattle and sheep newly acquired every autumn to save the drudgery of stock keeping in the warmer months, so that true domestication of herds was impossible.

The tribe settled near Bromley, near the country of my childhood. That was unimportant. But the settlement had the beginnings of permanence. During those years there were no expeditions to other towns. The young men went hunting and were away sometimes for many days, but the settlement was home. I kept apart from the main area of occupation, as much from choice as from exclusion. I stayed in a cottage on its own at the outer limits of the village and withdrew into my bitterness.

I never hunted at all during those years. Wretched years. Timeless. Meaningless. I never fished. I never loved. I did not take part in tribal activities. I was a dead man. Pip, ever loyal, looked after my material needs, made sure that I ate and that my clothes were adequate, and also that my children were not neglected. At first both Paul and Pip together made my well-being their responsibility, but I was vindictive to Paul, so malicious in my invective, so completely unreasonable to any approach of his, that he forsook me, and no one could blame him for that. But he persevered for many months, even years perhaps, for I can recall his face in the summer: sad, pleading eyes, the crowsfeet deep and grey; a rawboned, brown face, hair very thin and silver, and I knew he could not see too well at close quarters, for he would lean back to focus his eyes. A stooped and weary man. And there is the remembrance of a winter face, with his beard tugged by the wind and ice in his brows.

Mental sickness is not insanity. I was not by any means

insane. Just a hateful man. I drove my friends away, my wife —for Lee finally left me, too, I think in despair and pain. Only my children remained. Sometimes fearful, I believe, sometimes uncomprehending, but there with me, always there. They knew that I loved them in spite of my aloofness and my irritability, and they came to me in the night, snuggling against me for warmth and security. Life still held that for me. But Pip stuck by me. Dear Pip. His head as bald and his beard as black as ever, but not a laughing man any more, no longer the irrepressible clown. He mourned for Barry, I knew that, but in the isolation of my own bitterness I deliberately ignored his pain. He made no attempt to cheer me, and for that I was grateful. He no longer philandered. I think Lee went to live with him at the last, and that was a kindness of the little man, but the poor girl was destined for her own personal loneliness, and for that I am sorry. I am sorry for my indifference to her after the death of Lian, for she deserved much better treatment. She was a kind and loving woman, with the gift of beauty in her voice, but she never sang again.

Then one day Paul came to me. I had not seen him for so long that even my dullness of mind was capable of some surprise. 'Pip is ill,' he said. I remember turning away indifferently.

'Good God, man!' he cried in uncharacteristic anger. 'Didn't you hear me? Pip is ill. He is very ill. I don't think that I can save him.'

Something did move then in the pit of my stomach. An emotion did stir. 'What is it?' I asked.

'I'm not sure. I haven't seen it before. Some form of cholera.'

I turned and looked at him. Thought came slowly to my mind. Even the implications of that dread word took time to register. 'Just Pip?'

'No. Many others, if you're interested.'

I nodded and turned away. I heard him go, could feel the anger in him. He hated me then as much as I hated him.

The first thing to do was to evacuate my children from the infection. I went to find them and discovered that Paul had already instigated severe quarantine conditions. Every apparently unaffected person had been moved about a mile away from where the sick were bedded down in a makeshift hospital that had once been a church. Paul toiled. He had fires going with pots of his witches' brews simmering over them. He had to feed the fires, prepare the herbs, treat the patients and cook food without any assistance. There were seventeen sick persons in the building, nine women, three men and five children. Two of them, I discovered later, were already dead when I arrived. Paul just had not had the time to bury them. He noticed me. He said nothing, simply nodded in the direction of Pip's bed. I had already seen him. I went over.

Pip was not aware of my presence. He was aware of nothing outside his own fevered mind. His face had lost its fullness. His teeth were bared. His eyes staring blankly at the ceiling.

'He's dead!' I said aloud.

'Not yet,' was the clipped reply.

I knelt beside Pip. Philip Quincey-Jones. And I peered into the pits of his eyes. There was a glint in them yet. He lived still. There was spittle on his beard. His skin was odorous. One of the greatest biochemists of his age, a great mind, a fount of humour, a fun-loving, lusty little man, dying in a private torment, his intellect withering and wasted and futile.

'Pip,' I called gently. 'Pip, it's me. Jeff.' He registered no response. I did not want him to die believing I had not come. I touched him once, on the side of the face, but he could not feel. I stood up then and turned to the next bed.

I went the rounds not knowing how to help. There were two dead, a woman and a boy. I carried them out one after the other. The ground was hard, but I felt so vicious, so grim, suddenly awake and feeling emotion strong within me, that I did not cease attacking it until I had dug a great pit more than four feet deep. I rolled the corpses into it. I had known the woman well. The fat one, we called her. She had had a delicious fullness of figure when we first met her, one of the Mekan women, but complacency and child-bearing had settled that fullness into a pleasant corpulence. I had known that rounded body myself in the early days, before acquiring Lian, and so had Pip, and Barry, too, in latter years. Her name had been Vari, and now she was dead. It was then that sadness came to be as I began to shovel earth over her.

'Don't fill it in,' Paul's voice came from the doorway behind me. 'Not yet. Others will die soon.'

'Can you save any?'

He shrugged and turned inside.

'Only Pip,' I prayed. 'Just save Pip.'

That night I buried two more in the grave. Children. Then I filled it in. I dug another. In the morning Paul went off to examine the rest of the tribe. He was exhausted, that was quite evident, but he could cope with exhaustion. I had watched him during the night and knew his main problem was his eyesight. He was having trouble examining the patients. There was nothing we could do about that. He came back with three more sick. He kept them in another building and treated them separately. While he had been away another woman had died.

Pip died that afternoon. I buried him, heaping his body on top of the woman. I did not fill in the grave. There was room for two more. The ground was terribly hard to dig.

The whole seventeen died. Paul only managed to save the three he had isolated on the day of Pip's death. This phase of mortality lasted four days in all. Yet the epidemic endured for three or four weeks. It seemed that Paul, in spite of the limitations of his vision, had hit upon an infusion that contained the disease if he was able to detect it early enough. He never spoke of it. I did try once to ask him what had caused the outbreak, but he either did not know or simply declined to tell me. He had become the cold one then, and as I had no inclination towards reconciliation, so it remained. It was ridiculous, the last two surviving members of our own time deliberately indifferent to each other. But the past etches deep scars upon one's sensitivity, and I was content to leave our relationship so.

My period of sickness was over. My soul would never live again, but I did become aware of my environment once more, and of my responsibilities. It was too late. The tribe had alienated itself from me. They were afraid of me. The tremendous faith they had once held in my leadership, a faith that had led them to accompany me in unquestioned trust upon the frenzy of the ocean and into the bowels of the ocean floor, was now but the ashes of fear. There was a new generation guiding the tribe's destiny. Young men and young mothers, rejecting such refinements as the cart, and even the bow and arrow. Spears and strength were enough in their arrogance. And they were strong and arrogant, and proud, too, youth in absolute harmony with the environment. Natural man. In lots of ways it seemed that that was how mankind was intended to be, if one accepted the concept of intent. They were the same physically as man of the old time, but so different in their cultural outlook, products undoubtedly of the needs of the age, fitting as we had never fitted. It was impossible that they would accept the authority of Paul for much longer, if indeed they ever had. My time of authority had already passed. Paul's had not long to run. Our impact had been small in terms of forward guidance, very small indeed. Only one of our technological innovations had stuck: the humble needle. The women still used a needle, perhaps more truly described as a bodkin, to sew their hides together. Technological man, and two of the finest of that species, with the knowledge of space travel, television, genetic control, and a thousand other achievements at the fingertips of their minds, had only managed a bodkin as their testament to mankind.

The weeks drifted by following the epidemic. The tribe would not absorb me, but I was content enough. I had all that I required. My children and I would spend the days together. We hunted and fished and harvested. They were delighted that I had resumed such activities. Kerry was a big boy by then, nine or ten years old, and clever. Cleverer in the art of the field than I was, but a quiet and serious boy, having adopted his mother's silent ways. He was devoted to me and to his brother Smudge. Smudge was all noise. He was laughter and chatter and squeals. Just being alive was a sheer delight for him. Jenny had reached the age of awareness of arriving womanhood. She was charming, the softness of her chest delightful with the promise of a fullness to come, but shy and submissive, with magnificent dark eyes. She worshipped Kerry, but from afar. He was unaware of it, but was kind to her. This, then, was my family and my world. Sometimes John, but no other.

It was winter when I grew sick, physically sick. Paul did not come to me. It was possible that he never knew of it. They were days of fever. Wild dreams. Lian came many times. Sometimes Barry. They were distorted figures and no comfort to me. My two boys stayed with me; they fed me broth and bathed my head, and did in their ignorance and anxiety all that they could. Later they told me that twice I had died, since to them unconsciousness and undetectable breathing were the signs of death. Once I lay unmoving for over twelve hours. Poor children. They watched what they believed to be my corpse for all that period, holding their hands, afraid of my lying so still, knowing grief so young. Then I moved and that was a miracle. To them it was inexplicable, a return from death.

That sickness lasted, as accurately as I could discover, fifteen days in all. For many more days I was weak, but gradually my strength came back. When I finally felt recovered enough to venture far from my home I learned that the tribe had truly deserted me. From what my children told me, it was Paul who had persuaded the tribe to move on. Either he had feared another epidemic, which suggests he must have known of my illness, or he had been the victim of a younger man's decision. I prefer to believe the latter. Anyway they were gone and I did not care.

I did not need the tribe.

I needed no woman.

I did not want Paul.

Chapter Twenty-two

I suppose that I am old now. Sixty, perhaps? I really do not know for sure. A few days ago Kerry found a piece of broken mirror and I was able to look at my own face for the first time in many years. I am not yet all grey, but certainly more grey than brown now. My hair is very long, untrimmed, uncombed and dirty. My beard has less grey than my hair, but that, too, is an unruly mass that could do with a good wash. All there was to see of my actual face was my large hawked nose and the deep lines like furrows angling away from my eyes. I had grey eyes, though that colour is hard to discern now. They looked to me like tired eyes, tired and defeated. I did feel an emotion as I viewed the reflection of my face again, it was one of intense dislike for the dirt. In my youth I had been a fastidious man, and that early layering of ethic surged to the fore, dominating anything else in my emotional retreat. I resolved to have a bath, a real, hot bath. I have been planning it for days. It will require many pots and a big fire. There is an old cast iron bath tub that is still serviceable in a house close by. Soon I will have that bath. Maybe tomorrow.

Seven weeks have passed since the news of Paul's death was brought to me by John. When he came, Jenny came with him. I see far too little of my daughter and my heart warmed to see them both. John is a fine young man. He is as his father was, like Oa, tall and proud and defiant. I wonder if Oa still lives. I think John is destined for leadership one day. Jenny embraced me, indifferent to my grime, and she lingered in my arms, unashamed of her affection and her delight. She is quite lovely. She has Lee's beauty. Kerry is much taken with her in the discovery of his adolescence. I suppose she is not too young by prevailing standards. Of course they are half-brother and sister, but I feel no inclination to interfere in their young attraction. Perhaps she came to see Kerry as much as me.

So Paul is dead, and I am the last. John said that he was killed in an assault by the western people, but I do not believe that. The westerners have not ventured into our territory again since the winter of the Windsor expedition, although I think our young men have wandered westwards on occasions. They have a boldness and courage that is almost rashness. I wonder if the thought of conquest has entered their ambitions. So be it. I have no influence on their future path, and that is probably to the good. Conquest could mean unity and trade and co-operation. Perhaps conquest is the first step on the road to a new civilisation. But I wonder about the truth of the death of Paul. I cannot know for sure, but I suspect he may have been killed by one of the young men, possibly Kip, or even John himself. I am sure that a son of Oa's would be capable of such ruthlessness if it served his purpose. We had once seen a leader slain in Bordeaux because another needed to assume leadership. Was Paul's death within such a context? Shall I be next?

At first I was afraid, not with a dominating fear, but a small nervousness on the fringes of my thinking. I am the last of an alien culture, the final reminder of an authority that was, so perhaps in some way a threat to any new claimant to leadership. I shall have to die; somehow I am sure of that. After John left, taking Jenny with him, Kerry went part of the way with them to sound out the intentions of the tribe. He informed me that the group was considerably larger than it had been. It seemed that it had absorbed many of the local peoples, so perhaps conquest had already begun. Yet it did seem that I still posed a dilemma to them, whoever the leaders were, and the problem was rather more delicate than it might seem. There was still some lingering but very strong feeling of awe associated with my presence.

'They are all around us, father,' Kerry told me.

'I am here if they want me, son,' I responded. But suddenly, having said that, I did not want to die. Not yet. I want to see Kerry and Jenny and Smudge grow up into beautiful people and have beautiful children. And that is the nature of my fear. It is a fear of deprivation, the deprivation of looked forward to pleasures, rather than physical fear. But I am afraid of any more pain, as well. I have had enough.

Then Kerry made a surprising statement. He said: 'They will not come for you. They are afraid to.'

'Why is that?'

'They tell stories about you. You are the man who controls the sea and the wind and the snow. They say you cannot die.'

'What nonsense. You don't believe that, do you, Kerry?'

'I have seen you die, father. And yet you came alive.'

So the legends continue, and now the defeat of death is added to the other exaggerations. Well, perhaps the legends will survive. Legends have a tendency to endure where facts may fade quickly. At least they might buy me a little more time. I remember the legendary heroes of my upbringing, Hercules of Greek and Roman mythology, Samson and Noah of the Old Testament, Gilgamesh of ancient Ur. Am I to join those glorious ranks?

So the idea came to me. Scholars of my own time had deciphered the ancient writings of man, the cuneiform script of Ur and Erech, cities that flourished before the Flood, and they had revealed many possible truths behind the legendary stories. It was conceivable, in spite of Barry's predictions to the contrary, that civilisation would evolve once more, that erudition would be prized as it had been in our day. Pip had believed it would, he had believed that people would learn to read and write again, and there would be scholars once more, and archaeologists interested in the origins of their kind. Then I decided to pen this story of the last men of a remote age. Soon it will be finished and I shall bury it in an airtight jar like the Dead Sea Scrolls, in a nearby manhole that is an ideal spot for calculated preservation, protected from the elements and corrosive materials.

Looking from the window opening of my house, I can see the skyline of London, still much as it always was. The degradation and the decay is not visible from here. It is late spring now and the sun is friendly in a clear, immaculate sky.

* * *

The manuscript is finished. I cannot resist the temptation to add a postscript, because writing this has been a bitter sort of pleasure. It is the only contact with the written word that I have had for a long, long time, and it means more to me than I can easily explain. What does it matter? My thoughts are old, and I see our mistake was to cling to devices such as written characters which are so utterly symbolic of a different era. Yet I cannot deny the great pleasure words still give me. One cannot so readily discard the indoctrinations of one's childhood.

I cannot see the men who are waiting for me. Perhaps they are not. Perhaps they still hesitate. Fear is gone now, at least momentarily. Here is the jar, a large earthenware pot purloined from the British Museum. It looks of Eastern design, heavily glazed and strong. I have dropped it twice to make sure. I have clay ready to seal it. There is the manhole. And there sits Kerry watching me with eyes of love. I ache to embrace him, but he would not understand. I am not in the habit of openly demonstrating my affection for him, but there is no need. We are very close. Smudge is poking a stick down a molehill not far away. He is too big to carry now. I wish Jenny were here.

All that is left to do is to seal the jar and bury it. Then take my children by the hand and walk off into the sunshine.

This moment is exquisite. No men for as far as the eye can see. They are there, of course, but only birds are visible. They are lovely. They sing and flutter, and they are happy to be living. Without them this would be such a quiet place.